# THE FOOL

ALEX SCARROW

GrrBooks

# INTRODUCTION

**Author's Note**

The events in this book take place at the same time as the police investigation in *The Vanishing*, with Jay Turner's story beginning five days before the disappearance of Audrey Hincher.

# 1

Jay Turner watched the woman as she mooched her way around the Harrods shop at Gatwick Airport's North Terminal, idly picking things up and inspecting them before putting them down again and moving on. She lingered beside the perfume counter, spritzing her wrists with several samples and giving them the sniff test. Nothing in Harrods seemed to take her fancy this morning and she wandered out, across the departure lounge's main concourse and into Reiss.

He'd done the best he could to disguise himself – tall, muscular, head shaved to the wood, and sporting a constant five-o'clock shadow, his options were limited to wigs, hats glasses and fake beards. Today he was modelling his 'intermediate distance' disguise: a long-haired wig and stick-on goatee. He'd nipped into a toilet cubicle to put them on after he'd checked in and passed through the cattle grid of bag-screening and the magnetic scanner.

He'd been relieved when his passport was handed back to him at the check-in desk, without klaxons wailing or an armed response unit descending on him. As he'd suspected, the story that had been fed to him about being on some MI5 watch list for life had been an exaggeration. MI5 clearly had better things to spend their limited budget on.

Jay was even more relieved that his bag had not been selected for a random search after the scanning. His modest collection of wigs, facial-hair pieces and a bottle of skin adhesive would have certainly raised a brow, and he'd devised a convoluted story involving an American woman he'd met online and was going to meet in person for the first time.

'She, uh... she likes role-play sex,' was going to be his awkwardly whispered confession. The wigs and beards were part of his playful alter-ego, Randy Cyrus. The cover story, he figured, was too naff and embarrassing to be fictional. If he'd thought about it a bit more, he'd have packed a dildo and some lube too.

He wandered nonchalantly across the departure lounge towards the same store as his target – Kerry Wakefield. He glanced around for her husband, Malcolm – or Mack, as he'd insisted Jay call him – and spotted him sitting at the nearby Juniper & Co bar, tapping away on his phone. He wondered if Mack, in turn, had spotted him. Mack was well aware that Jay would be tailing them this morning. He was equally aware that Jay was catching the same flight to Miami, Florida. Of course, the Wakefields were going to be in the first-class seats, and Jay would be in cattle class at the back. But that was fine. Jay didn't want Kerry to get used to seeing his face during the nine-hour flight across the Atlantic.

If Mack had figured the bulky man with long brown hair and a goatee, striding towards Reiss, was Jay, incognito, then he was doing a good job of not showing it. The bald, bull-necked, round-shouldered businessman seemed more than happy to leave Jay to keep eyes on his wife while he got on with his various business deals.

'*I know she's been cheating on me, shagging* around,' he'd said to Jay when they'd first met. '*I just wanna prove it. I want evidence.*'

Jay had been shadowing Kerry for the last two weeks, getting to know her behaviour patterns, her body language and the way she moved. She was tall, slender, and yes... very attractive – if a collagen-pumped gym bunny was your type. Kerry Wakefield had a tense energy about her and was always fidgeting, always glancing around as if some invisible ghost kept blowing on her bare neck.

As Jay entered the store and made a show of examining the expensive wristwatches, his thoughts circled back to Sam and the very real possibility that this job he'd taken on might well have put some serious wear and tear on their relationship. The tone of her texts had transmuted from conciliatory, trying to convince him to come back home and talk things through, into messages with more of a 'well, screw you' tone to them.

And he couldn't help wondering if her frustration might have led to another supposedly 'work-related' drink with that South African shrink, Dr Pienaar.

His brother Karl had told him he was a complete twat for taking the job. That it had sounded dodgy as hell, that Jay was pushing his luck trying to catch a flight when MI5 had specifically warned him that he shouldn't, and that messing Sam around like this was asking for trouble.

'You're a fucking fool, Jay,' he'd said.

'I'm gonna be back home in twelve weeks' time with nearly a hundred K in cash, mate,' Jay had replied. 'She won't think I'm such a fool then, will she?'

## 2

'I s it okay if he stays with us for a while?' Boyd repeated Emma's question.

Emma nodded hopefully.

'Of course!' he replied, reaching for his morning coffee. 'It would be good to catch up with him.'

'It won't be just for a few nights, Dad...' Emma said. 'I mean, it'll be for *a while*. He's lost his flat. The landlady wants him out so she can refurb it and sell it on.'

'Can't he just look for another flat?' Boyd asked.

'That's just it – there aren't that many places going spare in Hastings, and those that are, are ridiculously expensive,' she explained.

'I thought he was doing well,' said Boyd. 'What's the phrase you used...? *Properly minted?*'

'Yeah, Dad, he's doing well *for a musician*,' Emma said. 'That sort of money can't compete with some rich twat from London who wants a weekend shag pad.'

'There's space for him here,' said Charlotte. 'We've still got two rooms upstairs that are doing nothing particularly useful.'

'That would be really helpful,' Emma replied. 'He'll need one to store his stuff.' She turned to Boyd. 'If that's okay, Dad?'

Boyd pondered that for a moment. It wouldn't be so bad. It might be nice to have Dan around. Another male in the house, and a pleasant one at that. And if Dan was living here, Boyd would be able to keep an eye on him. He'd be able to see for himself that Dan was putting Emma and their twenty-week-old daughter, Maggie, first. The truth was, Boyd was sympathetic to Dan trying his luck with his band. You only ever got one bite at that particular cherry, and you either went for it or spent the rest of your life wishing you had.

'All right,' he said at last. Then he smiled. 'Do you think he'd let me noodle around on one of his guitars?'

Emma grinned. 'He'd love that. You could jam together.'

Charlotte looked at Boyd wryly. 'You can still play the guitar, can you, Bill?'

He shrugged. 'It's been a while,' he admitted. 'I expect it'll be a bit embarrassing for all concerned.'

'Only if you sing, Dad,' Emma said, laughing.

'I'll spare you all that,' he promised.

Boyd resumed eating lunch while Emma continued trying to shovel Weetabix mulch into Maggie's tiny mouth. She was resolutely refusing to cooperate.

It definitely would be nice to have another chap in the house, he thought. Especially Dan. He might be a bit of a muppet sometimes, but he was polite, had a good heart, and they could talk music. It was a funny old thing, Boyd mused. Music fads seemed to run in circles and, from what he was hearing, the young musos of today were reaching back to his time, the eighties and nineties, for inspiration.

He nodded. 'Yeah, tell him it'll be dope to have him stay,' he said.

Emma pulled a face.

'Dope?' enquired Charlotte.

Boyd grinned.

## 3

Jay had lost eyes on Kerry and Mack as he stood in the non-US Citizens line, waiting his turn to be scrutinised by the Customs and Border Protection officer. Mack and Kerry had VIP passes, of course. With Kerry being American and Mack being her husband, they'd been promptly waved through after a cursory glance at their passports.

Not to worry. Mack had given Jay their address in Palm Beach and told him that he should allow himself a couple of days to get settled somewhere nearby and to buy any kit he needed, before resuming his discreet surveillance of Kerry.

Jay had booked a motel room. It was next to a small retail park just outside West Palm Beach, in an area called Jupiter. It had amused him to note that Google Street View had shown it to look a bit seedy and rundown, but the photos on the Jupiter Plaza website had been Photoshopped to make it look like a buzzing, vibrant business hub.

Once he'd checked in at the motel, he was going to need his 'booking agent' Ronni Kirk's assistance. Ronni was a PI herself, based up in Connecticut; however, their paths had

crossed at a surveillance seminar in Croydon of all places...
They'd clicked.

Kind of.

Ronni had networked while she was over in the UK and
picked up a few connections. One of them had been
Malcolm 'Mack' Wakefield. Wakefield was after someone
experienced in tailing to watch his wife while they were over
in the States, but he wanted a fellow Brit, not some Yank. He
wanted someone he could talk plainly with, somebody he
could 'get' – *one geezer to another.*

So Ronni had passed the job on to Jay. There were a few
items of kit that he needed to source in the US, such as
personal and car trackers. He had no idea how many cars
Kerry had at her disposal, nor how many handbags she
regularly used. So he figured he was going to need at least a
couple of each. Since he was over here under false pretences
– not a tourist, but actually *working* – he didn't want to leave
too much of a paper trail. Ronni could order the kit online
and have it delivered to his motel room.

With a start, Jay realised that the CBP officer was now
waving forward. The wig and goatee were safely packed
away in his hand luggage, and he was back to looking like
his passport photo: hair shorn down to his scalp, his jaw
peppered with freshly clipped bristles. The officer was
female, which might be helpful. He'd deploy some of his
natural charm. Perhaps deploy a little playful flirting, play
up his British accent. The ladies over here loved that, right?

He stepped up to the booth and handed over his
passport.

'All right, love?' he said, grinning at her.

She eyed him for a moment, before glancing down at his
blue passport, then back up at his grinning face.

'Please don't smile, sir,' she said.

He dropped the grin. She pressed the open passport down onto her scanner, then studied the monitor in front of her. Jay tried to hide his anxiety. The watch-list thing hadn't been an issue at Gatwick, but that didn't guarantee it wouldn't be an issue on *this* side of the pond.

'Why are you visiting the United States?' she asked.

'To see the sights,' he replied cheerily.

She raised a brow. 'More specifically, sir?'

'Um, Disney World. Universal Studios, the beach,' he replied. 'You know, all the tourist stuff...'

She didn't look particularly impressed with his answer. 'And where will you be staying, sir?'

'I've got a motel booked,' he answered. 'You want to know where?'

She nodded. He pulled up the address on his phone and read it out for her. She tapped the details into her terminal. 'Will you be visiting anyone you know?'

'I don't know anyone over here,' he replied. 'I'm a first-time visitor to the US... actually.'

He tacked that last word on – *actually* – and tried to make it sound as Hugh Grant as he could. Maybe she didn't like Essex accents and would warm to a more foppish and softly spoken tone.

She remained stony-faced. 'How long are you planning on staying, sir?'

'A month,' he replied.

'Do you have a return flight booked?' she asked.

He did. Ronni had told him to make sure he booked that. If he had to stay the full three months, it would be a few hundred bucks wasted, but it was Big Deal she'd impressed upon him, because it clearly demonstrated that he had an intent to leave the country again. He pulled out his tickets to show the officer.

She checked the details and entered them into her terminal.

'What's your profession?' the border officer asked next.

*Time for a white lie.* 'Antique furniture restoration,' he said.

'And how much money do you have available to you during this visit?'

'Huh?' He resisted the instinct to pat the money belt that was wrapped tightly round his waist, beneath his baggy sweatshirt.

'Do you have sufficient funds to see you through your stay here, sir?' she asked.

'Ah, yeah... yes. I'm sufficiently funded,' he told her. 'Worry not.'

She frowned at him suspiciously. Maybe he was overdoing the Hugh Grant thing.

'I'm sorted, *love*,' he added.

Then, at last, she returned his passport, her stony face animated with the tiniest trace of a perfunctory smile.

'Welcome to the United States, sir.'

∽

As per Jay's booking, a Nissan Pathfinder was ready for him in the Hertz Car Rental lot. The Hertz lady had handed him the keys and given him his first-ever all-American 'Have a nice day, sir!'

Jay dropped his suitcase and carry-on bag into the boot, then climbed into the driver's seat and familiarised himself with the dash and the unnecessarily complicated touchscreen, before finding the climate controls and switching the AC on. He settled back and mentally remapped his muscle memory to deal with the fact that he was sitting on the 'wrong' side of the car and was going to be driving on the 'wrong' side of every road for the next few months. He'd driven automatics, no problem. Any idiot could drive one. It was like driving a go-kart. But this other-side-of-the-road-thing was making him anxious already.

'It'll be a piece of cake,' he assured himself. If the little old ladies and rheumy-eyed old boys of Florida could manage it, so could he. He tapped in the zip code for his motel and hit 'Go' on the screen.

'Right then... Let's have it,' he muttered, slipping the Pathfinder into reverse and easing his way slowly out of the parking bay. He exited the Hertz lot and turned onto his first stretch of proper American highway, straight as a slide rule and ludicrously wide.

After totally ballsing things up at the first intersection and invoking a chorus of horn blasts from the cars behind him, he made his way onto an exit ramp that took him onto the I-95 heading north, towards West Palm Beach. Kerry and Mack Wakefield would be on the same road, probably well ahead of him, given their five-star VIP treatment.

As he drove conservatively, hugging the right-hand slow lane like a safety rail, Jay gazed out at the scenery – or lack thereof. From the highway, Florida was as flat as a snooker table. To his right, looking down from the raised highway, he passed an endless procession of artificial lagoons and mini marinas, lined with terracotta-roofed apartment blocks all elbowing each other for waterside space. Beyond the oncoming traffic on his left, he spied the chessboard grid of the suburbs, every square on the board painted with a different shade of turquoise. Pools were like back-garden trampolines over here. Everyone, so it seemed, had one. The lagoons on the right soon became golf courses and endless strip malls: large white shoebox buildings floating within a sea of glinting windshields and bonnets.

On the flight over, Jay had spent some time pondering how best to deploy his spoils when the job was done. Mack had guaranteed him a minimum of $90K for three months' work, roughly £72K in English money. He'd also said there'd be a bonus if Jay managed to photograph her with her tongue down some other guy's throat. It seemed to Jay to be an *obscenely* big fee for the job he was doing. But then Mack was obscenely rich and seventy-two large was probably chump change for him, particularly if Jay's work gave Mack enough evidence in a divorce case to show a Florida judge that his wife had been shagging away behind his back.

Mack wanted rid of Kerry... as quickly and as cheaply as possible. He wanted to avoid a hefty divorce settlement – and a little compromising material could work wonders.

Jay's plan for the money oscillated between throwing the lot into a down payment on some Hastings property together with Sam, or putting the money into some business venture. Bricks 'n' mortar was safe, but if he wanted to set up his very own PI enterprise, he was going to need some capital.

After an hour or so, the satnav indicated he needed to take the next highway exit. This time there was less flapping around and he felt that he did more of a competent job as he swung onto the 706, heading west towards Lake Okee-chobee. The road was flanked on either side by yet more golf courses, but very quickly the manicured greens and sand bunkers gave way to a coarse wilderness of stunted cypress trees.

The satnav informed him that his destination was coming up on the left. The online booking site had described Harry's Rest Stop as 'a cheerful traditional motel, perched on the edge of a vibrant plaza'.

Jupiter Plaza was a couple of acres of sun-baked tarmac, populated on three sides by single-storey business units, which surrounded the central car park. Jay drove over to the far side, where a Harry's Rest Stop sign blinked limply in the late-afternoon sun and parked his Pathfinder in one of the spaces marked for motel guests.

He turned the engine off, let out a deep sigh of satisfaction and stretched to release the driver's tension in his arms and shoulders. There it was, his first experience of driving abroad.

Anywhere.

And, apart from his bit of dithering at the first intersection, he thought he'd managed just fine.

# 4

---

'Sorry, Sam...' Boyd said. 'Run that by me again.'

'I said he's left,' she said.

'Jay?' Boyd asked.

She raised a brow at him.

Boyd looked up from his punnet of chips. Lunch today had been her shout. She'd said that there was something she'd needed to talk to him about, and on the way down to the pier she'd bent his ear about the additional courses she thought she should be put forward for as a newly promoted detective sergeant. He'd assumed *that* had been the sum of it.

'Jay?' He repeated. '*Left?*'

She nodded.

Boyd frowned. 'What do you mean, he's left?'

Sam sipped her coffee. 'As in, he's packed a bag and shipped out.'

Boyd paused, his next chip already dipped and in danger of dripping ketchup onto the table. 'But... wait, I thought you guys were good?'

Okeke shrugged.

Death, taxes and Jay's unflinching loyalty to Okeke were the only three certainties in life; he'd come to learn. 'Christ. It's not another woman, is it?' he asked.

She smiled. The idea seemed vaguely amusing to her. 'No. It's worse. Fragile masculinity.'

'Care to elaborate?'

'To be honest...' Okeke sighed. 'It's been a bit of a thing since we first got together. I don't think Jay's ever been comfortable with the fact that I'm the major breadwinner.'

'Oh? I thought he rather liked that,' said Boyd. 'Tinkering around with his hobbies... knowing the bills will still get paid.'

'He's changed,' she replied. 'I don't know if it's some sort of mid-life crisis...' She glanced at Boyd. 'That PI job, helping out with that government spooks thing last year... He thinks he's ready to run his very own PI business.'

Boyd glanced her way. 'And you *don't?*'

She shook her head. 'A few NVQs, a bit of job experience and a couple of courses do not make you Sherlock Holmes.'

He chuckled. 'Jay certainly doesn't lack self-belief, does he?' He popped the drooping chip into his mouth before one of the seagulls hovering overhead saw it as an open invitation.

'Oh, but he does,' said Okeke. 'That's the problem... he *acts* all confident. Which means he leaps into things without thinking them through.'

They sat in silence.

After a few minutes, Okeke broke the silence. 'Also... things got complicated recently.'

*Ah.* Boyd raised his brows. *Complicated* never meant anything good. 'Go on.'

'Remember the psychiatrist who treated Lucy Coleman?'

The South African one, he recalled. 'Dr Pie... Penner...' Boyd's mouth involuntarily sagged. 'Sam, don't tell me you _'

'Fuck, no!' she replied. 'But Jay? He's added two and two together and come to the conclusion there's *something* going on there.'

He studied her face. *Sam would be honest with him, wouldn't she?*

'Look,' she continued, 'he's uncorked a whole bunch of insecurities, right? Stuff he's been bottling up. And it's pushed him into some kind of frantic quest to prove himself.'

She locked eyes with Boyd. 'That's *it*. He's on some *quest* to make a point. He's gone rogue.'

'*Gone rogue*,' Boyd echoed. 'What do you mean?'

'He's ditched that PI job he had and picked up a free-lance job, for starters,' she said.

'Doing what?' Boyd asked. 'I thought he was happy there.'

'This new job looks dodgy as hell,' she added.

'What's he doing?' Boyd asked again.

She explained that some rich-prick British businessman with a young American trophy wife was certain that she was cheating on him. He wanted three months of surveillance and Jay would be paid ninety thousand dollars for his troubles.

'*Cash*,' she added, reaching into her jacket for a fag.

Boyd covered the rest of his chips with his hand as a gull swooped low over their table. 'Ninety-K, *cash*?' He shook his head in disbelief. 'As in...?'

'As in an actual *bag of cash*. Off the record. No declaring it. No tax,' replied Okeke.

Boyd couldn't help wincing. That amount of unexpected

cash was harder to make use of than you'd think. Buying anything substantial or even depositing it in a number of different bank accounts could trigger money-laundering questions from any one of them.

'Christ, that does sound dodgy,' he said.

She shrugged. 'I've told him that over and over. That kind of money has a stink to it. But he won't... he *didn't* listen to me.' She lit her fag angrily and blew out a cloud of smoke. 'He's been back a couple of times to collect bits and pieces when I've been at work, but he's basically been holed up in a Travelodge over in Kent for the last few weeks.'

Boyd listened in shock. 'Jesus... why didn't you say?'

Okeke sighed. 'Because I didn't know what to call this, or how to deal with it.' She shrugged again. 'Is it us actually splitting up? Or is this Jay having a long sulk?'

'When did you last speak to him?' Boyd asked.

'Speak? About a week ago. I had a text yesterday.' She sipped her coffee. 'The job's in the US. He flew out this morning.'

'Hold up...' cut in Boyd. 'He's actually taken a flight?'

'Yeah.' She nodded. 'I was expecting a call from the spooks to say he'd been arrested at Heathrow or Gatwick. Or arrested as some terrorist over in the US. Or turned round at the border and put on the next plane back.'

'I'm surprised you *haven't* had a call,' Boyd said. 'That was –'

'Idiotic?' she supplied.

Boyd nodded. 'We got off lightly with MI5, Sam. *Very* lightly. We're lucky we still have our jobs. He's pushing his luck with them.'

'I know!' she retorted. 'That's what I'm saying! I think he's trying to make a point.'

'To them?'

'*To me!*' she snapped.

He looked at her. Confused now. 'What point?'

'I dunno...' Okeke sighed, a frown creasing her brow. She gazed out at the gulls dipping and rising in the onshore breeze like closely tethered kites. She finally found a way to say it: 'Making the point that he can put on his big-boy trousers, stand on his own two feet and do whatever he wants.'

## 5

The motel room was everything Jay had expected it to be from watching a lifetime of DVD bargain-bin horror movies and repeats of old cop shows. 'Traditional' was something of a hopeful euphemism. Walnut veneer was peeling off the corners of the empty wardrobe and writing desk, which had a faded and dog-eared copy of King James Bible in the drawer – naturally. The walls were lined with a pineapple-themed wallpaper that had been, once upon a time, lime green but was now a sickly jaundiced yellow. The TV was so old it had a channel dial on it.

He checked for Wi-Fi and, to his relief and surprise, there actually was some. And a handy wall safe. Jay lifted his shirt and peeled his money belt from his waist and stuffed it inside the safe, along with his passport. It was a relief to get the damned uncomfortable thing off. He'd wrapped it so tightly the seams had left an indent around his middle. He pulled a couple of twenty-dollar notes from one of the pouches and locked the safe.

The room was hot and stuffy, so he turned on the AC

unit beside the door. It rattled and gurgled as it clattered into life, but then settled down into a loud steady drone.

Mack had told Jay that there wouldn't be much to do today or tomorrow. Kerry would be way too tired to go anywhere, to get up to any mischief, so Jay might as well get comfortable and familiar with his surroundings.

He decided to give the local area a quick recce. He opened the motel door and stepped out onto the shaded terrace that ran along the front of the dozen or so motel units.

There was a small, tanned, dark-haired boy sitting on the steps to the terrace a few doors along, playing with some action figures and making his own sound effects. The boy looked up at him.

Jay grinned. 'All right?'

The boy smiled, nodded and returned to the climactic battle scene he was enacting. Jay went down the steps, into the late afternoon sun. The damp heat of Florida was already feeling oppressive. He headed to the middle of the car park and completed a circular scan to take it all in. Jupiter Plaza's car park was surrounded on three sides by a dozen or so businesses: Captain Dan's Bait and Tackle, Jenny's Beauty Palace, Titan Hardware, Newton Office Supplies, Liquor Cabin, a 7-Eleven, a laundromat, a petrol station and beside it the obligatory McDonald's. He noted there was a FedEx and UPS drop point, which was handy.

A sudden gurgle from his stomach reminded Jay that he was hungry. He spotted a Mexican restaurant and a diner among the shops, and a small bar called Tanners on the far side of the car park.

He needed a bit of quiet to do some thinking and planning. A few days before the flight, Mack had dropped an information pack at Jay's Travelodge. It was a list of places that Kerry frequented when she was here in the States, and a rough itinerary of a typical week. She was a creature of habit. She visited the gym most mornings, a hair-and-nails place once a week, and ate out most lunchtimes with 'her girls'. She joined Mack a couple of afternoons a week at an exclusive Palm Beach golf club – *under sufferance*, he'd added.

Jay decided to give the diner a go. He went back to his room to pick up the folder of information, then strode across the hot tarmac of the car park. A cool blast of air greeted as he pushed open the glass door of the diner. It was relatively empty inside. Four old ladies wearing sun-visors and chequered golfing pants were at a window table, gossiping loudly as they played gin rummy. At another table, three teenage girls sat in a silent huddle, thumbing their phones.

Jay wandered over to the counter and waited until the waitress behind it had finished refilling the coffee maker before clearing his throat.

She turned round to look up at him.

'Oh, I am sorry – did not hear you come in. Can I help you?' she asked.

'Yeah. Do I order here or...' He trailed off, gesturing at the empty tables.

'Grab a table,' she replied. 'I will come over.'

Jay nodded and picked a table well away from the other customers. He pulled out Mack's handwritten notes was about to start reading when the waitress came over, pad and pen in hand. She was called Peggy, according to her name badge, which seemed a bit old-school for someone who looked to be in her twenties.

'What can I get you, sir?' She had an accent. Hispanic, Jay guessed.

'Ah...' He hadn't looked at the menu yet. 'Can you do, like, a fry-up?'

'Sorry?'

'You know, sausages, bacon, mushrooms, eggs...'

'Oh, like a breakfast?' she asked.

Jay nodded. 'Yeah. Something like that.'

She scribbled down his order.

'Oh, and beans too,' he added.

'Beans?'

'Yeah, you know... baked beans? *Heinz* baked beans?' Jay explained. 'Like, in *tomato* sauce?'

She giggled, then apologised, seeing Jay's confused face. 'Sorry, sir. The way you say that...' She repeated 'tomato' slowly, emphasizing the middle vowel: *to-maar-to.* 'You are from England?'

He nodded. 'Hastings.'

Her brows knitted together. 'I do not know this. Sounds old.'

He laughed. 'All of England's old, I s'pose.'

She smiled. 'You on vacation here?'

'Yeah.' *Keep to the script, mate*, he told himself. 'I'm seeing the sights of Florida. The beaches – I heard they're the best here...'

She nodded. 'They are. Where are you staying?'

He pointed across the car park. 'Over there.'

She seemed surprised and failed to mask an unguarded wince.

'I'm on a tight budget,' he clarified.

'Uh-huh... it is *cheap*.' She paused, then glanced down at her order pad. 'I go ask if we can do you the "baked" beans. What to drink, sir?'

'A coffee, please. And an orange juice. That'll do me, thanks.'

She nodded and went to get his order sorted.

Jay opened the folder again and resumed rereading Mack's briefing notes. He needed intel on Kerry's gym and the beauty salon, and on the places where Kerry met her girlfriends for lunch. He needed to do some research and work out where he could best position himself in order to keep a constant and discreet eye on her. Her gym – the Barre Wellness Centre – in West Palm Beach overlooked Palm Harbor Marina. It didn't look anything like Hasting's White Rock Gym; it was more like a luxury spa with some top-end gym equipment thrown in as an afterthought. It also looked ridiculously exclusive. Jay doubted very much if they'd let just anyone wander in. So, if Kerry was carrying on with some totally ripped personal trainer in there, Jay would have to wait until they hooked up elsewhere to find out.

Her regular salon was called Marielle's Beauty Fusion. Again, it was expensive and exclusive, but it appeared to be on a busy main street with a wide, windowed front that should afford Jay an opportunity to keep eyes on her fairly easily. She could, of course, be carrying on with one of the hairdressers, but he doubted Kerry was the kind to go for some flouncy stylist called Lorenzo.

The restaurants she visited most often looked like the kind of places that you'd have to book months in advance. They were, again, very pricey and equally exclusive. And almost certainly not where she'd choose to meet her fancy man. Palm Beach's VIPs probably all knew each other and, of course, tongues wagged no matter how much money you had.

'Here you are, one *Full English*.' The waitress, Peggy, set the plate down on the table, along with a cup of coffee. 'That is what you call it, yes? Our chef, Austin, tells me he had it in London once.'

Jay cleared away the notes he'd been making and smiled up at her. 'Yeah. Spot on. thanks!'

In addition to the eggs and meat, the chef had served up a couple of slices of fried bread and some grilled tomatoes – and what looked like actual legit Heinz baked beans. Austin clearly knew his stuff.

After Peggy had brought over a glass of orange juice, Jay dug out his notepad again. He had a short list of things he needed. Things he could quite easily have sourced back in the UK, but hadn't wanted to have in his bags, in case they'd been searched.

He dialled Ronni's number.

'Kirk and Hepburn Detective Agency.'

'It's Jay,' he said.

'Thought it might be,' she replied. 'You over here now?'

'Yeah. All settled in and sorted,' he told her.

'Did you have any problems getting in?' she asked.

'No,' he replied. 'I got a load of questions from the US border officer, though.'

'Yeah, that's normal these days,' Ronni told him. 'If you'd come from any place south of the equator, you'd probably have been bag-searched too. You didn't bring anything suspicious with you, did you?'

'No,' Jay assured her. 'But I've got a shopping list of bits I need you to get for me, if you wouldn't mind.'

'Sure,' she said. 'I'm guessing you need a burner phone and some trackers, right?'

'Yeah. Decent ones with a good range,' Jay said. 'I've done a bit of research online. I can send you a link for the kit I'm after.'

'Sure. Make sure it's a US supplier, right?' she said.

'There's a UPS Access Point just across from my motel,' said Jay. 'I'll text you its location.'

'Cool. You know our access points are automated over here, right? They use touchscreens. It'll want to scan your passport. You sure you wanna do it that way?'

Jay hadn't thought about that. He'd assumed there'd be some bored store assistant who'd glance disinterestedly at his face and passport, and that would be it.

'Or you can just give me the address of your actual motel room, Jay,' she added.

'Yeah... maybe that's a better idea,' he agreed.

'Relax. I'm not going to come down from Connecticut in the dead of night to molest you like Nosferatu.'

He could hear the grin in her voice. He felt his scalp prickle. Ronni *was* attractive if you liked a woman lean, mean and keen, and if he hadn't been with Sam, she might even have been his exact type, except for the fact that she was just too damned *predatory* for him. She reminded him of one of Jurassic Park's velociraptors looking for a quick meal.

'Uh... right, please don't,' he said.

'Relax. You had your chance and you blew it,' she chuckled. 'If you send me the links now, I can get those things delivered to you tomorrow.'

'Tomorrow's Sunday,' said Jay.

'And?'

'Well, does everything still, you know, still *happen* in Florida on a Sunday?' he asked, surprised.

'What? On Jesus Day?' She laughed. 'Presbyterians and Mormons may all be flocking into churches tomorrow morning, but, trust me, you can still buy yourself an assault rifle or a set of golf clubs if you want to.'

'Right,' he muttered.

'Glad you decided to take the job,' said Ronni. 'This'll be the easiest money you ever make.'

There was a brief silence, then...

'How much commission are you getting?' Jay asked.

'That's none of your business, Turner,' she replied.

'Fifteen, twenty per cent?' he pressed.

'Does it matter?' She sounded prickly. 'If you make him happy, he may use us again. Or, better still, recommend us to some of his rich-ass buddies.'

'I'll do my best,' he said. 'Lemme send you these links and we can crack on.'

'You do that.'

He ended the call, quickly copied and pasted links into a text message and made a start on the massive fry-up in front of him.

Peggy returned twenty minutes later to take away his cleared plate.

'You happy with what Chef made?' she asked.

The sausages had been frankfurters. The bacon had been a gammon steak, but the fried bread, fried egg, grilled tomato and beans had been on point and more than made up for it.

'Yeah, great, thanks. Good job,' he said.

Peggy smiled. 'I tell Chef.' She took away the plate, then came back to wipe the table. She turned to go, but then paused. 'You say you staying at Harry's?' She nodded at the motel across the car park.

'Yeah.'

'How long for?'

He shrugged. 'A few weeks or so.'

She smiled. 'So maybe we'll see you here again?'

He nodded. 'If the rest of your food is this good, for sure.'

Peggy nodded at the motel again. 'I am staying there too. The cabin on the end.' She narrowed her eyes as she gazed across the car park. She suddenly scowled. '*Madre. Idiota.* He should not be playing *outside*,' she muttered under her breath.

Jay turned to glance out of the window. She was staring at the small boy on the steps.

'I tell him – *inside*,' she huffed.

'He's... *yours*?' Jay asked.

She nodded. 'Jorge.'

The young boy was still playing with his action figures.

'He's on his *own* over there?' said Jay.

She didn't answer. He turned to look up at her and saw her frowning at him, an expression of irritation in her eyes at the implied judgement in his voice.

'I have no choice,' she replied eventually. 'It is just me and him.'

'You have no family? No friends you can ask to –'

She shook her head and muttered, '*Más vale estar solo que mal acompañado.* I work here, so I can keep my eye on him.'

Now it was Jay's turn to frown. 'But... he's alone? All day?'

She winced and repeated, 'I have no choice.'

*Shit.*

Jay had a day to kill. There was literally nothing useful he could do until the gadgets and gizmos arrived outside his motel door. He could do his research from one of the deckchairs out on the porch.

'I can, you know, watch him now, till the end of your shift, and tomorrow,' he said. 'If you want? And you can work and watch us both.'

Her anxious expression instantly melted away. 'You would do that...?'

'I'll watch him, yeah.' He smiled. 'I've got some trips I

need to plan, but I might as well do it out there and enjoy the sun.'

She squeezed his shoulder, almost desperately. '*Muchos grácias.*'

'Nah, it's uh... it's no trouble, Peggy.'

She tutted. 'Not Peggy. I do not like to use my real name here,' she explained. 'I am Sylvie. What is your name?'

'It's Jay.'

'Thank you, Jay.' She pulled a Nokia out of her apron pocket. 'I will call Jorge. I will tell him he is allowed to speak to you.'

# 6

'Thanks, guys,' said Dan. 'You know... for agreeing to put me up.' He nodded at the Chinese take-away that was spread out across the dining table. 'And for the food.'

'No problem,' said Charlotte. 'Are you still ready to move in? Sunday, two weeks from now, right?'

Dan nodded. 'Yeah. I got most of my stuff packed in boxes already.' He shrugged. 'Not that I've got that much stuff.'

'How much music kit have you got?' asked Boyd.

'Uh, just a couple of guitars. A Strat and an acoustic,' Dan replied.

Boyd raised a brow. 'Is that all? I thought you had a whole studio of stuff.'

Dan shook his head. 'Nah, it's not really necessary. I've just got my laptop, an audio/digital convertor, a mic. That's all you really need to write stuff these days,' he explained.

'Oh,' Boyd replied, a little disappointed. He'd been half expecting – half hoping, even – that the spare room at the back of the house would be transformed into something resembling a proper recording studio, with a mixing desk, monitors, effects racks and maybe even some funky acoustic-damping panels on the walls.

'How are things going?' asked Charlotte. 'With your band? The Mad...'

'Mad Priests. Yeah, good.' Dan nodded as he helped himself to some sweet-and-sour prawns.

'And how about your European tour?' said Boyd.

'Uh, yeah, man... It was proper mental,' Dan replied. 'Insane, you know? Crazy packed.'

Emma looked at him. 'I thought some of the gigs were a bit... sparse?' she queried.

'Well, yeah,' Dan said. 'I mean... there were some duds, for sure. Like, ones where no one really knew much of our stuff. But... mostly it was crazy.' He shovelled a loaded fork into his mouth and continued, 'I mean, proper crowds. Especially the gigs we did in Denmark.'

'You know, your band mates are welcome to drop by,' said Boyd. 'If you need to do a bit of rehearsing or writing.' He glanced at Charlotte, who looked a tad wary at the suggestion. 'I mean, not full-on drums and all that, but if you need –'

'Nah, it's okay,' Dan replied. 'We're pretty tight at the moment. We've been gigging solidly for sixteen weeks.' He grinned. 'And stuck in the back of a van together. It's nice to have a break from each other, you know?'

Boyd nodded. He vaguely remembered that feeling. It was all fun at first, but after a few weeks the novelty wore off and everyone's feet began to smell.

'Well, if you need another guitarist to bounce ideas off...' he said hopefully.

'Oh, good God,' said Emma, wincing. 'Please don't encourage him, Dan.'

Dan smiled at her. 'Don't worry, Ems – it'll be good riffing ideas with your dad. He's cool.'

Boyd couldn't help but allow himself a smug grin, directed her way.

'Playing along to some old Beatles songs for a chuckle is one thing,' Emma replied, 'but I don't think Dan needs you as a co-songwriter... or his muse.'

'*Beatles?*' Boyd replied. 'Christ. How old do you think I am?'

'Hey, the Beatles are cool', offered Dan.

'Nirvana, Pearl Jam, Chilli Peppers,' continued Boyd. 'That was my era. Foo Fighters too.'

Dan nodded in agreement. 'They're dope, actually.'

'See?' Boyd spread his hands. 'Totally *dope.*'

Emma buried her face in her hands, then turned to look at Dan. 'You're creating a monster. You do realise that, don't you?'

## 7

On Sunday morning, Jay left the diner having finished his breakfast of American pancakes and maple syrup. Another first for him. They had been Sylvie's recommendation and were bloody delicious.

He spotted a delivery van lingering on the motel's forecourt. He jogged the last fifty yards to catch it before the driver could leave a 'We tried...' card under his door. As he got closer, Jay noticed a FedEx box outside his motel door, and Jorge was standing guard beside it. Jay nodded at the driver, to indicate that the box was his and it was all good. The driver waved and pulled away.

'I look after it for you, sir,' said the boy as Jay approached.

'Thanks,' Jay replied, absently ruffling Jorge's dark hair.

'What's in it?' Jorge asked.

'Some things I need,' Jay said, stooping to pick up the box.

'What things?'

'Toiletries,' Jay answered.

'Huh?'

'Toothbrush. Toothpaste. A shaver...' Jay said, pointing at his fuzzy jawline. 'Look, Jorge... I've got to do some work inside. I'll come out in a bit, okay?'

The boy nodded.

'You go and watch some TV in your room, yeah?'

Jorge nodded again and Jay let himself into his own room. He dumped the box on his bed and opened it.

Ronni had got him *exactly* what he was after. He took out a pair of magnetised car trackers. He'd dithered over whether or not to order three, in case Kerry had regular access to two or three different cars, but at $450 a pop, it felt like overkill. The gadgets and gizmos were coming out of the advance payment from Mack, so Jay had some wiggle room, but every penny spent over here meant less to take home to show Sam.

There were another two trackers in the box: micro devices designed to be slipped into pockets and handbags. They were cleverly designed to look like coins, the size of watch batteries – small enough to tumble to the bottom and hopefully remain unnoticed. The kind of non-descript shrapnel that a well-travelled person might accumulate in the bottom of a side pocket. They had cost him a further $350 each.

He'd also ordered a personal surveillance bug, the size of a key fob, that acted as an audio recorder and included a built-in Wi-Fi module. The micro trackers could connect to its local network if they lost their 4G signal. That little marvel had set him back another $700.

Finally, there was a cheap Android phone with a pay-as-you-go SIM card. From this point on, his iPhone was going to have a long, switched-off holiday.

Jay unboxed everything, downloaded the required apps, and then set them all up as per the instructions. He grinned with delight as the various trackers appeared, one by one, on his phone's screen as pulsating green pegs.

*Proper legit spycraft kit.* He smiled. Provided he could sneak these little beauties into Kerry's bags and cars, he'd be able to tail her discreetly. Even when she went inside a building and lost connection with the phone network, the Wi-Fi bug could take over.

'Kerry, love...' he muttered to himself, 'I'm afraid there's going to be no escaping me.'

He sent Mack a specifically worded text message, as agreed, to give Mack his burner number.

Your package has been delivered. And is ready to collect!

Mack clearly was at a loose end, as Jay's phone buzzed on the bed almost immediately.

He picked it up and answered. 'Jay.'

'All right there, mate?'

'Yeah. I've got everything I need,' Jay replied.

'You ready to resume watching her?' Mack asked.

'Yep. I'm good to go.'

'Good man.'

'Is she at home today?' Jay asked.

'Yeah. And staying home by the look of it. She's still in her dressing gown and slippers, and watching some reality shit on Bravo. Tomorrow, she's got an appointment at her regular beauty place –'

'Marielles,' Jay said.

'Good,' replied Mack. 'You've been doing your homework.'

'What time's her appointment?'

'She doesn't book. She just turns up. They'll shuffle appointments for her. But she said she's going in for eleven. She'll be driving her red Lotus Elise.'

Jay jotted that down.

'Marielles has got VIP reserved parking right outside the window,' said Mack. 'If you're going to bug her car there, you're going to have to be very careful.'

'I'll be discreet,' replied Jay. 'It's a two-second job. You know what her plans are after that?'

'I dunno,' said Mack. 'She does what she does. She might have lunch somewhere. Do some shopping. I haven't grilled her because obviously I don't want her thinking I'm on to her.'

'No, that's fine. Once I've got her car bugged, I'm good,' Jay assured him.

'What about when she's on foot?' asked Mack. 'Mind you, the lazy bitch never walks anywhere.'

'I've got that covered,' said Jay. 'I've also got personal trackers. Discreet ones.'

'How're you gonna get one of those on her?'

It was a good question. Jay was going to have to be opportunistic about that. If her jacket was over the back of a chair in a restaurant, he might be able to drop one into a pocket.

'I'll find a way,' he said.

'Well, you're the pro.'

There was a pause. Jay heard Mack's footsteps echoing in a hallway.

'The offer still stands, mate,' said Mack. 'There'll be a big cash bonus coming your way if you get a picture of her stuffing her tongue down some bloke's throat.'

'That's the goal,' replied Jay.

'Good man.' Mack laughed. 'Well, enjoy your Sunday. Work starts tomorrow.' With that, he ended the call.

With his work done for the day, Jay emerged from his motel room. He walked along the porch and peered into the ajar door to Sylvie and Jorge's room. The boy was sitting on the floor with his plastic figures nestled on his crossed legs while he gazed, glassy-eyed, at a nature programme about pelicans on the TV. Jay realised the boy's viewing choices were limited. The motel rooms basically had a mini menu of free channels: little more than the local news and a ton of shopping channels.

He glanced towards the McDonald's.

'Hey, Jorge?'

The boy looked up.

'Fancy a milkshake?' Jay pushed the door wider and nodded at the Maccy D's.

Jorge nodded vigorously. 'But I gotta ask Mama first.'

## 8

J ay easily spotted Kerry's bright red Lotus Elise parked in the row of diagonal slots in front of Marielles, just off the main drag, Clematis Street. Her car was sandwiched between a Tesla Model Y and a Lincoln Navigator. All three were spotless and gleaming in the mid-morning sun.

He parked his Pathfinder further down the road at a parking garage. Luckily it had a ticket machine that still took quarters alongside the tap-and-go card reader. He wanted to keep as cash-centric as possible, so that – should the unlikely happen and he found himself being forensically scrutinised by some Homeland Security minion – there'd be no digital payment trail. Nothing tying him to anything or anywhere. These days, being a completely cash-oriented person looked a little suspicious too, but he figured it was the safer option.

He walked back up Clematis Street towards Marielle's, and as he drew closer, he realised that he *wasn't* going to be able to actually observe her while she was inside. The front window was smoked, affording him only the faintest outline of the receptionist's sun-lit back, standing behind a reception counter.

'Figures,' he muttered.

The car tracker was still in his backpack, which he'd slung over one shoulder. That was stupid. He should have got it out earlier and slipped it into the one of the pockets of his cargo shorts for a quick duck-and-drop. He spotted a health-food store nearby and decided to head there so that he could sort himself out inside. Maybe he could buy some groceries, he thought, so he'd have a shopping bag in one hand and look more like a stay-at-home-dad than a hitman.

Jay emerged from the shop five minutes later with a paper bag stuffed with healthy snacks and six-pack of energy drinks. They weren't just *props*... He'd binge it all later. He released a bag handle as he passed Kerry's car, and his snacks and soda cans clattered to the ground. He made a show of cursing and sighing, then he squatted to gather them all back into the shopping bag. With one hand, he rounded up his goods; with the other, he dug into a pocket and whipped out the car tracker – a black box, the size of a cigarette packet. He slid the switch to ON and quickly reached out beneath the back bumper of her car. The tracker's magnetic base clunked noisily against something as it latched on. Jay gave it a quick tug to be sure it was stuck on firmly. Then, happy it wasn't going to drop off at the first speed bump, he completed the task of shepherding his goods back into the paper bag – reminding himself that all six of those energy drinks were probably going to explode in his face when he opened them in his motel room.

Job done, Jay stood up, muttering and cursing for effect, then carried on his way back towards the parking garage.

*Nicely done there, Jay*, he told himself. *Nicely done.*

He returned to his Pathfinder, got in, pulled out his

phone and opened the car-tracker app. Straight away, there it was: a green pin pulsing gently on the map. Last night he'd read the manual cover to cover. The pin pulsed green when it was in standby mode. It switched to red when its motion sensors detected it was moving. A 'lightning' icon beneath the pin meant the tracker was on a low charge. A full battery was supposed to last four weeks before needing a recharge. So... if he was going to be doing this for three whole months, he'd need to replace the tracker a couple of times, at least. He made a note of what he was wearing. The next time he did this, he'd make sure he wore something different.

He slapped the car's AC on and settled back in his seat. There was nothing to do now but wait for Kerry to finish whatever she was having done in Marielle's and potter along to her next stop.

His mind idled back to yesterday afternoon and the McDonald's he'd had with Jorge. The lad had been both grateful and excited to be taken there. As they sat with their milkshakes and chatted – before Jorge got itchy feet and dived into the play area – Jay learned a little of the seven-year-old boy and his mother's situation.

They were illegals. Jorge had used the word casually, as though it was any other common-place noun: banana, cookie, car, house, illegals. The way Jorge said it sounded as though he was saying 'ill eagles'.

Jay's general awareness of migrants, immigrants, refugees... *illegals*... was – he was ashamed to say – limited to a snapshot recollection of Rishi Sunak's image next to a poster depicting brown faces crowded into small boats. He knew even less about the situation in America. But Jorge was giving him one hell of an education. Life for them was about staying off the radar, *all the time*.

So, Sylvie was working illegally at the diner, cash in hand, and Jorge was being left alone in a motel room all day. Presumably her employer was well aware of that. Presumably they were also paying her a low enough wage to make the risks worthwhile. And her home was that motel room. He wondered if her boss owned the motel too. In which case it made perfect sense, given that it seemed Jay, Sylvie and Jorge were the only ones resident at the moment. Rooms sitting empty – might as well be put to use housing cheap imported labour.

He'd asked the lad about school.

Jorge simply shook his head. His 'school' was the TV set in the room: documentaries about pelicans, bible stories, the local news station and episodes of *Sesame Street* from forty or fifty years ago.

*Jesus.* Jorge's and Sylvie's world seemed like some dystopian near-future sci-fi movie. Like the *Terminator* movies...always having to stay one step ahead, or one step below the grid. Jay couldn't imagine a migrant child in Hastings being *left entirely alone* with a telly for eight-hour shifts without hordes of well-meaning social workers converging like hungry pigeons, desperate to be seen dealing with the situation.

Or maybe there were plenty of children like Jorge hidden away in the UK?

He'd watched as Jorge played with the other kids in the play area, forging instant and transient friendships as names were exchanged and game rules agreed upon. His mind idled its way back across the Atlantic, to home.

*One day.* Hopefully sooner rather than later. He and Sam would knock a sprog out.

With his big payday, maybe having a kid was something they could look at doing sooner rather than later? Sam could carry on with her career as soon as she'd had the baby, if that's what she wanted to do. He'd be just fine as a stay-at-home dad, dabbling in a bit of PI work on the side.

Hell, a wriggling sprog in a papoose would make for the perfect disguise anyway.

## 9

K erry's pin started pulsing red just after half twelve, rousing Jay from his wool-gathering.

'It's showtime,' he muttered.

Kerry had finished at Marielle's and was on the move. He pulled out of the parking garage, following the pin at a respectable distance.

She crossed the bridge over Lake Worth Lagoon to reach Palm Beach, the eastern and seaward side of the city, where all the nice, exclusive beaches were. It wasn't long before she parked at a restaurant called La Casa Amarilla.

Jay glanced at the restaurant's private parking and spotted a total of zero parking spaces available, as well as an intimidating number of security cameras mounted on poles along its front. He cruised onwards and found a multi-storey parking garage several blocks down. He parked, then doubled back on foot, tapping the restaurant's name into Google as he walked.

As he expected, La Casa Amarilla was a members-only establishment: a restaurant with its own pool, patio seating and a private strip of beach. He scrolled Google Maps' satellite view to get the lay of the land and pondered whether he could gain entrance from the beach, but there was a privacy screen that ran all the way down the sand and a little into the turquoise surf to deter any determined paps, or overly curious peasants, from mingling with their elite guests.

He guessed he could try swimming round the barrier and emerge from the surf as though he was a patron who'd just gone for a quick dip. But he suspected they probably had their very own lifeguards watching out for that very ruse.

*The front door it is, then.*

Mr McGuire – his boss up till a few weeks ago – had told him that good, old honest-to-God blagging was still a very effective technique, despite everything being computerised and digital these days. Particularly with exclusive places like this one. Receptionists, concierges, doormen and the like were used to their pampered clientele constantly forgetting their membership cards, or not bothering to book ahead at all. The trick, McGuire had explained, was sounding enti-tled and difficult enough for them to want to avoid any hassle.

Jay quickly evaluated his reflection in the smoky glass of the restaurant's main entrance. He wasn't scruffy, but he wasn't dressed particularly smartly either. He'd have to lean into that.

'Today, Matthew, I'm going to be...' he muttered under his breath, 'Mr Celebrity Arsehole.'

Jay boldly stepped into the cool interior and ambled straight past the hostess, as though he'd already been in once and had just nipped out for a quick vape.

'Can I help you, sir?' the hostess asked politely.

He ignored her.

'*Sir!*' she said, more loudly.

Jay slowly turned round and offered her, what he hoped looked like, a smile with a strict time limit on it. 'Hey.'

'Sir.' She beckoned him over. 'Is there something I can help you with?'

'Yeah,' he began with a long, slow drawl. He wasn't going to bother trying an American accent. Or even a posh British one. *Fark it... A bit of Cockney would do nicely. A bit of Danny Dyer.* 'Yeah, love. I'm just meetin' my manager for a drink.'

'Your manager's a member?' she asked.

'Yeah, 'course,' Jay replied.

She tapped her screen. 'Their name, please, sir?'

*Shit.*

He was tempted to use Mack's surname. But if the hostess decided to let Kerry know 'her guest' had arrived, the game would be up. He should have given himself five minutes to google some likely member names.

'D'Angelo,' he blurted.

'D'Angelo?' she repeated, then swiped away at her screen. 'Ah. She's already in.'

He tried to stifle his surprise that he'd luckily scored a direct bullseye.

'Would you like me to take you to her, sir?' she offered.

'Nah.' Jay shook his head and gave her a wink. 'I'm good, thanks, love. Been here plenty of times before.'

He turned away from the hostess, to head in the direction of the restaurant.

'I'm sorry, sir,' she called out. 'You still have to sign in as her guest, I'm afraid.'

He sighed. 'Really? I thought you lot was changin' all that?'

She pressed her lips apologetically as she flipped open the guest book and held out a pen.

'If you insist,' he grumbled as he took the pen and

scrawled in the book. She turned it round, then her eyes flickered wide for a moment. 'Mr Statham?'

Jay glanced at the name he'd absently filled in. *J. Statham.*

'Yeah,' he replied. For some unknown reason, his accent thickened. ''E's me older bruvver, innit? I'm James.' He grinned. 'Younger, better-looking.'

She offered him a slightly disappointed smile as he started to walk away. 'Have a nice day, sir.'

He pushed his way through a pair of bamboo-cane saloon doors and took in the restaurant. It was large and bright with bamboo furniture, woven palm partition screens and several large rotating fans overhead. Half-scale ivory statuettes of near-naked 'African' villagers stood on mahogany plinths. He wondered what the hell kind of brief the interior designer had been given.

He spotted Kerry Wakefield immediately, sitting at one of the outside tables, under the awning, near the pool. She was chatting to three other women about her age – and with the same Botoxed appearance. He wondered what the collective term for WAGs would be... A waggery? A bitchery?

Jay was mindful that the hostess might still be watching him and that he needed to find a table quickly. Preferably one with a solitary woman sitting at it. His eyes rested on a table that had been recently vacated, with a coffee pot, cup and saucer, and a plate dusted with pastry flakes. That would do nicely. He hastened over and sat down. If any staff members looked his way, he was just a guy waiting for his friend to return from the restroom, or from paying the bill.

He picked up a cup from a neighbouring empty table as he breezed past, sat down and placed it on the table before him. It held the dregs of a cappuccino in there. Perfect. Now,

satisfied that he was a touch less conspicuous, at least for
the next few minutes, Jay made like he was gazing absently
out at the pool and the cordoned-off beach area beyond.
But, in fact, he was watching Kerry Wakefield. Closely.

◇

SHE WAS busy gossiping with her friends; all four of them
were drinking frothy smoothie cocktails through straws. A
waiter approached their table with a tray of plates. It was
salads all round, clearly a light lunch. The waiter lingered.
There were questions. Jay could guess the kind...

*Is this* vegan *mayo?*

*Is there any mango on my plate? I'm allergic to...*

*Hey, can you get me some....*

Christ, those women looked like hard work.

Jay decided the distraction of the waiter was something
he could work to his advantage. He got up, sunk a hand into
his pocket and felt for the small, slim micro tracker.

He strolled onto the patio, as though he was heading
towards the private beach to look at the gently rolling surf.
As he approached Kerry's table, he eased the tracker out of
his pocket and veered slightly to the right, so that he'd be
walking closely behind her chair. Kerry had removed her
jacket and placed it over the back of her seat. Perfect.

As he drew closer, he needed a reason to linger, if only
for a moment.

'Mate?' Jay said to the waiter, resting a hand on the back
of Kerry's seat.

The harried-looking man glanced his way.

'Can I have the bill, yeah? When you've got a moment?'
said Jay.

The waiter smothered an irritable frown. 'Of course. What table are you at, sir?'

Jay turned to point at the table he'd been sitting at a moment ago. He let go of the tracker at the same time. The tracker missed Kerry's pocket by an inch and settled on the seat of her chair. Just beside her bottom.

Just then, she sat back and her bare shoulder brushed the knuckles of his fist, which was still resting on the back of her chair. She twisted in her seat to look up at him irritably. Their eyes met.

'Hey? Do you mind?' she snapped, glaring at *his* hand on the back of *her* chair.

He withdrew his hand quickly. 'Sorry, love.'

'Your table, sir?' asked the waiter again.

'Errr... that one,' said Jay, pointing.

'I'll have someone come over.' The waiter turned back to the women to ask if there was anything else they needed, while Jay quickly stepped away and headed towards the beach.

*Shit.* He wondered if she could feel the tracker beneath her bum. If so, was she going to pick it up? Inspect it closely? Or just throw it away?

Well, that was 350 bucks wasted if she decided to toss it into the pool for good luck.

*And double shit.* He'd committed his first, unforgivable blunder.

He'd made direct eye contact with her.

## 10

'You clumsy fuckin' twat,' Jay muttered to himself as he angrily clicked through the channels on his motel TV. Mid-afternoon was apparently the time for Old Testament Bible stories and deals on garden furniture.

Earlier, he'd idled by the pool at La Casa Amarilla for a while, wondering whether or not he'd be able to retrieve his expensive micro tracker. However, it had quickly become apparent that Kerry and her friends had settled in for the afternoon, so Jay had decided to cut his losses and bail out before she could spot him and get another good look at his stupid face.

Once was bad enough.

Not for the first time, he questioned whether he'd bitten off more than he could chew. Ronni had bigged him up massively to Mack as a 'pro with experience'. Of course she had – she wanted whatever commission she was getting, and, as far as Mack was concerned, he was paying top dollar for that pro.

Shit. And Jay had been doing so well: fitting the car

tracker, blagging his way into an exclusive members-only club... He'd been on a goddamned roll. He'd even begun to convince himself that he was Ethan Hunt on his very own Mission Impossible.

*Well*, he thought, *I've muffed it all up now, haven't I?*

Would Kerry go home tonight and tell Mack she'd had to deal with a rude Brit who didn't understand the concept of personal space?

He'd been getting too bloody cocky, that was the problem. Eight months at McGuire's PI agency and a couple of courses under his belt – and all of a sudden he was an expert?

*Bloody idiot.*

He wanted to hear Sam's voice... and it really didn't matter what she said, whether it was a bollocking for not answering her calls and texts or tearful relief that they were finally talking again.

Jay powered up his personal phone and was about to call when a nagging doubt stopped him.

*MI5.*

Those sneaky, snooping bastards with all their sneaky, snooping software. Had they lobbed something onto his phone so they could listen to his calls? Check in every now and then to make sure that he, Boyd, Sam, Charlotte and Emma hadn't suddenly formed some dangerous terrorist cell?

But then... he'd managed to leave the UK and enter the US without setting off international alarm bells. Maybe using his own phone would undo that good luck?

He picked up his burner phone instead. It would show up on Sam's screen as an unknown ID. But she'd *know* it was him. She'd answer, for sure.

He tapped in '*67' to withhold his number, then followed

it with the UK country code and Sam's number. He listened as the call blipped and bleeped through various digital gateways, until finally it started to ring...

## 11

The microwave was old and noisy and droned like an old Lancaster Bomber. Okeke thought she'd noticed an intermittent pulsing coming from it for the first time – probably a new warning that it was finally time to shell out for a replacement before the bloody thing exploded.

But then it pinged... Job done. And that buzzing kept on going. By the time she'd figured out that it was her phone vibrating and rushed into the lounge to pick it up, the call had ended.

She checked the screen to see who'd called: *Unknown*.

Okeke knew instantly who it was. Jay. It *had* to be.

'Fuck!' she snapped. She unlocked her phone and quickly tapped out a message to him.

Jay? Was that you? Withheld number? Try again. I'll pick up this time!

She turned up the call volume on her phone, then sat down on the couch and stared at the TV. It was just gone 8 p.m. She was catching up on last month's *Pottery*

*Throwdown*, but it was impossible to concentrate, knowing that Jay had tried to call her.

She waited fifteen minutes, her dinner growing luke-warm in the microwave.

'Shit', she muttered eventually. Maybe it hadn't been Jay after all. More likely a cold-caller trying to sell her loft insulation.

Okeke pocketed her phone, returned to the kitchen and programmed the microwave for another minute to reheat her dinner.

As it droned noisily once more, she forced herself to stop worrying about the big idiot for five minutes. He was a grown adult. He was going to have to look after himself now.

## 12

That Friday afternoon, Jay found Mack Wakefield sitting in a booth at the back of O'Connor's – a supposedly British pub, just off Elizabeth Avenue. It seemed that 'British' and 'Irish' were interchangeable terms for whoever had decorated the place. There were Toby jugs hanging on the wall next to silver horseshoes and clovers. Jay noticed a portrait of the late queen hanging on the wall next to a photo of Gerry Adams, who was shaking hands with a sandy-haired US President of decades past. The poor queen would be turning in her grave.

Mack was watching football on a wall-mounted TV. *Proper* football, that is... the kind that involved kicking a proper spherical ball around a pitch.

Jay made his way over. 'All right?' he said.

Mack looked up. 'Ah... Jay, mate. I'm just watching Everton giving Coventry an absolute spanking.'

Jay glanced at the screen. Everton were three–nil up.

'I'm gonna grab a pint,' said Jay. 'Can I get you anything?'

Mack nodded at his nearly full pint. 'I'm OK, but get me some pork scratchings, will you?'

Jay returned five minutes later, set down his beer and tossed a couple of packets of pork scratchings onto the table.

'I'm surprised they've got those here,' he commented.

'They import them specially,' replied Mack, as he opened the packets. 'Adds to the ambience, right?' He glanced around at the decor. A framed tartan quilt hung on one wall and a red dragon was in a frame on the wall opposite. 'Though, fuck me, I dunno which bit of Britain this is supposed to be.'

Jay glanced around. 'Looks like all of it to me.'

'How're you doing?' asked Mack. 'All settled in now you've had a week?'

'Yeah. All good,' said Jay.

'So...' Mack tossed a piece of pork gristle into his mouth. 'How's my soon-to-be ex-missus been behaving this week?'

'So far, nothing unduly suspicious,' replied Jay. 'She's been to the salon a couple of times, lunched with her friends three times this week, done a bit of shopping. That's about it.'

Mack pulled a face. He looked disappointed. 'Well, it's early days yet.'

'Right.' Jay nodded.

He had felt anxious turning up empty-handed at their first update meeting. He had some pictures on his phone of Kerry having coffee with her friends, of her inspecting a dress in a very expensive boutique, of her getting in (or out) of her Lotus. He had them to hand so that he could show Mack he was actually doing his job. But there was nothing that Mack was going to get excited about.

'Look, uh, Mack,' said Jay after a moment of silence. 'One thing that's a bit of a problem is that a lot of the places where she goes are, you know, *exclusive*. Members-only kind of thing.'

Mack nodded. 'And?'

'Well...' Jay shrugged. 'I can't get in. So I can't see what she's getting up to when she's inside. I mean... I managed to blag my way into one restaurant at the start of the week.'

'Which one?' asked Mack.

'La Casa Amarilla.'

He nodded. 'They're letting things slip there.'

'But, since then, I've had no luck,' Jay added. 'I'm stuck with snooping from the street.'

Mack snorted. 'You're the *pro*, sunshine. Go and figure it out.'

Jay nodded. 'Um, see... there *is* a way I can still keep tabs on her. I've got this...' He dug into the pocket of his khakis and pulled out his Wi-Fi bug and set it on the table.

Mack looked at it. 'A key fob?' His face suddenly creased into smile. 'Or are you gonna tell me that's a spy gadget?'

Jay nodded. 'It's a bug. Ideally I need it dropped into her bag,' he explained.

He pulled out his burner phone, swiped to the bug app and showed it to Mack.

'I can listen live on my phone,' he explained, 'record the audio or download the recordings using the app.'

Mack picked up the bug and inspected it closely. 'Amazing! Bloody incredible what they can pack into these things nowadays, eh?'

Jay nodded. 'The thing is, I need your help.'

Mack narrowed his eyes. 'I'm not paying *me* to spy on her. I'm paying *you*.'

Jay nodded again, sheepishly this time. 'I just can't get close to her. I've already had one direct interaction with her.' He relayed the moment at La Casa Amarilla. 'She made eye contact. Once is not good. Twice is bad. Three times you're pretty much burned.'

'That's a thing, is it? *Three times?*' Mack asked.

'Yeah. Plus, look... you've got a better idea what jackets, shoulder bags, handbags she's likely to wear the most.'

'Hmmm...' Mack rumbled as he leaned back in his seat. 'I'm not too keen on having listening devices wandering in my gaff, Jay.' He leant forward. 'I have business meetings at home. Ones that are *very commercially sensitive*. You get my drift?'

Jay nodded, then tapped on his phone and turned it round to show Mack the screen once more. 'On the app I can set up blind zones and active zones. The bug knows when it's outside or inside a zone and will either wake up and alert me or stay dormant, depending on what you've told it to do. So, look, I can set up your home as a blind zone. Whenever Kerry steps inside, it switches off and I stop hearing what's going on. You want me to do that?'

Mack nodded emphatically. 'Yes! I would bloody want!'

'No problem,' Jay assured him.

'So how would I know if you changed that?' he asked. 'Hmm? How do I know you haven't switched it back on and started listening in on me and Kerry in our home?'

'I wouldn't,' replied Jay, managing to sound a little hurt. 'You're my client. I've been hired to spy on your wife, not you.'

Mack raised a brow, not entirely comforted.

'In any case, I'm bound by client confidentiality, Mack. Right? Anything I learn about you...' Jay mimed locking his lips and tossing away the key.

Mack still didn't seem entirely convinced.

'Look,' said Jay, 'if I get a bad review from a client – say, on Trustpilot – I'll never get any more work as a PI, will I?'

Mack shook his head and chuckled. 'It all boils down to

that these days, doesn't it? What number of stars you got in a review?'

Jay nodded. 'It really does.'

Mack picked up the bug and checked it over. 'All right then. Why not? She's got a Hermès bag that she uses most of the time, even though she's got about a hundred others. I can slip it into a side pocket.'

Jay sipped his beer. 'Once she steps out of your home, I'll get an alert and then I can remotely listen to whatever she's doing.'

Mack glanced down at the devices in his hands. 'Is it expensive, this kit?'

'Very,' replied Jay. 'Please don't lose either.'

Mack nodded, then tucked them both into the breast pocket of the flowery shirt he was wearing and buttoned down the flap.

'So…' Jay looked around the virtually empty pub. Apart from the barman and one other patron propping up the bar and watching the football match, they had it to themselves. 'This seems a good place to meet next week. Same time?'

'Can't do next Friday,' said Mack. 'I've got business meetings going on over that whole weekend at the house. How about the Monday after?'

Jay nodded. 'You're the boss. Whenever you want's good for me.'

'Monday, then – that'll be the twenty-ninth of April,' Mack confirmed. 'This place is even quieter on a Monday.' He glanced at Jay and grinned. 'If you can imagine that.'

∾

JAY GOT a three-word text from Mack at about five in the evening as he was having an early supper in the diner.

Packages safely deposited.

Good. Going forward, he'd be able to hear what Kerry was up to, even if he lost sight of her. He couldn't help having a bit of a play with the app on his phone as he ate alone. Right now, checking its location on the map, the bug was within Malcolm Wakefield's designated blind zone. Kerry was home.

Jay's finger hovered above the 'DISABLE BLIND ZONE' button. He was sorely tempted to activate the bug, if only to test how good it was at picking up sound. Mack would never know he'd done that, and Jay would get an idea of how effective it was.

But... it wouldn't be *professional*.

Jay withdrew his finger and went back to eating his supper.

## 13

On Saturday morning, at eight o'clock, Jay's phone buzzed him awake to let him know that Kerry Wakefield had moved out of the blind zone. He checked the car-tracker app and saw that her Lotus was still at the Wakefields' house. So she was driving a different car, or she was being driven. He switched to the bug's app and activated the mic.

The audio that suddenly flooded into his headphones was piercingly loud and he frantically dialled down the volume on his phone. He could hear music, which he vaguely recognised as 'Poker Face' by Lady Gaga.

In the background, he could hear a male voice and recognised it as Mack's. The music abruptly stopped.

*'No, we're not putting that shit on, Kerry.'*

*'Aw, come on – don't be such a grumpy old man.'*

*'My car, my choice, love.'*

Jay heard him fumbling, rustling. Then a radio station came on – a talk show, or maybe a news station. The volume was low.

Kerry sighed like a teenager. *'Oh God... Boring.'*

Jay decided to mute the bug. She was with Mack, so there was nothing to be gained by listening in, plus flipping the device back to sleep mode would preserve its charge.

He dragged himself out of bed, got dressed and emerged from his motel room, stepping out onto the terrace. Jorge was sitting outside, wearing a T-shirt, shorts and flip-flops with white socks. He was playing with his action figures once again. Sylvie, Jay could see through the diner's window, was already working the breakfast shift.

'All right there, little man?' he said to the boy.

Jorge smiled up at him. 'Morning, Mr Jay.'

'You had any breakfast yet, Jorge?'

The boy shook his head.

'Fancy a McBreakfast?' Jay said, nodding at the McDonald's across the forecourt.

∾

JAY KEPT a watchful eye on his phone's screen while they ate in silence. The bug was still in sleep mode, conserving its battery. It looked like Kerry was now in the middle of a golf course – with Mack, Jay assumed.

'You playing a game on your phone, Mr Jay?' Jorge asked.

Jay looked up at Jorge, whose cheeks bulged like a hamster's as his mouth worked on the Egg McMuffin he was holding.

'Yeah, kind of,' he replied.

'What is it?' Jorge asked.

'You know *Pokémon Go*?'

Jorge grinned with his mouth full. 'Gotta catch 'em all!' he spluttered.

'Right. I'm sort of playing a game like that.'

Jay slurped his coffee. His Sausage McMuffin was long

gone and he was toying with the idea of ordering himself another. Jorge, on the other hand, was a meticulous chewer and a painfully slow eater.

'How's your mum?' Jay asked.

Jorge finally finished his mouthful and then slurped on some Coke. 'Stressy.'

It was odd. Jorge sounded just like any other American kid, while his mum had a strong Hispanic accent. He guessed Jorge must have learned all or most of his English from the TV.

They lingered at the McDonald's for most of the morning, both of them getting their money's worth out of the play area. While Jorge plummeted repeatedly down the slide, returning every now and then, hot and sweaty, for a slurp of his Coke, Jay kept one eye on the boy and the other on his phone.

As it was, nothing much happened. Mack and Kerry spent the morning and lunchtime at the golf club, then returned home. Jay drove Jorge to a public part of the beachfront – DuBois Park – and let him splash around in the warm water, before returning him to his motel room for Sylvie's mid-afternoon hour-long break.

~

THAT EVENING, after taking himself out for supper at a downtown noodle bar, Jay returned to Jupiter Plaza. He paused outside the motel door and gazed across the car park at the flickering lights of the bar, Tanners. He was tempted to round the night off with a cold beer, but instead told himself that he'd probably be better staying completely sober and car-ready, just in case.

An alert pinged on his phone. Kerry was outside the

blind zone. He checked the car-tracker app and saw that her Lotus was moving. Hurrying into his room, he switched to the bug app and activated the mic.

Over his phone's speaker, he could hear the soft purr of her car's engine, but nothing else. There was no Lady Gaga and no Mack this time. Jay listened and watched the tracker pin as it inched its way along Rosewood Boulevard, finally stopping in a car park, in front of a 7-Eleven.

*Okay*, Jay thought, *so she's got a late-night hankering for Oreos or something?* He heard her pull on the handbrake and turn the engine off. Then he heard some very loud rustling.

*That's her fumbling in her handbag.* He hoped to God she wasn't going to find the bug, that Mack had done a good job of burying it at the bottom. The rustling suddenly ceased and was followed by a long pause.

*Shit. She's found it.*

Then he heard her voice. 'Ryan, it's me.'

*Ryan? Who the hell was Ryan?*

Jay hit 'Record' on his phone , then jotted the name down.

'Yeah...' said Kerry. 'I can't talk for long. I told Mack that I was desperate for some chocolate.' She chuckled nervously. 'So I'd better go back with something.'

There was a pause as she listened.

'Monday?' she replied. 'Sure. What time? Um... He's got a morning Zoom call at eleven with his business guy back in the UK. He's usually a couple of hours on the call with him.'

*Halle-fucking-lujah!* At last he had something he could play to Mack. He made a note of the time and day.

'Same place?' she said.

Jay held his breath, hoping she'd say the 'where' out loud.

'No?' she replied. 'Where then?'

Another pause. 'Pan's Garden? Where's that?'

Bingo. Jay grinned as he scribbled that down.

'Okay. I'll be there... Sure... I'll be super careful.'

Another pause.

'Uh-huh. Just nervous. You know? Listen, Ryan... I swear he's got his eye on me. He was more chilled when we were over in the UK, but now we're home again I think he suspects I'm seeing someone or something...' There was a brief silence before she continued. 'I'm getting really nervous. I'm not sure I can carry on seeing –' She listened for a while, then: 'Right.' She sounded unhappy. Almost tearful. 'Okay.'

The call ended and he heard the deafening rustling again as, presumably, she dropped her phone back into her bag, then he heard the car door slam and the bleep of the locks being activated.

Jay stopped the recording and smiled. He'd recorded her saying 'Ryan' several times, and that Monday meeting sure as hell sounded promising. If he could just snap a picture of her kissing her fancy man, then *ker-bloody-ching*.

# 14

Pan's Garden, where Kerry would be meeting Ryan, was a public park on Palm Beach island, thirteen miles south of where the Wakefields lived. The park was very small, about half an acre, but with plenty of nooks among the bushes, shrubs, trees and wildflowers. Jay arrived at 10 a.m. when the park opened, an hour before Kerry and Ryan were due to meet, to familiarise himself with the place.

It had a very zen vibe going on. There was a bronze statue of a naked cherub with two dope pipes, accompanied by the sound of solar-powered mini-water features and soft meditation music that was being played around the walled garden from a speaker somewhere.

There was no entrance fee, just a suggested donation of $5 at the kiosk by the gates.

Jay only had twenties on him and was buggered if he was going to donate one of those. He patted himself down for some loose change and managed to muster a dollar and a quarter in loose change. He tossed them into the money basket as he entered the park, the rattling indicating that he'd at least thrown something in.

A sweet old lady was sitting inside the kiosk, reading a paperback. She glanced up from her book at the sound of his coins landing in the donation basket.

'Good morning, sir,' she croaked.

'Mornin',' he replied.

'Oh, are you British?' She beamed and lifted her book up. 'I'm just reading a detective book set in Britain. You know a place called Edin-burrow?'

Jay smiled at her delightfully wayward mispronunciation.

'Edinburgh,' he replied, pronouncing it as *Eh-dun-bruh*. 'Yeah, it's in Scotland.' He looked around. 'Is it normally this quiet in here?'

She shrugged. 'It's a Monday morning, my dear, and I've only just unlocked the front gate.' She beamed again. 'You're our first visitor today.'

He nodded. 'Good.'

'It's a peaceful spot,' she said. 'A nice place to get away from all the hurly-burly out there.'

He glanced over his shoulder. *Hurly burly?* They were in a peaceful suburb, lined with hibiscus plants and palm trees.

'Do you mind if I just head in?' he asked her.

She nodded. 'You go on and have a wander, my dear. Recharge your spiritual batteries.'

Jay turned to his left, deciding to take a clockwise route along the terracotta-brick path to get his bearings. He wanted to identify where Kerry and Ryan were likely to pick to sit together. Presumably it would be somewhere with a bit of privacy, someplace where they could get intimate, if that's what they were planning.

Five minutes later he'd completed his recce – the walled garden, despite its deceptive dead ends and nooks really was tiny – and he was back beside the kiosk and the bronze sculpture.

The woman looked up from her book. 'You leaving already?' she asked.

'No. I just wanted to see what's what,' Jay replied. He pointed ahead. 'I'm gonna go and have a sit-down, I reckon.'

She returned to her detective book and Jay headed over towards a gazebo in the middle of the garden that gave him shelter from the sun and a pretty good 360-view of most of the grounds. He'd have eyes on the entrance, the kiosk and the bronze statue of the naked kid smoking two crack pipes. He'd also be able to see when Kerry arrived and which way she decided to head with her man.

Jay had brought a glossy gossip magazine from a convenience store to hide behind. Plus, he'd put on a baseball cap and sunglasses, given that she'd eyeballed him once already. He sat down in the shade, opened it and made a show of casually flicking through it. It was only twenty-five past ten. He checked the car-tracker app – Kerry was just turning onto the Interstate 95. She was about half an hour away, still. He'd definitely overestimated how much time he'd need to check the place out.

～

Jay was in danger of being sucked into a salacious article about the Kardashians when he reminded himself he was meant to be watching the entrance. Just as he glanced up, he spotted Kerry Wakefield enter the gardens.

She was on her phone. But without her handbag.

*Bollocks.* No handbag meant no bug.

She was lingering beside the gates, presumably telling Ryan that she was here. Jay watched as she finished talking, pocketed her phone, looked around and then strode purposefully towards the south side of the garden, where, thanks to his earlier recce, Jay knew there was a bench beneath the low-hanging branches of a willow tree.

Very discreet and tucked away. Good. She and Ryan would hopefully feel emboldened and secluded enough to indulge in a little tongue hockey.

Jay checked his watch. It was five to eleven. So far this morning there had been two visitors to Pan's Garden. Ryan, presumably, would be the third.

At bang on eleven, a man entered the park alone. He appeared to be in his mid-thirties, athletic and well groomed, with dark hair and a nicely defined jaw. If Jay was pressed for a descriptor, he'd have said it was the kind of jaw that wouldn't look out of place on a junior doctor in *Grey's Anatomy*. Or a Gilette ad.

Ryan strode along the terracotta path towards where Kerry was waiting for him. Jay waited until he'd turned into the secluded area beneath the willow tree before getting up and emerging from the deep shade of the gazebo.

Jay crept along the path until he reached the point where it branched off towards the willow tree. He stepped off the path and into a flower bed, from which tall phallic-looking pink flowers emerged and swayed gently in the breeze like patiently waiting triffids. He carefully wriggled his way into a dense thicket of pampas grass and some other belligerent thorny shrub that scratched and scraped at his bare calves, until finally he could see the pair of them through the foliage.

Kerry and Ryan were sitting close to each other on the bench.

Jay reached into his pocket, pulled out his phone, swiped on the camera app and began filming them. He zoomed in on their faces, his eyes focused on the screen. Kerry was doing all the talking. Ryan was shaking his head, nodding, then shaking his head again.

Then Ryan looked down at something. Jay angled his phone to see what had caught Ryan's attention. It was her phone. She was holding it out to Ryan, almost thrusting it at him as though she wanted him to take it from her.

It wasn't the same one she'd been using in the entrance, Jay noted. That one had a red leather case.

*What's going on here?* he wondered.

Jay aimed his camera back at Kerry's face. She'd started sobbing. Her shoulders heaved and her head drooped. She looked like a woman hearing some bad news.

*Okay, I wasn't expecting that. Maybe it's the secret phone they used for each other.*

He watched as Ryan reached for her hand and held it in his, caressing it softly. Comforting her. This encounter very much had the look and feel of a him-dumping-her scenario. Jay continued to film them as Ryan ran a hand up Kerry's bare arm and squeezed her shoulder affectionately.

So there it was... Mack had been quite right. His trophy wife *had* been cheating on him, but now, it seemed, her studmuffin was calling time on her. Jay wondered if that news would change Mack's intentions towards her. If Mack decided to confront her with the break-up footage Jay was getting right now – and if Kerry demonstrated contrition and batted her eyelids enough – would Mack reluctantly give her a second chance?

Malcolm Wakefield didn't seem like the kind of bloke who handed out second chances.

Ryan gave Kerry a hug, a peck on the cheek and got up from the bench.

She glanced up at him, rubbing tears from her eyes.

He spoke. It looked to Jay as though he'd said, '*You gonna be all right?*'

She nodded unconvincingly.

Ryan emerged from beneath the shadows of the willow tree onto the terracotta path and left Pan's Garden. Jay continued filming Kerry. Presumably Mack was far less interested in who Ryan was, and more interested in how his wife felt about him.

She was still sobbing. Jay stopped recording. He had what he needed.

A few moments later, Kerry got up and left the gardens too, the confident swagger she'd had the other day at Marielle's and La Casa Amarilla a thing of the past. She seemed as though she had the weight of the world resting on her shoulders. She looked defeated.

## 15

Kerry Wakefield kept herself extremely busy for the next few days. Jay guessed that was how she was dealing with her broken heart – checking in with her girlfriends, getting in some serious gym time.

*She shouldn't have been cheating, then,* Jay told himself time and again as he studied her listless face from afar, watching the sudden thrown-on smile for her friends, before her expression fell back into a forlorn pondering. From what his bug was picking up, she hadn't mentioned the break-up to anyone. He had no doubt that that kind of gossip would be all over Palm Beach within a day.

Still, he felt a little sorry for her, though it was hard to know where exactly to place his sympathy. She'd been cheating on Mack, that much was obvious. She married him because he was rich and because he could give her the lifestyle she wanted. In Jay's opinion, it couldn't possibly be down to his looks or his charm. But she just looked so sad.

He wondered how Mack would respond to the footage when he showed it to him on Monday: Kerry sobbing her heart out over some stallion who had a face that could sell veal to vegetarians. Surely that had to be painful to watch.

*Christ.* Would Mack cry? That would be bloody awkward. Maybe he'd just be mightily pissed off. On balance, Jay wasn't sure which was better. He hoped to God that Mack wasn't the type to take his rage out on Kerry physically. While this job was an absolute gift, Jay wondered how he'd feel returning to the UK with $90K only to find out that Kerry Wakefield was being beaten black and blue by her husband just as his plane took off.

As the week progressed, Jay couldn't help feeling slightly guilty that he was continuing to stalk the poor woman, recording everything she said and did. And, maybe, that's how he messed up – pondering the rights and wrongs of what he was doing – because, on the Thursday, he blew his cover...

∾

HE WATCHED Kerry pull into the VIP parking area of the Jupiter Beach Galleria, hop out and head inside.

Jay parked further away, then ambled to VIP section, which was overlooked by CCTV cameras and one very bored security guard on the far side, who was sitting on a plastic garden chair and thumbing his phone. Jay decided this was probably as good an opportunity as he was going to get to change the battery on the car tracker.

It would be a thirty-second job. If that.

As he approached Kerry's car, he ducked out of view between her Lotus and the neighbouring SUV. On all fours, he groped beneath the rear bumper of her car and finally found the fag-box-sized tracker. Its attachment magnet was insanely strong, but with a hard tug he wrenched it off.

Within a few seconds, Jay had replaced the car tracker with his second one, fully charged and good to go. He managed to attach it to the underbelly of her Lotus but, on examining it, decided it was protruding too low and might get knocked off by a speed bump. He slid back under, wrenched it loose and placed it in a recess where it stuck out less and was just starting to pull himself back out from underneath the car when he heard the soft scrape of a shoe. He twisted on the ground to see bare feet and beautifully manicured toenails, in expensive sandals, followed by ankles and the hem of Kerry's flowery summer dress.

'What the fuck do you think you're doing?' she barked.

Jay wriggled out from beneath her Lotus, knocking the sunglasses off his head as he emerged, hands raised in apology.

'Uh...I uh... I dropped my...' *Shit*. He couldn't think of a damned thing. Fortunately, he spotted his sunglasses, which had landed just behind the car's wheel arch. He picked them up and waved them at Kerry. 'I dropped *these*.'

'Why were you fucking about under my car?' she asked.

Jay did his best to look apologetic. 'I told you. I dropped these and they landed under your car. Stupid of me, I know...' he said, slowly getting to his feet.

Her brows locked together as she studied him. 'Wait,' she said. 'I know you. Yeah... I've seen you somewhere before.' Her frown deepened.

'Nah,' replied Jay. 'Nah, I don't think so, love.' He leant heavily on his Danny Dyer accent, ready to launch into some meandering bollocks about being just a simple tourist *'avin' a bit of a wander-abaht.*

Kerry shook her head. 'No. No... I've definitely seen you,' she replied, her voice hardening. 'Have you been *following* me?'

'What?' Jay's eyes bulged. 'What? No!'

She pulled open the driver-side door, reached into the side pocket and produced a phone. She held it up at him and, before he could turn away, she'd taken his picture.

'So now I've got your face on my phone, asshole.' She waggled the phone at him.

'Hey, I was just getting me sunglasses back!' Jay protested.

Then he noticed something. The phone. It didn't have a red cover. It was the other one: the one she'd been trying to press into Ryan's hands on Monday in Pan's Garden.

'If I set eyes on you again,' she threatened, 'this is going up on all of my socials... and I'll go to the police and I'll tell them you're some goddamn pervert who won't leave me alone!'

'Listen, love,' Jay tried again. 'Like I said –'

'No. *You* listen,' Kerry spat. 'You need to back up from my car right now or I'm dialling 911!' She tapped the phone's screen to show that she was deadly serious.

Jay raised his hands again in complete surrender.

'Bloody hell! All right! All right!' He turned and strode away from Kerry.

He wondered if he should demonstrate a bit of righteous indignation, shout something back at her, because if he had been just Touristy McTouristFace having a nosy at the nice cars and had clumsily kicked his glasses beneath her very nice red Lotus, then he'd be quite rightly angry.

Instead he beat a hasty retreat.

## 16

'Might as well have stayed a bouncer,' Jay grumbled sulkily to himself.

Jorge looked up from playing with his action figures for a moment, then resumed the important Final Battle Between Good and Evil.

*What a fuckin' idiot*, Jay continued scolding himself. What he *should* have done is follow her into the mall and checked that she was busy trying on a dress, or ordering herself a latte, before doubling back to her car to fiddle with it.

It was basic. Bloody. Common. Sense.

Now, not only would she be watching for his face every time she set out from her seafront mansion, she was probably going to tell Mack all about the creepy English dude too. Jay glanced at the burner phone in his lap. That's what he was waiting for: a call from Mack. A very pissed-off Mack. Jay could well imagine what he'd say: *'Fucking amateur! I thought you said you were a bloody pro!'*

In all likelihood, Mack would tell him that the contract was over and he could stop wasting his time. That Jay could damn well piss off home and go back to tracking down stray cats for old ladies.

He wondered whether he should give Mack a call – beat her to it, so to speak – and let Mack know he'd been burned. That, as a *professional* PI, having been compromised, he couldn't in all good conscience continue with the job. Jay decided that was probably the best way to go. Because surely, *surely*, she was going to mention it over dinner tonight. He got up out of his deckchair and headed into his motel room.

Mack answered quickly with a gruff 'Yeah?'

'It's Jay.'

'I know.'

Mack sounded pissed. *Shit*, Jay thought. She must have spoken to him already.

'I've got bad news, Mack...' he said.

There was a pause.

'Kerry caught me fumbling around under her car,' Jay continued.

There was another pause.

'Are you telling me she knows you're a PI?' Mack asked.

'No,' Jay replied. 'Actually, I think she thinks I'm some sort of pervert. But the point is, she knows my face and she'll be looking for it every time she goes out. Wigs, fake beards, hats, sunglasses ain't going to cut it any more.'

'Bollocks,' huffed Mack. He sounded more disappointed than annoyed.

'Right,' said Jay. 'I gotta be professional about this, Mack... I can't do the job you hired me to do. Not any more. Not now I'm burned.'

Mack let out a long sigh.

'But I do have some intel for you,' Jay went on. 'She *was* seeing a bloke called Ryan, but she's not now.' Jay relayed to him what he'd seen in Pan's Garden and told Mack that he had it all recorded on his phone.

'Fuck! I knew it!' Mack hissed. 'That explains a lot. She's been grumping around the house all week with a face like a smacked arse.'

'Obviously, I'll write this all up in my report, before I head back. And I'll give you what I recorded on a memory stick,' Jay said.

'Yeah, that'll be useful down the line,' Mack replied. 'But hold on, Jay... don't pack your bags just yet. I still want you around. Look, Kerry's as dumb as a rock. You might have to get a bit more creative to keep from being spotted, but she's no Sherlock Holmes.'

'But it's over with her and this bloke,' said Jay. 'She's –'

'It might be or it might not be,' Mack said. 'Or she might be about to chase down another bit of cock. Who knows what she's capable of. I want you to keep watching her.'

'You're sure?' Jay asked, hardly believing his luck.

'Yeah...' Mack paused and lowered his voice slightly. 'I *like* workin' with blokes I can trust, see? You was *honest with me* just now. Telling me she'd clocked you when you didn't have to. You could have lied, mate. But you didn't. I respect that.'

Jay grinned to himself. That wasn't the response he'd been expecting from Mr Wakefield. 'Well, if you're sure...'

'I'm sure. Like I said, I like lads I can trust,' Mack said. 'Ain't much of that going around these days.'

'All right. Well, that's great. Thanks,' said Jay. 'What about our next update meeting? Do you still want to meet on Monday?'

'Hell yeah. I wanna see this bastard who was shagging her,' Mack said. 'And you know what? I wanna see her reaction when he dumped her.' He snorted. 'Bit of bloody karma, eh?'

Jay emerged a minute later from his motel room feeling relieved. Very relieved. Somehow his honesty about the rookie screw-up had resulted in him getting a big fat *attaboy* from Mack.

He sat in the deckchair and watched Jorge's Good Guy finish smashing the living daylights out of the Bad Guy.

From now on, Jay pondered, he was going to have to put more distance between himself and Kerry. And still keep doing his job.

It was easy money. The easiest he'd ever made.

A thought suddenly occurred to him. 'Hey, Jorge?'

Jorge stopped playing and looked up at him.

'Does your mum ever get a day off work?' Jay asked.

'Tuesdays. Sometimes,' Jorge replied.

'What about this coming Tuesday, after the weekend? Is she off then, do you know?'

He nodded.

Jay smiled. 'How would you an' your mum like to go to Disney World or something?'

Jorge's loud whooping turned several heads across the car park.

## 17

It was later that night, while he was watching the news on Fox – the news anchors were debating President Biden's re-election campaign bid and Trump's trial – that there was a knock on his motel-room door.

Warily, Jay got up from his bed and approached it. Earlier, he'd been watching a documentary about criminals who targeted tourists, particularly those with obvious hire cars parked outside their motel rooms.

'Hello?' he called.

'It is me? Sylvie!' came the reply.

Jay opened the door to find her clutching a brown grocery bag in her skinny arms. She was still wearing her pastel-pink uniform from the diner.

'Jorge told me about Disney. I wish to say thank you very, very much,' she said. She nodded at her grocery bag. 'I have this for you.'

Jay took the bag and peered inside. It contained a six-pack of ice-cold beers and a couple of packets of nuts and crisps.

'I know it is not much, but...' Sylvia said tentatively.

Jay smiled. The cold beers would do very nicely. 'Nah...
it's perfect, thanks.'

Sylvia pressed her lips together and looked as though
she was about to cry.

'You okay?' he asked.

She nodded quickly and swiped at her eyes. 'You are so
very kind to Jorge and me.'

'Don't worry about it,' Jay replied. 'I've got the time spare
and it's been fun.'

'But Disney World,' she whispered. 'It is so, so *expensive*.'

'It's not that bad,' he replied. Then he added, 'I've always
wanted to visit, but I'd look a right mug going on my
own, eh?'

He set the grocery bag down on his bed and pulled out a
couple of beers. 'Will you join me?' he asked.

Sylvie raised a solitary finger. 'Only one. I must start
early tomorrow.'

They took their beers outside, onto the porch. He pulled
up a deckchair for her and she sat down. He settled into the
deckchair beside her, unscrewed the cap on his bottle and
clinked it against hers.

'Cheers,' he said, smiling.

'*Salud*,' she replied.

He took a hefty and welcome slug of cold beer, then
wiped his lips. They sat in silence for a moment, gazing at
the empty car park, which was illuminated by fizzing amber
lights and the blue glow of the petrol station's sign. He
sighed and listened contentedly to the distant sound of
passing traffic and the steady chirruping of cicadas.

'Why are you here in America?' he asked eventually.
Instantly realising that might have sounded a bit harsh, he
added, 'This is no life for the both of you. You working all
hours, Jorge stuck in that motel room all day.'

Sylvie took a sip of her beer. 'It is this... or back home,' she said.

'Mexico can't be that bad, surely?' Jay asked.

'I am from *Guatemala*. But yes. It is bad there. *Very* bad. Dangerous.' She looked at him. 'There is no law. Corruption is everywhere. It is a little better with Arévalo, but still very dangerous.'

'Who's –' Jay began.

'Our new president. He wants to fix the corruption, the gangs, the violence. But...' She shook her head. 'Bad people are the ones who run our country. And this will never change.'

'What about Jorge's dad?' Jay asked. 'Is he back there? Or here? Can't he help you two?'

Sylvie's face hardened. 'I do not talk about the father.'

'Why not?' Jay asked.

'He is a bad man,' she whispered. 'I was only seventeen. He was our neighbour. An important man in our village. When I told the local police... what he did to me, they told him and then he sent a man to *kill* me.'

'Jesus!' gasped Jay.

'I had to run...' She paused. 'I go to Mexico. But there was no help, no money... I was homeless, so I entered America.'

'Sylvie... I'm so sorry,' Jay said.

'De nada.' She shook her head, taking another slug from the bottle. 'I am strong. I do what I can for Jorge. But...' She sighed. 'I cannot put him in a school, you see? Or ask for any help because... you know... the government...'

'Because they'd deport you?' Jay asked.

She nodded. 'I try to help Jorge. I teach him to read and write. And when I have time I teach him other things. But...' Her voice tailed off.

'But it's not enough,' he finished for her.

She shrugged.

Again, they sat in silence, sipping their cold beers. Then she spoke. 'Jorge likes you very much.'

He smiled. 'He's a good boy. A very smart boy.'

'Jay.' She glanced his way shyly. 'I also like you.' Her eyes lingered on his. 'Very much.'

If things had been different, if he'd been another Jay Turner in another universe, he might well have tiptoed through that figurative door she was holding open. But he wasn't. He was here, in this world, and he had Sam. Or he hoped he still did.

'Look,' he began awkwardly. 'Uh...I... uh... I like you too, Sylvie. But...'

She understood where he was going. Embarrassed, she quickly glanced away, finished her beer, set the empty bottle down on the terrace and got up.

'I should go to bed now. I get up early,' she said.

'Right.' Jay nodded, raising his beer. 'Thanks again for –'

She shook her head and squeezed his shoulder. 'No. I thank you for being kind to us. Jorge is so excited.' She smiled and nodded goodnight.

He watched her go and gave her a little wave as she opened the door to her room. She waved back and the door closed behind her, leaving Jay alone with his thoughts.

## 18

J ay took advantage of a quiet start to the morning to finally get some laundry done. When he'd packed and left Sam to go off on his epic get-rich quest, he'd stuffed only a week's worth of clothes into his bag and had been recycling those for the last seven weeks. The generous application of Lynx every morning just wasn't cutting it any more. As he watched his clothes tumble in the suds, he considered it might be time to buy some new ones. He had the money. He didn't need anything expensive or flash – a Walmart would do.

In fact, if he was going to continue to watch Kerry, albeit from a greater distance, a new set of clothes and a complete new look would be sensible. The clothes bouncing around in the washer were a mix of Marks and Spencer's, F&F and Next. He wondered if at some level undetectable to him, but obvious to anyone who 'did fashion', they'd marked him out as an outsider. It might not be a bad idea to buy some local clobber so he'd blend in better.

The slow tumble accelerated to a fast spin and there was nothing but a dizzying blur to watch, so Jay checked his phone to see if Kerry was on the move. She wasn't. Her pin was firmly stuck in her mansion. It was accurate to three yards, suggesting she'd chosen to stay at home this morning, probably lounging around the large kidney-shaped pool.

Jay switched from map to satellite mode and found himself staring at a pretty decent aerial view of the Wakefield residence. The garden looked to be about an acre and a half of well-kept lawn, shrubberies and flower beds, leading down to a patch of cordoned-off beach and a pontoon. Very nice. Like every other property on the seafront of Palm Beach, it had to be worth tens of millions.

Malcolm Wakefield, an ex-truck driver from Kent, had done remarkably well for himself. Jay respected for self-made blokes. Genuine rags-to-riches fellas. Sometimes you just had to take a chance in life. And this was exactly why he was here.

After taking his laundry back to his motel room and grabbing lunch at the diner, Jay looked up the nearest Walmart and drove over to kit himself out with a wardrobe of clothes that would hopefully make him look more *Floridian*.

He wasn't surprised to find that Walmart stocked a range of MAGA gear. The ubiquitous red baseball cap, T-shirts that loudly and proudly screamed a selection of three-word slogans. He threw a plain white baseball cap and a couple of T-shirts into his trolley, mindful that he'd not wear them in front of Sylvie or Jorge, and only while out and about in disguise. He added a pair of chinos, jeans, a smart jacket, trainers and a six-pack of pants and socks. Then, for good measure, he threw in a sleeveless khaki hunting jacket with pockets a-plenty.

Before heading for the checkout, he found himself lingering in the gun section, mesmerised by the large range of firearms and accessories on open display. It seemed utterly bizarre to him that he was looking at enough fire-power to equip a small army, but when he turned round he would be staring at pink plastic garden furniture and camping equipment.

~

THE NEXT DAY, Saturday, the shopping plaza was at its busiest. The car park was full of grey-haired customers: the gents migrating over towards either Captain Dan's Bait and Tackle or Jupiter Hardware, the ladies to Jenny's Beauty Palace.

Jay wore his new Walmart clothes and Jorge had already done an amusing double-take, telling him he looked like a gringo. Jay had laughed and told him he wanted to blend in.

'Just like a spy, Mr Jay?' Jorge had asked.

Jay had nodded, mock serious. 'I'm on a top-secret mission.'

Kerry's car-tracker pin was hopping around like a blow fly this morning. Jay recalled Mack had said something about having business meetings over the entire weekend. Presumably she was out and about getting supplies: beers, snacks or whatever Mack and his business buddies needed to fuel their various strategy meetings.

Jay watched as Kerry stopped at a Publix supermarket, then drove on to a place called Grey's Deli. She was then back at home for several hours over lunch. He wondered if Mack was putting her to work as his trophy wife. Jay also wondered whether Mack had decided to confront her about her infidelity. Maybe she was now scurrying around, playing the dutiful wife as penance for her sins.

By mid-afternoon, though, her marker was in motion

again and heading back to the mainland, before heading south on Interstate 95. Jay watched as her pin slid along the highway for five minutes before it occurred to him that the last time she'd taken that route, she'd been heading towards Pan's Garden.

Ten minutes later, Jay was in his Pathfinder and on the I-95, pushing at the frustratingly low speed limit to try to make up the distance between them.

$\sim$

HE PARKED on the street just outside Pan's Garden. There was a sign warning that he'd need a resident's permit to park or face a hefty fine. He decided to risk it. According to his tracker app, Kerry had the bug with her, and she was already in the garden, in the same place as before. This time round – and if she was meeting Ryan again – Jay would be able to hear them. As he crossed the road, he pushed in an earbud and activated the bug.

'– I really can't do this.' It was Kerry's voice. It sounded as though she was already with someone, hopefully Ryan.

Jay swept past the kiosk and quietly made his way along the terracotta path towards the willow tree.

'Listen, Kerry...' A man's voice, presumably Ryan. 'This is it. This is really important.'

Kerry's voice: 'There's so many of them. They scare me, Ryan.'

Jay stepped onto the flower bed, pushed his way through the phallic flowers and into the thicker pampas grass beyond. He crouched down, shuffling forward the last few feet until he had eyes on the couple, who were once again sitting on the bench beneath the willow tree.

Ryan's arm was around her shoulder. 'I know. It's a big

ask, Kerry... I know.'

'I'm terrified that Mack's going to find out,' she said.

'He won't,' Ryan replied. 'Not if you're careful. Not if you just act natural. Smile, flirt... do whatever Mack expects you to do for his guests, okay?'

'They're creepy, Ryan... I mean, really creepy. One in particular – Carl, I think – an old, skinny, short guy who just doesn't take his eyes off me.' A pause. 'I think he knows.' Kerry sounded tearful.

'Relax,' said Ryan. 'Men with power are like that. They think they own everyone. They think they can have any woman they want.'

'It's not like that. He's not... undressing me. He's...' She began to sob.

There was a loud rustling sound that obscured what she said next. Jay could see Kerry was fumbling in her handbag, looking for something.

'... time. There's so much...' Ryan was saying, but all Jay could hear was Kerry's damned hand fumbling around inside her bag.

Jay cursed under his breath. *Come on – put your pissing bag down, love.*

She pulled out a small packet of tissues, tore it open and pulled one out.

'Listen to me,' continued Ryan, grabbing her hand. 'You've done great so far. Just a little more time, that's all. We're nearly there.'

Kerry dabbed at her eyes. 'How much longer?' Then she buried her face in her hands. 'I'm freaking out, Ryan! Do you get it? I'm fucking scared!'

'I know, I know...' He squeezed her shoulder. 'But this is important. We've got most of them there, right?'

She nodded. 'I think it's all of them...' She delved into

her bag again, and once more the deafening rustle in Jay's ear obscured what Ryan was saying.

'We're so close to –' He was talking as she pulled out some sweets and started to suck on one.

'What if Mack finds my burner, huh? What if he goes into my stuff, finds it and asks me why I've got a second phone?' she asked.

Kerry had to be talking about the phone without the leather cover, the one she'd pulled out to take a picture of Jay.

'He won't. Not if you're careful with it,' Ryan assured her. 'Where do you keep it?'

'In my walk-in closet. Among my shoes. It's in one of my ankle-highs,' she told him.

Ryan nodded. 'Okay.'

'But I'm telling you… I swear Mack's on to me,' she said. 'I caught a guy snooping around my car. I didn't tell Mack, though.'

'What?' Ryan exclaimed.

'It was a few days ago, Thursday,' she told him. 'I came back out from the mall and there was a guy crouching by the back fender.'

Jay felt the hairs twitch on the back of his neck.

'What was he doing?' Ryan asked.

'It looked as though he was hiding from me. I thought he was a bum or a pervert so I told him to fuck off, but now I'm thinking –'

'What did he look like?'

'White… Tall. Muscular. I think he might have been a Brit – he had a weird accent,' Kerry said. 'And I swear, Ryan, I swear I've seen him somewhere before. I took a picture of him.'

Ryan held out his hand. 'Let me see.'

'No. Not on my phone. On the burner. I didn't feel safe bringing it with me.'

'Can you send it to me?' he asked.

She shook her head. 'There's no cellphone signal at home and no Wi-Fi. The landline isn't working either. It's been like that since last night. I think there's a problem in the area.'

Ryan stroked his chin. 'That might not be a coincidence. If the whole club is at Wakefield's place, that could well be a security measure. A digital blanket. If you need to contact me, you'll have to leave the house.'

Kerry looked at him. 'That's what worries me. I can't call for help if something bad happens. What am I going to do?'

'Listen, nothing's going to happen. Okay?' Ryan assured her. 'No one suspects anything. They just see you as Mack's eye candy. If any of them had any doubts about you, Mack would have sent you away for the weekend, right?'

Kerry gazed in Jay's direction, her eyes settling right on the cluster of pampas grass that he was huddled in. For a moment, he thought she'd spotted him. It seemed as though her eyes had caught his and he found himself holding his breath. At last, she turned back to Ryan.

'*Yeah. Maybe,*' she said.

'*Okay.*' Ryan stroked her hand. '*It's going to be fine.*' He smiled. '*And it's not for much longer. Just get through today, tomorrow and tomorrow tonight, yeah?*'

Kerry nodded. '*The last of them should be gone by lunchtime tomorrow... hopefully.*'

'*Then –*' Ryan smiled – '*surprise, surprise, I bet the phone signal and the Wi-Fi will suddenly be back to normal.*'

She nodded.

'*As soon as you have a signal,*' he continued, '*send me that photo and I'll see if I can ID this guy for you.*'

## 19

That evening Jay picked up a pack of bottled beer from the 7-Eleven and a couple of Big Mac meals, and ate dinner in his room. He'd let Jorge come in to watch TV, so that he could keep an eye on him for Sylvie. The lad had found an old black-and-white war movie on one of the channels – *The Green Berets* – and was stuffing French fries into his face while John Wayne was busy teaching the Vietcong about the American Way with his machine gun.

While Jorge watched the movie, Jay – earbuds in – was listening to what he'd recorded earlier. One thing was absolutely clear to him now: Ryan wasn't just Kerry's lover. He seemed to have some kind of hold over her. What was it that she was doing for him? That was the question. Why was she spying on Mack? Was she spying this weekend on the businessmen that were staying over?

And what the fuck was this Ryan guy after? Was it some kind of scam? Was he some sort of con artist who had Kerry over a barrel and was using her to unlock some corporate intel?

Or was she doing this more willingly? Neither coerced nor blackmailed but a co-conspirator? Mind you, she hadn't seemed that willing before, when she'd tried to hand back the burner phone. It seemed to Jay that she'd had a definite case of cold feet.

And what the hell was it with the 'ID this guy' thing? Was Ryan some sort of cop? The FBI? Or worse... working for some foreign intelligence agency? Shit. If Mack had some foreign gang pissed off with him for some reason, would that put Jay in the firing line too?

Jay's mind drifted to another problem. He had a contractual obligation to Mack, to let him know what he'd overheard in Pan's Garden. To let him hear what he'd recorded. Kerry had looked and sounded terrified, and Jay even felt sorry for her. But, he reasoned, Malcolm Wakefield wasn't exactly Tony Soprano. He wasn't going to have his own wife whacked and dumped in a reservoir.

Mack needed to know that there was more to Kerry than playing around with some guy. He decided to drop Mack a quick text. It might not get through if Mack was sitting in a black spot, but if he nipped out for a fag or something, then Jay's text would possibly land then.

He tapped out a quick message.

K made another trip to the garden to meet R today. Got audio. Don't think she's cheating. Think it's something else. Call me.

He sent the text, and a moment later a ping sounded.

It was a notification to say that his text had not reached its intended recipient.

'Hmmm...' Jay mumbled to himself.

'What's up, Mr Jay?' Jorge asked.

He glanced up from his phone to see the boy looking his way.

'Ah, nothing,' Jay said. 'I think... I've got a problem with my phone.'

'Oh.' Uninterested in Jay's tech issues, Jorge turned back to his fries and war movie.

~

LATER THAT NIGHT, after Sylvie had returned from her evening shift and put Jorge to bed, Jay once again shared a beer with her on the porch.

Thankfully, there was none of the awkwardness of the other night. Sylvie had got the message loud and clear that he wasn't hanging out with Jorge to ingratiate himself with her. That the kindness came from a genuine place, with no strings attached. And, while it was obvious that Sylvie clearly wouldn't have minded Jay being her knight in shining armour, that wasn't what this companionship was about. It meant they could sit more comfortably in each other's company, side by side in their deckchairs, listening to the soft bump of rock music from Tanners and the hiss of passing cars and not feel the need to fill the silence with small talk.

After their beer, he bid her goodnight and finished the remaining two bottles while watching an old Hitchcock movie about two random men on a train planning the murder of each other's wives.

## 20

On Sunday morning, Jay woke up with a desperate urge to get back into his usual gym routine. Since there wasn't a gym at the plaza, he made do with his own customised Travelodge workout: table-pull ups using the desk, press-ups with his bare feet up on the wall, and, finally, jogging round the car park several times to get in some long overdue cardio work.

Mid-morning, he returned to his motel room and took a cold shower. It had become unpleasantly warm and humid, and by the time he'd finished his run at 11.20 a.m. the sweat was rolling down his bald head and building up in pools above his thick brows.

Ten minutes later, he emerged from the bathroom, feeling like a champ, to find that his phone had been pinging away. He swiped the screen and saw that Kerry's Lotus had emerged from the private perimeter of Mack's beachfront property, and her pin was now making its way westwards along the 706, away from Palm Beach and heading inland.

Straight towards him, as a matter of fact.

He checked to see whether Mack had received his text yet, but still there was only the single 'message sent' checkmark; no 'message delivered' tick. He wondered how the hell Mack and his business buddies could conduct any kind of serious deal without access to the internet. Or perhaps it was a welcome relief for them? A digital detox of sorts, a break from pestering PAs, business managers and lawyers.

Jay dressed hurriedly, grabbing his kit of wigs, hats and hoodies in case he needed to follow Kerry on foot, and then jumped into his Pathfinder.

Kerry's car tracker showed that she had driven past the Jupiter Plaza just a few minutes ago. Jay joined the 706 and began following her from a discreet distance. There was no need to get too close; he had her car's location marker and she was five miles directly ahead of him. Five miles was a good distance. It gave him enough time to see which way she was going and, if she turned off somewhere, a chance to quickly pull over and check where she might be heading.

At the end of the 706, the green pin turned right, onto the 710 – apparently called the Bee-Line Highway – then swung down an exit ramp and onto a road heading southwest. He reached the same junction five minutes later. He crossed the four lanes of highway and was soon bouncing on a potholed road flanked by tall, skinny cypress trees and spiky undergrowth. He caught fleeting glimpses of the sunbaked marshland beyond. *Swamp*, he corrected himself. In America... they called it a swamp, didn't they? As in 'Drain the swamp!'

The road they were now on – the 76 – headed straight west until it eventually hit a huge lake. It was the furthest Kerry had travelled from Palm Beach since the bug had been planted in her bag.

Jay found himself driving alongside a canal with an

endless orchard of oranges or tangerines on the other side of the road, when he realised he was gaining on Kerry and slowed down a bit. Then he saw that she'd come to a stop. He pulled over with two miles between them.

'What's this, then?' he muttered to himself.

Kerry's car tracker remained static for about five minutes.

*Is she meeting Ryan in the middle of nowhere?* Jay wondered, but then she began moving again. Or more precisely... her handbag began moving. The car tracker remained where it was.

*Shit.* That complicated things.

Jay wondered what he should do. Follow the handbag? Or stay with her Lotus? It was quite possible, she'd driven over a fallen branch and knocked the tracker off. But that seemed pretty unlikely. The stubborn bugger had been a challenge to wrench off when he'd replaced it with the fully charged one.

Then he recalled a soundbite from the surveillance course last year: *A moving target is higher value than static one.* That piece of wisdom had come from the ex-KGB bloke who'd looked as if he'd have happily strangled his granny for the right price. It was sound advice, though, and Jay decided to follow the bug. Maybe she'd met Ryan, ditched her car as an extra measure of caution and was now riding with him to some other location.

For some reason.

Jay allowed the gap between them to build up to a comfortable five miles once again. He wondered whether she was doing a runner. It was quite possible that *something* had happened last night or this morning. Perhaps she had been found out, and had grabbed her keys and fled? That scenario made some sense and would explain why she'd swapped cars.

Her marker turned left at the lake. When Lake Okee-chobee finally came into view and Jay, not used to the scale of American geography – indeed, not used to the scale of anything outside East Sussex – was stunned to see that it wasn't so much a lake as an inland sea. It was so wide that the far side was invisible beyond the horizon.

'Fuck me, that's big,' he gasped.

Kerry was heading southwards, skirting the lake. He continued tailing her as they passed through a small town called Pahokee, with a marina on one side full of skiffs and motorboats, and fishing tackle shops and churches on the other. The town thinned out and the endless orchard of orange trees returned to his left. the lake channelled into a wide canal on his right. Beyond the canal lay a blanket of mottled green. He realised he was looking at the actual glades of Florida, where bearded dudes in camo fishing jackets drove those speedy hovercraft through thickets of reeds in search of crocs... or drug drops.

After about ten miles, Kerry took a right onto a road that took her across the canal and closer to Lake Okeechobee, past a place called Slim's Fishing Camp. She showed no sign of stopping there, though. Her pin had taken a turn north-wards, heading further into the wilderness. Taking the same turning, Jay discovered they'd left the world of tarmac behind and he was now driving along a dry rutted dirt track.

'What the actual fuck is this?' he muttered.

Finally, the pin stopped. Jay – aware that he was now in such a remote bit of wilderness that the rumble of his Pathfind-er's engine might give him away – found a turn-off and parked his car, deep in the reeds and invisible from the main track.

He climbed out of the air-conditioned comfort of the car and into a wall of cloying humidity, complete with a cloud of buzzing mosquitos.

# 21

Jay picked his way along the dirt track, checking his phone every few minutes to make sure Kerry's handbag pin wasn't suddenly on the move again.

Either side of the dried track, the ground dipped away, quickly becoming wetter. One side leading to actual swampland, the other to patches of lake water.

'Shit,' he muttered under his breath. He remembered he was in croc country. Or was it alligators? He could never remember which was which.

*Oh, the irony of it.* There was Sam worrying that he was going to be led astray and commit some minor felony in the US or invoke the wrath of the British intelligence services, when in actual fact he was likely going to end up a croc's dinner.

He advanced more slowly along the track, his eyes frantically scanning the reeds for any patiently waiting, wide-open, tooth-lined mouths. The track curved to the left, and as Jay rounded the bend he finally spotted the rear of Kerry's mud-spattered Lotus.

*What the actual fuck?* He'd expected to see a different car. Whichever car Ryan drove.

He ducked down into the reeds, one of his booted feet splashing into a pool of shallow water. 'Bollocks,' he whispered.

Through the reeds, he watched the Lotus. He opened the bug's app to see if he could hear anything. There was a rustling, the sound of movement, but no conversation.

*So what happened to its tracker?*

It was unlikely that it had fallen off. Maybe Ryan had been savvy enough to check it out. Perhaps he had spotted the device, removed it and tossed it.

Through the mud-spattered rear window of the Lotus, Jay could see the silhouette of a head in the driver's seat. But it didn't look like Kerry's – there was no perky, bobbing ponytail and no large Victoria Beckham-style sunglasses pushed up on top of her head. And no sign of any one in the other seat.

The figure's head moved around in a methodical manner. It was a bloke, for sure, and it appeared that he was searching the car for something. After a few minutes, the driver-side door swung open and a man climbed out.

It wasn't Ryan.

Instead, it was a bald man with a sandy, slightly ginger beard. Stocky and muscular, he moved quickly and economically.

The man walked once round the car with a rag in his hands, wiping the door handles and the roof above the doors on both sides. Then he leant into the open front passenger-side window up and reached for something inside, then tucked it into the belt of his trousers.

*Shit. Was that a gun?*

The man reached in again and emerged holding a small

one-gallon jerrycan. He uncapped it and emptied it inside the car, sloshing petrol over the dash, the front seats and the narrow rear seats. He stepped back, rounded the front of the car and tossed something into the driver's side, then slammed the door shut.

A moment later, there was a soft *whump* and the car's interior instantly filled with flames. Ginger Beard went to the rear of the car, bent down to put his shoulder against it and began to push the car forward. It rolled slowly down the sloping ground.

Jay realised that Ginger had picked this spot because it had a ramp for small recreational boats. The Lotus effortlessly slipped down the concrete and splashed into the murky water.

Ginger kept pushing the car until he was waist-deep in the water, and the buoyancy caused by the air trapped inside the car allowed it to float. It bobbed in the water while the flames continued to rage within. Finally, the car's bonnet dipped below the surface and, as the windows sank below the water line, a froth of smoke-filled bubbles churned in the lake water.

Ginger emerged, dripping wet. He looked around a couple of times, presumably checking to see if there were any witnesses, then began to stride towards the track – and towards Jay.

Quickly, Jay stepped deeper into the reeds, hunkering down even lower into the water, desperately hoping he wasn't about to have an encounter with something nasty.

Ginger marched past, rounded the bend and disappeared from view.

Jay waited another couple of minutes before emerging from the swampy water and hurried across the ground towards the boating ramp. The roof of Kerry's car was still faintly visible beneath the water, the vibrant red now a rectangle of muted amber.

Jay realised he'd been holding his breath from the moment he'd stepped out from the reeds.

'What the hell?' he wheezed.

For the first time, an unsettling possibility occurred to him. The possibility that Kerry might well be inside the car. Maybe whatever she'd been up to with Ryan had been rumbled.

And she'd been dealt with.

By whom? By *Mack*? That thought suddenly made him feel queasy. Mack might be a bit of a geezer, but, bloody hell, he wasn't a cold-blooded killer!

On the other hand, this could easily be a random thing. Jay was in America, right? Weren't random carjackings the norm here? They always happened in films: '*Hey there, sugar tits. Nice car.*' *Blam!*

RIP Kerry Wakefield: wrong time, wrong place.

He needed to check. He owed it to Mack to check if that's what had just happened.

Jay looked around. He was alone. He pulled off his T-shirt and cargo shorts. His boots were already soaked and caked in mud so might as well stay on. He was damned if he was going to split his foot open stepping on some jagged rock or discarded beer can.

He waded into the water towards the submerged vehicle. Bubbles were still appearing on the surface either side of the roof, popping and releasing thin tendrils of smoke from the car's interior.

It was filling up. Quickly.

Jay took a deep breath and ducked under the surface to check inside. The fire had been quelled. From the sunlight spearing down through the green water, Jay could see that the inside was a twisted mess of blackened springs. A blanket of smoke that had yet to escape hung in a pocket of air hugging the underside of the car's roof.

There was no sign of a body. *Thank fuck for that.*

Jay surfaced, sucked in a fresh gulp of air and took another downwards plunge to take another look. She definitely wasn't there.

He surfaced once more and paused, listening to the whisper of a breeze moving through the reeds nearby.

*All right... what the hell do I do now?*

What about the boot? He tried to push away the unwelcome thought. He really, *really* didn't want to check in there. Because, well... shit... that's where bodies always ended up, right? Stuffed into the boot of cars pushed into lakes?

He *had* to look. He dived down and fumbled for the latch, successfully pulling the boot open. To his relief, the only things inside were a bag of golf clubs and a spare tyre. He surfaced again, swiping the water away from his dripping face.

'All right... okay,' he gasped, relieved. 'Nobody's dead.'

The most obvious explanation then, at this point, was that Ginger – perhaps some local smackhead – had managed to flag Kerry down and nick her car.

*And the car tracker?*

Jay could answer that too. *So maybe Ginger was a smackhead with a bit of common sense.* He'd quite rightly checked to see whether a luxury car like this might have something on it that would allow police to track it down and... voila. There it was.

Jay waded out of the water and sat on the boating ramp to catch his breath. The Lotus would surely be found the next time someone decided to launch their boat. So he needed to think. Was there anything in the car that he needed to retrieve?

Her handbag? Well, that was almost certainly a pile of charred leather now.

The bug? That was almost certainly a lump of melted plastic and metal.

Jay decided he'd lingered beside the water for long enough. He pulled his T-shirt and shorts back on. He needed to head back to his motel room and update Mack on what the hell had just happened. He also needed to know that Kerry was okay. On the way back, he'd pull over where her Lotus had stopped earlier, to check that she wasn't stranded there, hidden from the road.

Or worse.

While he was there, he'd try to retrieve his discarded car tracker. Its pin marker was still dutifully pulsing on the app. And it hadn't been cheap.

## 22

J ay returned to his Pathfinder and retraced the route that he'd driven earlier. Soon, he was now closing in on his pinging tracker. As the distance dwindled to the final fraction of a mile, he found himself at a layby along a deserted road. He parked and got out.

There was literally nothing out here. A bit of gravel and dirt on either side of the two lanes of shimmering tarmac and beyond that a carpet of reeds and cypress trees, their roots descending into brackish dark water. He scanned the road for anything that looked like his very expensive tracker but it was nowhere to be seen.

So it hadn't just fallen off in the road, then.

Ginger must have tossed it out into the swampland.

'Thanks, mate,' muttered Jay. That was several hundred bucks he wasn't going to get back.

More importantly, though, there was no sign of a stranded Kerry.

Presumably Ginger had jumped her back in Palm Beach. Maybe even right outside the Wakefields' gated entrance.

Perhaps Kerry was now sharing her traumatic ordeal with Mack over a consoling champagne.

All the same, he decided to give the area a quick once-over. He crossed the road and found himself staring down at a drainage ditch that ran parallel to the road. It seemed to be fulfilling a secondary role as a favoured location for fly-tippers. Along its length, he could see bulging bin-liners and damp cardboard boxes, rolls of carpet and the rusting springs of an old burned mattress poking from the stagnant water like gnarled twisted fingers.

He tried to push away an unwelcome thought.

*I'm going to find a bloody body out here, aren't I?*

Because the debris-choked ditch looked like the perfect place to find one. He was going to stumble across a rotting corpse covered by writhing maggots – perhaps some low-ranking drug-gang guy, snatched by rivals, capped in the head and dumped with the rubbish.

*Jesus... you watch too much Netflix, mate.*

Jay decided against picking through the mucky trash. As far as the tracker was concerned, it could be yards away in the reeds or inches away from his boots in the muddy water and he'd never even know. With the money Mack had already paid him, he could afford to take the hit.

He was about to turn round and hasten back to his car when he caught a glimpse of coral pink. He stopped dead.

His eyes found the dash of colour again.

It belonged to the toe of a pink trainer, emerging from beneath an unfolded, crumpled cardboard box that had once housed a washing machine. Jay realised with growing certainty that he *was* going to find a body – and it was going to be Kerry's.

He stepped down the sloped bank of the ditch, squatted beside the sheet of discarded cardboard and took a deep breath. The pink trainer was a Garavani, the logo in embossed gold foil. It looked expensive. And brand new.

And it was occupied by a pale, bare foot.

'Oh shit,' he muttered.

He lifted the sheet of cardboard away.

'Oh, fuck. Oh, fuck....'

Kerry's ankle was stone cold.

## 23

B oyd and Charlotte returned from walking the dogs and Maggie on the West Hill to find Dan sitting at the dining table, watching Emma working on the Sunday roast in the tiny kitchen.

'You moved in already?' asked Boyd, surprised as he pulled off his wellies.

Dan nodded. 'Yeah, Mr B, all done.'

'Blimey. That was fast,' Boy replied as he hung Ozzie's and Mia's leads on their hooks. 'I was expecting to find a van outside and a bunch of burly lads traipsing in and out.'

'Yeah, I don't like to have too much shit cluttering up my life.' Dan glanced at Charlotte. 'Sorry.'

'Oh, I've heard far worse,' she said, heading into the kitchen. 'Need any help with the spuds, Emma?'

Boyd shrugged off his anorak and lifted Maggie out of her buggy. 'Where do you want Maggie Munchkin, Ems?' he asked.

Emma poked her head into the dining room. 'Dan, you're up.'

Boyd handed the squirming package across to her dad. 'She's all yours, matey,' he said.

He set off down the hallway to look for his slippers. He remembered they were up in the bedroom and climbed the stairs. He paused at the top and listened for a moment, then – satisfied that no one was going to come up the stairs behind him – he went to peek into the spare room at the back of the house.

Dan's stuff amounted to little more than: a few cardboard boxes, which seemed to be full of DVDs, CDs and buff-coloured notebooks; a couple of bin bags stuffed with clothes; two guitars, a small practice amp and a quilt. Boyd found his slippers waiting patiently outside the bathroom, put them on and headed downstairs.

'Are you sure you've actually moved in, Dan? There's hardly anything up there!' he said.

Dan was bouncing Maggie on his knees. 'Yeah. That's me done.'

Boyd sat down and ruffled Ozzie's ears. 'I thought you had a whole flat full of stuff to move.'

'I had a big clear-out,' Dan explained. 'Plus, most of the big stuff in there came with the flat. So...'

Boyd shrugged and said, 'Fair enough.'

Two bin bags and a couple of cardboard boxes, though? Even for someone who liked life streamlined and uncluttered, it didn't seem very much to him. Maybe Dan had dumped a load of stuff at his mum's, though he knew from Emma that Dan's mother lived in a tiny flat over in Ore.

'You know we've got loads of space here, Dan,' he said, 'if there's anything at your mum's you need to move. I've got an attic the size of a flipping barn.'

Dan shook his head. 'It's okay. But thanks Mr, B.'

Boyd's brow knitted. 'Come on, Dan, just Boyd is good for me.' He glanced at Charlotte, who was busy preparing the spuds to go into the oven. 'But I think Char's loving the whole Mrs B thing.'

Charlotte laughed. 'Good grief. It's very J. B. Priestley.'

An hour later, Emma had Sunday lunch on the table. Boyd was impressed with her precision management of the whole process, assigning tasks to everyone to ensure that the roast (lamb) and the veggies, gravy, mint sauce, wine, Maggie and everyone's bums all landed in the right locations at the exact same time.

As Boyd poured out the Malbec, he was keen to hear more details of the Mad Priests' first European tour. It was something he'd have loved to have done – the whole band-in-a-van whistlestop-tour thing.

'What were the venues like? Big ones? Total dives?' he asked Dan.

Dan huffed. 'They were a bit of a mixture, really,' he said.

'You said you did a few larger venues...' Emma glanced Dan's way. 'For how many? Several thousand?'

Dan nodded.

'Nice. But I bet that was nerve-racking, eh?' Boyd said.

Dan smiled. 'Yeah, it was pretty terrifying.'

'I was happy playing bass,' said Boyd, 'and doing a tiny bit of backing vocals, but –' he shrugged – 'I was even happier not to be right at the front singing. *That's* pressure.' He nudged Dan's arm. 'Well done! It's not easy doing that, mate.'

'I bet it's a nice feeling having done it, though,' said Charlotte. 'You must be very proud of yourselves, you and the other boys.'

Dan nodded and smiled. 'Yeah. We did pretty good, all said.'

'Any funny anecdotes?' asked Boyd.

Dan looked up from his plate. 'Huh?'

'You know? Guitar-strap fails? Tripping over cables? Drummer accidentally hurling a drumstick into the audience?' Boyd chuckled as he sipped his wine. 'When we played the Rock Garden, back in the day, I did this daft power-chord jump when we went into our first big song and twatted my head on a beam running across the ceiling.'

Emma and Charlotte laughed.

'How small was this place?' asked Charlotte.

'Tiny!' Boyd grinned. 'Low stage, low ceiling. I misjudged the space and nearly knocked myself out.'

'Uh. Nothing like that happened to us,' Dan said, realising that all eyes were on him. 'We just kind of got stuck into it,' he went on. 'No real comedy fails as such.'

'Oh,' said Boyd, disappointed.

'I presume that tour has helped with your –' Charlotte shrugged – 'record sales? Or it's downloads now, isn't it?'

'Yeah, Mrs B. Touring is all good promotion. Kind of raising band awareness, you know?'

'Uh-huh,' she replied, meeting Boyd's eyes with a slight narrowing of hers.

Boyd had been expecting – hoping for – a long monologue of anecdotes, high points and low moments. But there was none of that. The last time he'd spoken to Dan about the Mad Priests, the lad had been so full of it: the number of Spotify plays they had, the Patreon subscribers, the TikTok followers and so on. Something was up.

'Well…' Boyd raised his glass and held it up. 'We are all very glad you survived your first tour abroad. To conquering the rest of the world, one gig at a time!'

'Yeah,' said Emma, lifting her glass. 'To headlining Glastonbury one day!'

Dan lifted his glass and clinked them all dutifully. 'Yeah. Glasto. That would be totally dope.'

## 24

It was gone five o'clock before Jay finally managed to get through to Malcolm Wakefield.

'Oh, Jesus, *finally*!' he blurted out.

'Jay? Sorry about the radio blackout,' Mack said. 'My lines have been down since –'

'Mack, I need to tell you something,' Jay interrupted. 'It's bad. Really bad.'

'What's the matter?' Mack replied.

'Mack, listen... Have the police been in touch with you?' Jay asked.

'No.' Mack's jovial tone vanished. 'Why? What's up?'

'It's Kerry...' Jay had practised three different ways to break the news and had decided on the straightforward approach. 'She's dead.'

'WHAT?' Mack exclaimed.

'Murdered,' Jay said. 'Shot in the head.'

'WHAT?!' Mack gasped again. 'My God! Fuck! When?'

'This morning. I've been trying to get through to you all bloody day!'

There was a long pause as Mack processed the information. 'Jesus... She... she said she was just going out.' He huffed dryly. 'She said... she'd had enough of being surrounded by boring old men and was going out to do some shopping, to have lunch with her girls.'

'She wasn't heading out to do any of that,' Jay cut in. 'This morning, I caught her tracker heading *away* from Palm Beach.' He gave Mack the bare bones of what had happened, neutral and flat – a police constable reading back a logbook entry. No theories, no speculation, just the facts... and then he gave Mack a moment to digest all that he'd shared.

At last, Mack spoke. 'And this man you saw... He definitely *wasn't* her fancy man?'

'Ryan? No. It wasn't him,' Jay confirmed. 'It was a stocky guy, bald with a ginger-ish beard.'

'Jesus...' Mack whispered. 'You... What... what do you think?'

'It could have been a random carjacking,' Jay offered. It was a possibility. 'I dunno. I mean, how often does that shit happen over here?'

'It does happen,' replied Mack, 'but this isn't Denver, for God's sake.'

'Her Lotus stopped on a really remote road,' said Jay. 'I mean, it was literally the middle of nowhere... and that's where the car tracker came off. It's possible that this was some opportunist thing. Someone looking for an easy win. Saw a woman on her own having a break from driving – just pulled open the passenger door and jumped right in with her.'

'God,' Mack said.

Jay paused, realising he hadn't offered any condolences. 'Mack... I'm really sorry to have to be the one telling you about this.'

'Thanks,' Mack replied. 'I'm... I guess I'm in shock. I... Jesus Christ... She may have been making a fool of me behind my back with this Ryan, but for fuck's sake *this*?'

'Look, Mack. There's something...' Jay wondered for a second if now was the right moment. He should probably give Mack some time to absorb Kerry's death first.

'Something? *What* something?' Mack asked impatiently.

Jay took a deep breath. 'If it's any consolation, I don't think she was seeing this guy – you know, *romantically*.'

There was another long pause. Finally Wakefield spoke again. 'Jesus. This is... *God*, this is just bloody horrific.'

To Jay, Mack's grief was coming across as genuine. He may have been scheming to catch Kerry out, to coerce her into a minimal divorce settlement, but clearly he still felt something for her.

'Mack?'

There was no reply.

'Mr Wakefield? I should probably report what I've found to the police. It's been a few hours already.'

'No,' Mack said abruptly.

'Huh?' Jay hadn't been expecting that response. 'No? Why not?'

'I'm thinking for your sake, mate,' Mack replied. 'Do you have an explanation for why you were out there? For why you were following her, huh? Think it through. If you go to the police with this, and then tell them you've been following her – stalking her, even – they're going to jump to the wrong conclusion.'

'Well, no. I'd tell them that it was a job,' Jay pointed out.

'A job? That's even worse, Jay. They'll conclude you were hired to hit her. Then they'll come looking for me too.'

Jay had been so busy this afternoon dialling and redialling Mack's number, and walking frantic circles around his motel room, that he hadn't done much in the way of forward-thinking. Mack was right. Saying '*Yeah, I found her body, but, hey, I didn't do it – though I was being paid to stalk her and my client was planning to ditch her... and...*' None of that was going to sound good, and once the cops had a prime suspect and a viable motive, they might not bother considering anyone else.

'Listen, *don't* fucking call them, Jay. All right?' Mack stressed. 'I'll report her missing.'

'When?' Jay asked.

'*Now*, obviously!' Mack said. 'When we've finished. It's been what... five or six hours?'

'Six hours since she left the house,' Jay confirmed.

'Well, that's long enough for me to start worrying,' said Mack. '*I'll* call them.'

There was a pause, then Mack asked, 'Is there anything of yours on her still, Jay? Your tech stuff?'

'My bug was in her handbag, but it's stopped working, so I'm guessing it's melted inside the car somewhere. My car tracker was pulled off and tossed into some nearby swamp,' Jay said.

'You sure this bloke didn't take her bag with him?' Mack asked.

'No, I'm pretty sure he walked away from the lake empty-handed,' Jay replied.

'Did you see him pocket anything?'

'No,' said Jay. 'But neither of my things are working anyway. He proper fire-bombed the interior. And the car tracker's lost in a swamp. I mean, I could go and wade around and try and find the fucking thing, but it'll be hard.'

'Hmm, maybe you don't want to draw attention looking for it.'

'Yeah. It'll run out of charge in a few weeks anyway.'

'Right,' Mack replied. 'So there's nothing else to connect you to her?'

'No. Nothing.' *Apart from a picture of my mug on her burner phone.* Jay was hoping to God that she hadn't had it on her. But if she had intended to drive it out of Wakefield's grounds to hand it over to Ryan, perhaps it was also a clump of metal and plastic, or the perp had found it and already factory-reset the damned thing to sell on.

'Okay, then,' said Wakefield. 'For Christ's sake, let's keep you well and truly out of the picture, okay? I'll report her missing and we'll go from there.'

'What do you want me to do now?' Jay asked. 'I mean, you don't need me any more, right? So it might make sense for me to pack up and head back to Eng–'

'Stay put! For your own sake! Just think about it,' said Wakefield. 'If the police do find anything on her, or if she told a friend she caught you messing with her car, skipping the country a few hours after her death is going to make you look as guilty as hell!'

There was that, Jay had to admit.

'And if *you* look guilty, then *I'll* look guilty,' added Wakefield. 'Listen. Just sit tight, Jay, all right? I'm going to call the local fuzz right now. And, of course, I doubt they'll lift a finger for a couple of days anyway.'

Jay heard him chug something. A whisky? A beer?

'Right. Okay,' he agreed.

The call ended abruptly. Mack was either done being polite or just done with trying to hold his shit together. Maybe the grisly, pug-faced bugger was sobbing his guts out as soon as he hung up.

Jay stared at his phone with a mind racing with of unanswered – and unasked –questions. So what *exactly* was he supposed to do now? Just hang around and wait for Mack to tell him when he could go home? Was he allowed to contact Mack again? Should he continue to use this phone? What about the rest of the money? *Was* there going to be any more coming his way? Because, technically, Mack now had what he'd wanted: no wife to pay out.

Which led Jay to another thought.

Could Mack somehow have been behind this? Boyd would no doubt be telling him right now that coincidences only happened in shit films and Aussie soap operas.

The needling thought began to flesh itself out. If Mack's plan had been to have her whacked, then all this crap about her cheating on him and having Jay follow her around, taking photos of her, had simply been a charade. Why would he have done that? Why would he have hired Jay to watch her?

The answer to that question came to him seven hours later as he lay in bed. In fact, the answer came to him via a dream – well, more of a nightmare, really. For some reason, Jay was on the run in some remote part of the USA with sheriffs, search dogs, swooping helicopters and swat guys all combing swamplands and cornfields for him. In his fevered dream he had become America's Most Wanted!

The nightmare woke him with a start, but it left him with a possible, or even probable answer.

*Stay put! Don't go anywhere, mate.*

What if Malcolm Wakefield had murdered Kerry himself, or, more likely, hired someone else – an *actual* pro – to do the job? And he'd had hired Jay to be the fall guy...

## 25

Okeke squinted at her watch. It was five past six. She groaned. *Who the hell would be calling this early on a Monday morning?*

She stubbed out her cigarette in the ashtray that was nestled on her chest. Before meeting Jay, before he'd moved in, the first fag of the day had always been the one in bed, beating her first coffee by an hour. When Jay had moved in, she'd broken the habit. Despite him also being a smoker, he wasn't a huge fan of sleeping in a bedroom that stank like an old Ladbrokes. She'd taken up her old habit again, now that he'd stropped off to be a Big Boy PI.

She blindly reached out to the side table and fumbled for the phone that was buzzing insistently like a wasp caught in a bottle. If it was DI Abbott with some dumbass 'How do I...?' question about LEDS, she vowed she'd stab him in both eyes with a pen when she got into work this morning.

Okeke held the screen in front of her bleary eyes. It was her personal phone that was making all the noise, not her work phone.

And it was an unknown number.

*Jay.*

She swiped to answer the call and paused in case it was a marketing chatbot.

'Babycakes?' Jay's voice rasped softly, quietly. It was almost a whisper.

'*Jay?*' she all but screamed. '*JAY!*'

'Yeah... it's me,' he said.

'What the – Where the –'

'Babes,' he cut in. 'I can't talk for long. I've gotta be quick.'

'Jesus Christ, Jay! I've been out of my mind! Worried sick about you! I've been –'

'Babes, shhh... Just let me... speak. I ain't got long.'

She heard him clear his throat. 'What?' she asked. 'Tell me.'

He cleared his throat again. 'I think... I might be in a spot of trouble...'

It took every fibre of will not to bellow '*I told you so!*' down the line. Jay didn't sound like his usual cocky self. He sounded shaken.

'What's happened, love?' she asked.

'I think I might have fucked up,' he told her.

'How?'

He paused. 'I got a nasty feeling, Sam, that I might've been a bit of a silly mug.'

'*What's happened?*' she pressed.

'You know the woman I was paid to keep an eye on?'

'The businessman's wife?' she said warily.

Okeke had a horrible suspicion that Jay was about to admit he'd been cheating on her. That the whole story about some Brit businessman paying him ridiculous money to watch his wayward wife was just a pack of lies to cover up an affair that he, Jay, had been having. She felt her hand tighten around the phone. The other balled into a fist so tight the skin over her knuckles blanched.

*I bet it's that Ronni he mentioned. I bet the dirty bastard's been shagging her ever since they met in Croydon last year!*

'She's dead,' Jay blurted out.

It took Okeke a moment to digest that. 'Sorry?' she asked.

'Dead,' he repeated. 'The wife. Murdered.'

Before she could stop herself, the words slipped out. 'Jay… what have you done?'

'Christ, Sam!' he exploded. 'Fucking hell! It wasn't me who did it!'

He explained what he'd witnessed yesterday. She glanced at her watch as he spoke and did some mental maths. It had to be one or two in the morning where he was. So yesterday for him too.

Jay concluded with an account of the phone call with his employer, Mr Wakefield.

'Well, he's right about one thing,' said Okeke. 'If you packed your bags and scrambled for the nearest airport right now, you'd look *very* guilty.'

'But at least I'd be back home in Hastings before they started checking out suspects,' he replied.

'That wouldn't help you, Jay. Not if they decided it's you that did it.' She didn't need to explain to him that the Yanks had a global reach when it came to arrest warrants, surely? Especially with the UK.

'You're doing the right thing, baby,' she continued. 'Just stay calm and don't do anything stup–'

'The thing is, Sam,' he cut in, 'I'm thinking that Mack might have done it.'

'Mack? The bloke who hired you?' she asked.

'Uh-huh. I'm beginning to think this whole thing was a set-up. I think he hired me to be the idiot who gets arrested, and he hired some other bloke to get rid of her!'

Jay's voice was shaking now. She'd only ever heard him like that once before, at Louie's funeral when he'd given the eulogy for his old friend.

'Okay, listen... Jay? Listen. That American *colleague* of yours, Ronni? She can vouch for you, right? She can tell the police that Mack approached her and then she approached you, right?'

'Yeah... I guess,' Jay agreed.

'Then call her,' said Okeke. 'Call her and tell her what's happened.'

'Okay,' he replied. 'Do you think I should go to the police?'

'Call Ronni,' she repeated. 'See what she advises you do. And listen, Jay. This is really important. The first twenty-four hours after a murder is the critical time. Don't do anything rash. Don't call anyone else. Don't go anywhere suspicious.'

'Okay,' he said.

'And I'm going to speak to the guv,' she continued.

'Yeah. Tell Boyd.' She could hear a pitiful lift in his voice. 'Do you reckon he can help?'

'It can't hurt.' She paused. 'And, to be fair, he does owe you.'

## 26

Ronni Kirk muted her TV, answered her phone and then listened to Jay spill out his whole story in one long, breathless word-salad.

'Okay, stop,' she said as soon as he paused for breath. 'Jay, shut up a second, will you?'

'Right,' he muttered.

'So let's just wind back a couple of steps here, okay? You mentioned two different guys. This Ryan guy who Kerry was meeting and then this ginger-beard guy who you witnessed firebombing and dunking her car?'

'Yeah,' Jay confirmed.

'And you're saying it's the ginger-beard guy who shot her?' Ronni asked.

'Yeah.' Jay paused. 'Maybe. I didn't actually see him shoot her, but he looked like a hitman.'

'He what... why?' She laughed. 'Because he was bald?'

'What? No!' Jay exclaimed. 'Because...'

'Relax, I'm just kidding,' Ronni said. 'So what about this Ryan guy? He sounds pretty suspicious.'

'It's serious, Ronni,' Jay huffed. 'It's not funny. Like I said, at first I thought Kerry and Ryan were having an affair, then the second time they met, it seemed more... business-like.'

'Business-like?' Ronni repeated.

'The pair of them were up to something, Ronni,' Jay said. 'Maybe scamming Mack. Maybe trying to find something he had, spying on him? I'm not sure.'

Ronni sucked air between her teeth. 'Jesus, Jay... What the hell mess have you stumbled into?'

'What the hell mess have *you* stumbled *me* into?' he replied. 'This was *your* booking!'

He had a fair point. She'd not exactly done all the due diligence she could have on Mack's background before passing the job to Jay. Mack had seemed like a dumb Brit with a lot of money and a huge, paranoid chip on his shoulder where his trophy wife was concerned.

'Look, this could just be a random thing, Jay,' she said. 'Just bad luck.' There was no reply from him. 'You disagree?'

She could hear him smacking his lips. She'd noticed that he did that when he was unsure of himself. Like the time she'd drunkenly suggested they should fuck and he'd suddenly morphed into a spooked, six-foot-tall toddler.

'Ronni... I'm... I've got real concerns about Mack,' he told her.

She checked her watch. It was nearly 2 a.m. Luckily she was a night owl. She struggled with insomnia and thanked God that she'd been born to live in an age with round-the-clock news channels and game shows to keep her company.

'Go on,' she said.

'What if... he planned to have her murdered all along?' Jay said. 'And he just hired me to be the dumbass who takes the blame for it?'

Ronni paused. It sounded far-fetched at first, but – as she thought about it – she realised that if Malcolm 'Call Me

Mack' Wakefield wanted his wife gone, that wasn't a bad way to go about it. Hire a killer so he could have his alibi. And a patsy so the police could have a quick result.

'Hey, listen, Jay, if the police come knocking, I'll vouch for you,' Ronni said. 'I'll lose my goddamn operating licence, for sure... but I'll vouch.'

'Thanks,' Jay said.

'But let's not go running to the police just yet. Okay?'

'Mack's told me to sit tight. Not to go anywhere, not to do anything and definitely not to approach the police.'

'To be fair, that's not bad advice,' Ronni replied. 'If you call it in, you'd be the first person they'd take a long hard look at.'

'Yeah. Mack said that too.'

'And if you've got hundreds of pictures of her all over your phone, you'll be even more of a suspect.'

'Yeah, I do,' he replied. 'I know... it's not a good look.'

'Right. But on the other hand,' she continued, 'you've been observing her from a distance, right? So there's nothing on her that would link her to you, like DNA, hair, fibres, prints?'

'My car tracker. But that got tossed out into the wilderness.'

'Shouldn't you go retrieve it?'

'It's at the bottom of some swamp, Ronni. I don't want to be spotted wading around looking for it. Anyway, in a couple of weeks or so it'll be dead. So...'

'Anything else?'

'She took a close-up picture of me,' Jay confessed.

Ronni sat bolt upright. 'What?!'

'She caught me messing around under her car. I'd just refitted the tracker,' Jay explained. 'She took out her phone and snapped a pic of me.'

'And where is that phone?' Ronni asked.

Jay explained that Kerry had one phone that Mack knew about and one that he didn't. Both phones would almost certainly have been on her. Jay had thought it through: if she'd been keen to send the photo to Ryan, or had been planning to meet him to hand over the burner phone, she would have had it with her. She might have been paranoid enough to hide it in the car somewhere. The best outcome, as far as Jay was concerned, was that the bloody thing had been on the back seat and was now a useless lump of melted plastic and warped silicon.

'It could still be readable, Jay,' Ronni pointed out. 'Smartphones have SD cards. You want to be absolutely sure the fire was hot enough to completely destroy them. But of course you thought of that, right?'

Jay sighed. 'Fuck... if it's still in her Lotus, what do I do? Should I go back and see if I can find it? But if I do that, I *am* gonna leave my bloody DNA all over the car. And someone might spot me.'

'How deep is it?' Ronni asked.

'It's just below the surface,' Jay said. 'If someone pulls up there to do some fishing or whatever, they'll see it.'

Ronni bit down on her bottom lip. 'The way I see it, you need to give the car another look-over. You really don't want some forensics tech discovering that phone. If it ain't there, then maybe Ginger took it, or it wasn't with her in the first place.'

'I'm thinking of getting the hell out of here right now,' said Jay in a panicked voice.

'*Don't*,' Ronni told him. 'Mack's right, if you light out of town, it's only gonna bite you harder on the ass later.'

## 27

Okeke spotted Boyd entering the CID floor and stood up to intercept him before he could get to his desk, dump his jacket and disappear to the top-floor canteen for a frothy coffee.

'Can I have a quick word?' she called across to him.

He glanced over at her. 'Can I just dump my stuff and grab a –'

'It's urgent,' she replied, lowering her voice.

'Urgent, as in it can't wait five minutes?' he asked.

She stood in front of him, blocking his way. 'Urgent, as in –' she lowered her voice so the others sitting at their desks couldn't hear – 'Jay.'

Boyd raised his brows and looked around. Minter, Warren, Rajan and Abbott were involved in some heated debate about whether cannabis should be pulled off the class C list and legalised in the UK, their voices carrying loudly across the deserted, amber-hued CID bullpen.

'Outside?' he replied softly.

She nodded.

~

OKEKE LIT up and blew out a cloud of smoke. Boyd could tell she was stressed – the hand holding her cigarette was trembling slightly.

'All right,' said Boyd, leaning against the wall beside her. 'What's the big man gone and done?'

He had been expecting some kind of brush between Jay and US officialdom. If not on his way into the country, then being pulled for driving on the wrong side of the road, or haplessly contravening some piece of state-level legislation: drinking a bottle of beer on the street that wasn't concealed in a brown paper bag, for example.

The Americans were weird like that.

She looked at him. 'Guv, he might be arrested for murder.'

'*Murder?*' Boyd gaped at her.

Okeke nodded. 'I told you why he went over, right? I'm beginning to think this Wakefield bloke was after a sucker... and he found one.' She relayed Jay's garbled story to him.

'So did Jay witness it?' asked Boyd. 'This woman's murder?'

'No. He was remotely tracking her car. It stopped someplace for a few minutes, then moved on and was dumped. He went back to where it had stopped... and found her body in a roadside ditch.'

'Christ. Do the local police know?' Boyd asked.

'He hasn't reported it yet,' she told him.

'But she has been reported missing?'

'I dunno. He didn't say,' Okeke replied. 'It only happened yesterday. He called me a couple of hours ago. He's absolutely shitting himself.'

Boyd shook his head. 'You said he saw the guy who nicked the car and then ditched it?'

'Yeah.'

'What did *you* advise him to do?' asked Boyd.

'I told him to sit tight. I told him I was going to talk to you about it,' she said.

Boyd shook his head again. 'Look, if you're after my advice... if this a set-up by this Wakefield fella, then Jay needs to go straight to the police asap. He needs to explain why he's over there and what he was doing. I know he'll get into some trouble, but that's better than saying nothing and the police being pointed in his direction by someone else.'

'But what about all the pictures of this woman that he has on his phone?' Okeke said. 'I'm not so sure that's the best thing for him to do. Maybe he should just get on a plane and come home...'

'Here's the thing, Sam...' Boyd said. 'If this Wakefield bloke is using Jay as his patsy, then who knows? He might already be helping the police with their enquiries? He might already be telling them that his wife had been worried about some chap stalking her in recent weeks.'

Okeke's face froze. 'Jay took the same flight as them,' she said.

'And that's not going to help,' replied Boyd, 'That looks about as stalkerish as you can possibly get. Wakefield could be telling the police right now that his wife thought she'd spotted her stalker on the same flight. And how long would it take them to get hold of the passenger manifest and pick out Jay's name on the list?'

'Fuck.' Okeke closed her eyes.

'Sam, I'm presuming he's gone and booked everything under his own name over there?' Boyd said. 'Car hire? Hotel? He didn't use an alias or anything?'

She nodded. 'I think so.'

Boyd pulled a face. 'What's he doing right now?'

'I told him to get some sleep. And not to do anything rash.'

He gave her a stern look. 'I'd give him a call immediately. And I mean *right now*. Tell him to get up and go straight to the police.'

She was conflicted. 'I'm not sure.'

'I'm *serious*, Sam. If he is being set up by this guy, Jay needs to get *his* story logged with the police as soon as bloody possible.'

'Right.' She started digging in her bag for her phone. 'Shit. Fuck. Okay.'

## 28

Sam's advice had been to sit tight and leave well alone. Ronni's had been to go back to the car. After staring at the four walls of his motel room for an hour, his imagination running riot, the only thing he could think about was the possibility of Kerry's secret phone sitting on the back seat of her car, waiting to be discovered by some bunny-suited forensics technician.

An hour before sunrise, he was back beside Lake Okeechobee, parked at the top of the boat ramp that descended into the gently lapping water. As he'd driven there, the urgency and necessity had built in his mind. If Kerry had been on her way to meet Ryan, she – one hundred per cent – *would* have had her secret phone on her: in her bag, tucked into a door pocket or beneath her drivers' seat. She *would* have had it with her, because she wanted Ryan to find out who the hell Jay was.

If the man he'd witnessed getting rid of her car really had been a hired hitman, then presumably he'd have searched the vehicle thoroughly, if only to be sure he wasn't leaving anything behind that might incriminate him.

However, if Mack had hired this bloke to kill Kerry *and* hired Jay so that he'd be the framed patsy... then there'd be something in that car, for sure, that would point the police Jay's way, wouldn't there?

The paranoia was driving him crazy.

And then there was that fucking car tracker. He just hoped it was going to be long dead before the local police ever got the idea – if they ever did – to knock on his door.

As soon as he'd got on the road, he could hear Sam's voice scolding him for pursuing this job in the first place. Telling him he wasn't cut out for this kind of thing. Reminding him that he was actually rather good at restoring furniture and that he might have been smarter sticking with that.

'Yeah, well...' he replied out loud, as though she was sitting beside him. 'It's easy to say that with the benefit of hindsight, babycakes.'

He'd left his iPhone and burner phone back at the motel room. There was nothing on him at all to log this incredibly suspicious early-morning dash to Lake Okeechobee. No flipping phone masts were going to incriminate him in some US courtroom months from now.

～

JAY UNDRESSED down to his boxers and a pair of trainers, then flicked-on the water-resistant torch he'd brought with him. He pulled out a pair of cheap kiddie swimming goggles that he'd bought for Jorge a few days ago and he'd left behind in his Pathfinder. He loosened the strap to fit his head as best he could, pulled them over his eyes and then waded into the chilly lake until his toes were just touching the bottom and his shoulders were under the water. The torch's intense beam shot a murky green shaft through the gloom and illuminated the car's passenger-side door in a diffused ring of light.

He fumbled for the handle and tugged it, but the door remained resolutely closed. Jay tugged again, this time bracing one foot against the side of the car, and the door gave an inch. It wasn't locked but presumably it had been stuck solid by some plastic fascia on the inside. He pulled the door harder and it jerked open.

Jay surfaced again and took another few breaths to ready himself for the next submersion. He tried the glove compartment first. Then, after surfacing again for another breath, he tried the area beneath the driver's seat and the footwell. There was no sign of a phone. On his next dive, he checked the door pockets on either side and felt along the rear footwell.

How on earth, he wondered, had he got here?

$\approx$

JAY RETURNED to his motel room as the McDonald's across the car park was serving breakfast to eager customers.

He collapsed onto his bed exhausted, smelling faintly of rancid water and even more faintly of burnt rubber and plastic. As he lay on his back, staring up at the sunlight stealing in through the gap in the curtains into his low-ceilinged room, he lifted his hand above his head and gazed with utter relief and a little exhilaration at the palm-sized prize of warped metal, plastic and cracked glass that he was holding.

'Got you,' he muttered wearily.

He'd had to prise the thing loose from the exposed

springs of the driver's seat. Kerry had hidden it by pushing it into the space between the seat and the backrest.

Ginger had missed it. Had he fucked up? Or was it intentional? Had it been left there to frame Jay?

Well, it didn't matter. Jay was satisfied that there was nothing left in Kerry's car that was going to link him to her murder. And the car tracker? Well... it was where it was. Hopefully an interesting archaeological find for someone centuries from now.

His eyes grew heavy. A shower, shave and general clean-up could damn well come after he'd grabbed forty winks.

## 29

Tyler Furman hated this section of the Chicken Run. Florida was relentlessly flat from side to side and down its entire length. He liked to think of Florida as America's giant flaccid dick, dangling above Cuba.

An hour ahead of schedule, he had a 7 a.m. delivery slot at Danton Poultry Processing, which was only a mile or so away. They didn't tolerate lateness there. If you missed your delivery window, you were likely to be waiting in their holding area with your thousands of chickens for a good number of hours, oftentimes the rest of the day. And by the time the spare end-of-day slots became available, you were looking at a fair number of dead birds in the back. Many of them dead from dehydration and heatstroke, quite a few simply pecked to death by their distressed cage mates.

He could see an apron of gravel ahead along this stretch of the 76. Admittedly it was on the far side and he'd have to pull left across the oncoming lane to make use of it, but he really needed to take a shit badly – and this highway was long, straight and, given this ungodly early hour, completely deserted.

Tyler steered his 18-wheeler to the far side and ground to a halt on the gravel strip. Two minutes was all he needed. One to dump his load, the other to 'sand and shine' as Gramps used to say. He'd run out of toilet paper, but he had a stash of KFC handwipes. His asshole was going to sting from the scented ethanol, but at least it would smell of lemons.

Even before his brakes had finished hissing, Tyler had jumped down from the cabin with his scented wipes in one hand and a flashlight in the other. He looked around for somewhere discreet to hunker down. He was lucky. There was a trench running alongside the highway. He could shuffle down the sloping ground and do his business down there, out of view.

Tyler was done within a couple of minutes and winced at the sting from the wipes.

He aimed his flashlight at the ground as he stood and pulled up his trousers. As he made his way back to his waiting truck and chickens, he stumbled on a loose rock and lost his grip on the flashlight. It rolled down the slope, stopping just short of the gross water in the ditch.

Tyler scrambled down the slope to retrieve it, cursing under his breath. He leant over to pick it up and, as he did so, spotted peeking out from beneath a sheet of cardboard that lay in the dark, brackish water – something pale and pink.

## 30

J ay was ten again; Karl was six. They were huddled together, listening to doors slamming and adults shouting. Well, their foster dad shouting. The other screaming voice belonged to their mum. The sound of slamming doors segued into a rhythmic thudding, which Jay's sleepy mind slowly understood to be a loud knocking on his motel-room door.

Emerging from a dream world, Jay took a groggy moment to pack the memories away – but they weren't real. They were memories of dreams of memories and, with each retelling, the story had become more distorted.

His eyes blinked open. He wasn't ten any more; he was thirty-six, and he was sitting up in bed, in a tired, threadbare motel room in America.

Sunday came flooding back to him. Kerry Wakefield lying dead in a roadside ditch.

Monday had been a blur of fatigue and panic, pacing around his room, avoiding his phones because he couldn't bear finding out whether Kerry's body had been found yet. Later in the afternoon he'd gone across to Tanners for a beer

– deliberately leaving his phones behind – to take his mind off things and had ended up staying far longer than he should have. He vaguely recalled stumbling back to the motel room at some point in the evening.

That hammering on his door right now could well be the police coming to arrest him for her brutal slaying. By teatime today, his mugshot could be on Fox News and BBC South East – and on the front page of the *Daily Mail* by tomorrow morning.

'Jay?'

A female voice. It was Sylvie.

'Mr Jay?' Another voice. Jorge.

Jay suddenly remembered. He'd promised to take them both out for the day.

'Just a second,' he called as he stumbled out of bed. The walls in this place were plywood-thin, the doors even thinner.

'Okay!' replied Sylvie from the terrace. 'We go wait on the steps.'

Jay pulled on a T-shirt and jeans and checked his phone. He'd missed several calls from Sam and one from Ronni. Both had left a voicemail message.

He checked Sam's first, from yesterday at 4.35 a.m.: *'Jay, I just spoke to the guv about your situation. He was pretty clear about his advice. He said you need to go straight to the police and let them know about the body. The longer you leave it, the more explaining you'll have to do. So I guess, I hope, you're doing that now... Call me when you get this. Love you.'*

Next was Ronni's message, left yesterday morning as well, at 4.39 a.m.: *'Jay, okay, I've been thinking about this. I suggest you get your ass over to that dunked car and double-check there's nothing in there that's going to lead the Feds to you. I'm thinking specifically about her burner phone with your ugly face on it. And I'm also thinking that if the guy ditched her handbag nearby with your bug in it, and if the police get their hands on it, the bug will have a serial number, which might lead them straight to me, since I ordered the goddamn thing. So, if you're not there already, get your ass in the lake and give the car a proper search, yeah?'*

Jay shook his head. *Christ.* Two gobby women with two entirely different pieces of advice for him, four minutes apart, right after he'd driven off to check the submerged car. If he'd left just ten minutes later, he would have actually taken those bloody calls and have spent yesterday flip-flopping between going and not, locked in an endless decision loop: a tiny Sam on one shoulder, a tiny Ronni on the other, both barking their contradictory wisdom into his ears.

Luckily he'd missed them both and taken things into his own hands. He glanced at Kerry's fire-damaged phone. It looked very much as though it was good for nothing now, except maybe as a piece of avant-garde art. But Ronni could well have been right. It could contain data that was perfectly intact and salvageable.

At least it was here in his hands. *His* shit was sorted. And maybe it was time to start acting the part of an innocent tourist while he waited for Mack to get back in touch and tell him he was good to go home.

He pulled on his hoodie, slipped Kerry's misshapen phone into one of the pockets and his burner phone into the other, in case Mack did have an update for him. He opened the door and stepped out onto the terrace, to Jorge's expectant face peering up at him: eyes wide, mouth dangling, holding onto a hopeful breath.

'Right!' he announced, jangling the Pathfinder's keys from his finger. 'I can't quite remember... where did I say we should go?'

'DISNEY WORLD!' yelped Jorge.

Jay grinned. 'Oh, yeah – that's right.'

Jorge jumped to his feet and punched the air. 'Yayyyy!'

Sylvie beamed at him. She was wearing a flowery pink cotton dress, her dark hair was down and longer than he'd expected it to be. She looked very pretty.

'Thank you so much for doing this for us, Jay,' she said.

'Hey, no problem,' he replied. 'I've always wanted to visit the House of Mouse.'

## 31

Detective Angela Durrant stood halfway down the bank to the roadside ditch. She watched the forensic technicians carefully place the dead woman in a vinyl-coated body bag.

'Can you give me a time of death?' she called out to them as they zipped it up.

'Not really,' replied the older technician. 'I can give you a ballpark answer.'

'I'll take *wild* for now,' replied Durrant.

He sighed. 'Twenty-four hours? Give or take.'

'Give or take what?'

He shrugged.

'Helpful,' she replied sarcastically, then shook her head. 'Well, she's not fresh. I can see that from here.'

Durrant turned away and clambered up the dirt bank. At the top, she paused to rub her left hip. Sixty years, twenty of those as a gymnast, had taken its toll on her joints, from the pelvis downwards. Apparently turmeric was a remedy for joint pains – either eaten or slathered on in lotion form. She'd even snort the goddamned stuff if someone told her it would make a difference to that persistent ache in her bones.

She picked out the nearest state trooper. 'Hey, where's our trucker?' she asked.

He pointed at the man sitting in the cab of an 18-wheeler truck, the driver-side door wide open, his legs dangling idly. Angela went over to him, eyeing the load he was hauling: a long, tall block of wire cages containing frantic, scrabbling hens. Feathers fluttered out to the ground like snowflakes. She glanced at the wretched birds and wished she hadn't. The vast majority of them had bald patches, scabs and open sores; some of them were clearly dead.

'You're the guy who found her?' she asked the man. 'Tyler Freeman?'

'Yup. Tyler Furman,' he replied.

She pushed up her spectacles and checked her notepad. 'Right. Say, Mr Furman? Can you hop down from there for a minute? I'm trying to look up but my back's killing me.'

He screwed the cap back on to his bottle of Diet Coke and jumped down.

'That's better,' she said. 'So, Mr Furman...'

'You're a cop?' he asked.

She pulled out her badge. 'Detective Durrant, Martin County Sheriff's Office.'

'Okay.'

'Mr Furman, I got a few quick questions. I don't want to inconvenience you any more than I have to,' she said.

'It's too late for that,' he replied. 'I've missed my delivery slot... I'm gonna be taking a lotta dead birds home with me.'

'I'm sorry about that,' she replied. 'Where've you come from?'

'Quincy.'

She winced. That was a fair way. 'I'm gonna ask you

some questions you've probably answered a dozen times already. Okay?'

'It was six a.m.,' he said, as if by rote. 'I pulled over for a bathroom break. It was... *urgent.*'

Durrant nodded. 'Understandable. When you gotta go, you gotta go, right?'

'Right.'

'And that's when you found the body?' she asked.

'Uh-huh. I went down into that ditch for, ahem, privacy...'

'And there was no one else around? You didn't see any other vehicles here?'

Tyler shook his head. 'I heard one of them forensics guys saying she got shot in the face? Is that right?'

Durrant nodded. 'Above the eyes. It was a single shot.'

'Jesus. Poor lady.' He shook his head again. 'Did her killer, you know, mess around with her?'

'You asking me whether she was raped first?' said Durrant.

He nodded.

'I don't think so,' Durrant replied. 'This doesn't look like *that* kind of a murder.'

She glanced back at the forensics technicians, now carrying the body bag towards the waiting gurney.

'Hey, guys,' she called out. 'That Jane Doe is going to our medical examiner over in Fort Pierce, right?'

Before they could answer, a voice behind her barked, '*No!*'

Durrant turned. A man in his mid-thirties was marching towards her, his car parked behind the CSI van. He reached into his jacket pocket as he approached.

'Special Agent James Ryan, FBI,' he announced, holding out his ID.

## 32

'**B**oss?'

Boyd looked up from his monitor to find DI Minter looming over his desk like an Easter Island edifice. He removed his headphones. He'd been listening to an interview Rajan and Warren had conducted with a scrote who'd brought in his solicitor with him last week. The solicitor had been running legal circles around them with what they could and couldn't do during the interview. It had been a whole load of bollocks.

'What can I do for you?' asked Boyd.

'You've got a visitor downstairs at the front desk,' Minter replied.

A civilian then, otherwise they'd be up here already.

'Who is it?' he asked.

'It's your Emma's fella, Dan,' Minter told him.

'Dan?' Boyd got up from his desk. 'What's he doing here?'

Minter shrugged and wandered back to his desk, job done.

Boyd left the CID floor and took the stairs down to

reception. He spotted the lad through the glass doors. He was outside having a fag. Boyd stepped out to join him.

'Are you all right there, Dan? What brings you over here?'

Dan turned to look at him. There was a somewhat guilty expression on his face.

'Is everything okay? Are Emma and Maggie all right?' Boyd asked, suddenly worried.

'No, yeah... They're fine,' Dan assured him. 'I just... Is it okay if we have a chat about something?' Dan pressed his lips together. 'I'm after a bit of... advice.'

Boyd checked his watch. It was nearly half twelve. As near as dammit to lunchtime.

'Sure.' He glanced up at the overcast sky. There were no heavy clouds, only the usual British, flat grey. His suit jacket would suffice. 'Do you fancy some chips on the pier?'

Dan's listless face split with a relieved grin. 'Yeah, that'd be cool. Thanks.'

～

'QUIT?'

Boyd paused the steaming chip midway to his open mouth. It was dangling on the end of the wooden fork – pretty dangerous, considering the feathered mafia gathered on the safety railing of Hastings Pier, watching them closely.

'Yeah,' replied Dan.

Boyd completed the chip's journey. 'But Jesus bloody Christ... *Why*? Why would you want to do something like that?'

Dan had been telling him about his recent tour, the glowing online reviews and the growing word-of-mouth support for the Mad Priests. Their songs were getting incredible numbers of downloads. 'Wonderful Day' was their biggest hit to date. Dan had even half-sung a verse and a chorus, and Boyd had had to admit that not only was the tune pretty damned ear-worm catchy but the lyrics were Morrissey-level dry... witty, even.

'You wrote that?' he'd asked, impressed. The lad had some talent.

'Why?' Dan echoed. He sipped his coffee and gazed at the railing, the menacing row of pigeons and the sea beyond. 'I don't really think I'm meant for this.' He looked back at Boyd and rephrased it. 'It's just not me.'

'Well, clearly it *is* you,' Boyd said. 'You've bloody made it, Dan. Or, at least, you're well on the way to making it.'

'I... I'm writing *fluff*,' Dan replied. 'Four minutes of meaningless shit.'

Boyd shrugged. 'So what? That's exactly what pop music is supposed to be.' He shook his head. 'Dan, mate, getting *any* degree of success in the music business is virtually impossible. And, for crying out loud, it sounds as though you and your band have actually cracked it. You'd be crazy to throw that away!' He dug his fork back into his punnet of chips and speared one. 'Does Emma know how you're feeling?'

Dan shook his head.

'What about your bandmates?'

He shook his head again. 'I haven't told Emma or them. I wanted to talk to you first.'

Boyd frowned. 'Me?'

Dan nodded. 'I want to do something that makes an actual difference to the world. What you do is cool. You make a difference. You catch bad guys and help people.'

*Christ*, Boyd thought. He hadn't been expecting a conversation like this – a dreamy-eyed musician wanting to throw away his one shot at stardom to become a *copper*, of all things, for crying out loud!

'My job's not all that, Dan,' he said. 'It's not just taking down bad guys and locking them up. It's paperwork. It's office politics. It's long shifts, late nights... It's not a fun job, I tell you. It's hard, often boring, and it's not particularly well paid.'

And it wasn't just that, Boyd mused. It was often frustrating and dispiriting watching scrotes walk away scot-free because the CPS couldn't guarantee *themselves* an easy win.

'And listen, Dan,' he added. 'Emma thinks you're a creative genius.'

She really did. At first, Boyd had wondered why she'd been ready to grant Dan a hall pass when it came to his fatherly responsibilities, but maybe she'd figured he was talented enough to deserve at least one good shot at success.

'I just wondered...' Dan resumed.

*Oh, Christ, here it comes...*

'... if you could help me get a job in the police?'

Boyd reached for his coffee and took a heavy slurp to buy him time to figure out the kindest way to politely say *no*. It dawned on him that maybe Dan was feeling this way due to some sort of post-tour fatigue. Or perhaps he'd had a falling-out with one of his bandmates and was feeling low about it. Give them a few days and they'd probably get over it, share a pint, and be besties once again.

The smart response would be to gently kick this police idea into the long grass.

'Sure, I can look into it, Dan...' Boyd replied. 'When I've got a bit of spare time, eh?'

## 33

J ay carried a sleeping Jorge into Sylvie's motel room. The boy was out for the count, exhausted after a day's worth of raging adrenaline, dopamine and sugary treats. Jay set him down on the camp bed beside his mum's bed and pulled a blanket over him. He patted his shoulder gently.

'I think he's going to sleep well tonight,' he said to Sylvie as he stood up.

She nodded. 'Thank you so much, Jay. You don't know how much this means to us both. Thank you.'

'You had a good time?'

She nodded again. In the amber light spilling in from outside, he detected a glint in her eyes.

'No one has *ever* been this generous to Jorge. Or to me...'

Jay felt a bit guilty being on the receiving end of such earnest gratitude. He'd had an ulterior motive to go to Disney World – to play the part of British Tourist, so that he could have a credible story in his back pocket, along with tickets and purchase receipts, to hand over if the police came knocking. Who the hell would be frolicking around in Disney World after committing a murder? If push came to shove, he might need to ask Sylvie to stretch the truth a little and give him an alibi that covered Sunday too. Would she? Would she lie for him? He shook his head. Sylvie and Jorge were undocumented immigrants. He'd be putting them in legal jeopardy if he got them involved.

A light touch on his arm jolted Jay from his thoughts. His ability to read female body language was rudimentary to say the least, but the long pause in the darkness, the gentleness of Sylvie's touch strongly hinted to Jay that she would meet him halfway if he picked this moment to lean forward and kiss her.

Devilish Naughty Jay whispered in his ear that it wouldn't be the biggest crime of the century. Sam had almost certainly been giving that Dr Pienaar the come-on. And Sylvie *was* very pretty. But Good Jay, Noble Jay – perched on his other shoulder – was busy telling him that Sam would never, *had never* cheated on him.

Jay reached for Sylvie's hand and squeezed it gently. Platonically.

'Jorge's a lovely lad. I'm just glad I could do that for him,' he said.

He sensed her wilting slightly.

'Hey, I'd better go,' he added.

She smiled sadly. 'I see you tomorrow?'

He nodded, turned and left her room, closing the door behind him.

He clomped along the terrace to his room, warily eyeing the wan, flickering sodium-tinted hue of the plaza's lights. If there were police sitting out there, ready to jump him, presumably they'd wait for him to confirm his identity by opening his motel room.

He paused by the door, dug into his jeans and pulled out his door key.

*Here goes.*

He pushed the key into the lock, turned the handle and opened the door, all the while listening out for the inevitable sound of approaching boots on tarmac and someone shouting, 'FREEZE!'

But none of that happened. Jay turned to survey the mostly empty car park before stepping inside and locking the door behind him.

'You're jumping at shadows, you knob,' he muttered to himself.

He grabbed the burner phone, to see if Mack had called. He had. There was one missed call from an hour ago. Jay dialled his number.

'That you, Jay?' Mack asked. 'Why didn't you fuckin' answer when I rang you?'

'I was out...' Jay replied, surprised by the anger in Mack's voice. He was tempted to add that he'd been out 'being a tourist... like you *told* me to!' But Mack didn't sound as though he was in the mood for any backchat.

'They've found her body, Jay,' Mack told him. 'Some trucker spotted her in the ditch early this morning. I got a visit from the police a few hours ago. I would have called you sooner but they came with an emotional support lady to sit with me. They've only just gone.' Mack sighed. 'I've been squeezing out fake tears for ages. It's been fucking exhausting.'

Jay wasn't sure how to react to the news that they'd found Kerry's body. Relief? Panic? And as for Mack... *fake* tears? Surely he had to be feeling *something* for his wife.

'How're you coping, mate?' he asked.

'I'm stressed,' replied Mack. 'And tired. I've got to drive

over to the morgue in Fort Pierce tomorrow morning – which is an hour's drive or so, by the way – and make a formal ID on her body.'

'Right,' Jay said, noting that Mack seemed more irritated than upset. 'What about her car? Have they found that yet?'

'Not yet. They're looking for her Lotus, but the cop who called me said they didn't expect to find it, though. He said being a luxury car, especially one that's not made any more, it's probably already in a shipping container heading to the Far East.' Mack sipped on a drink. 'Which suggests they're already putting this down to some carjacking with a bad ending.' He paused.

'I'm so sorry, Mack... She didn't deserve this,' Jay tried again.

'No, she certainly didn't,' Mack agreed.

Jay looked out through the blinds at the mostly empty car park and chastened himself for being quite so skittish. 'So, Mack, what do you want me to do? Stick around a bit longer? I was thinking about packing up my stuff and heading home.'

'The fuck you will!' Mack snapped. 'You stay put!'

'But –' Jay tried.

'But *nothing*,' Mack cut in. 'I've paid for your time so you're still on my bloody clock! You stay right where you are. You've been paid to do a job.'

'But she's *dead*,' said Jay. 'There's no longer a job for me to do. And if the cops are already sure it was a carjacking, we're good, right? I might as well head back.'

'Do you want the rest of your money, Jay?' Mack asked.

Jay really wasn't sure whether he should be holding out for the rest or beating a retreat to Hastings. Mack had given him thirty thousand dollars up front and the promise of the rest if he was happy with Jay's work. Sixty large was a lot of money to miss out on. It was tempting. And Mack didn't seem to have stitched him up so far.

'Uh...well, yeah. Yes, please,' he found himself muttering.

'Then go and visit Disney World or Universal Studios or something. You've got a return ticket, yes?' said Mack.

'Yeah, for May thirteenth. I've got a fortnight left –' Jay began.

'So, do me a favour,' Mack interrupted. 'How about you hold on until the end of next week, huh?'

Jay pondered that. A week and a half of sitting around for $60K? It *seemed* like the police were thinking the murderer was some professional car thief on the prowl for big-ticket cars. He figured he should be pretty safe. Mack might have a temper, but he'd kept his word where Jay was concerned.

'Okay,' Jay found himself saying.

'Good. Well, I'll come by before you head home and drop you off the rest of that money,' Mack promised. 'And no more calls from now on. Unless it's urgent – and I mean *extremely* urgent.'

With that, Mack hung up.

# 34

Mack dropped the phone into his lap and reached for his gin and tonic.

*What a day. What. A. Fucking. Day.* He didn't need stress like this. It was bad for his heart. And bad for his liver. He'd downed three double gins since the cop and victim advocate had offered their condolences for a final time, asked if he was going to be okay overnight and then left him to it.

Now that the police had departed, he didn't have to carry on acting the shocked and heartbroken husband. He could calm down a bit, settle his mind and order his thoughts.

Kerry, the cheating bitch, had been fucking some personal trainer or whatever called Ryan and now she was dead. Call it karma; call it divine justice. At least he was now out of the alimony hole, which would have cost him so much.

He'd reported her missing six hours after she'd left the house, saying that it was out of character and that he'd been unable to reach her on her phone. And he'd had multiple

Zoom calls throughout the day that provided him with a solid alibi. The only person in the world who knew he was lining his ducks up to divorce Kerry was Turner. And no one but himself, Turner and Ronni Kirk had any idea that the Brit was on the job over here.

If the police, somehow, became aware that he had a PI shadowing his wife, then maybe the sensible thing to do would be to just come clean. Because no husband planning to actually kill his wife would be dumb enough to hire someone to watch her back.

His phone vibrated in his lap.

He turned it over, half expecting that muppet Turner to be calling him back.

But it wasn't him. It was an unknown number.

'Yeah?' he answered cautiously. 'Who's this?'

'Carlton.'

*Carlton?* Dominic Carlton had been the unexpected plus-one who'd come along with Senator Bowman this weekend. A wrinkly little ex-CIA gremlin who now worked freelance as the senator's personal security.

It was Carlton who'd been responsible for the digital blackout at Mack's mansion over the weekend. He'd even walked around and unplugged all the landline phones that Mack had had installed in various guest rooms. The wrinkly little fucker had even hijacked Mack's welcome speech to the Mulligan Club, to remind all the gents attending, that their club had strict rules. Carlton had informed them that nothing was to be written down or tapped into phones as memos. There were to be no texts, no emails, no selfies, not even any pictures of Mr Wakefield's fine collection of porcelain figurines. And that there was going to be a digital blackout across Wakefield's mansion and grounds for the next twenty-four or so hours.

'Mr Wakefield,' said Carlton, 'let me be the first to offer you my condolences. Poor Kerry.'

'How did you–?' Mack began.

'I'm very well connected, Mr Wakefield,' Carlton cut in. 'It's my business to know things. So, like I said, my condolences. Your wife was a very pleasant hostess. Very personable. Very charming.'

'I... yes. I'm still in a state of shock,' said Mack.

'We need to talk about her,' continued Carlton.

Mack drew in a sharp breath, wondering what was coming next. But the wily old bugger said nothing. Clearly waiting to see how Mack would react.

'Is there something you want to share with me, Mr Wakefield?' Carlton asked. 'About Kerry?'

'Sorry?' Mack said, wondering if he was supposed to share that Kerry had been shagging some handsome buck behind his back and that he'd hired a PI to catch her in flagrante delicto. Or did the little bastard know something about Kerry?

'Okay,' Mack sighed. 'So the bitch was cheating on me.'

Carlton remained silent.

'I hired a PI to follow her, to catch her in the act.' Mack huffed angrily. 'I'm damned if I'm going to have to pay out a ton of alimony to some cow who's fucking someone behind my –'

'You hired a PI?'

'Yeah,' replied Mack.

'You hired someone to *watch your wife*?' Carlton paused. 'And you didn't think to share that with me?'

'I just wanted a few compromising pictures of her. That's all,' Mack said.

'Jesus Christ!' Carlton hissed.

'The PI. He's a totally solid bloke,' Mack said. 'He's just –'

'You fucking idiot!' snapped Carlton. 'She wasn't cheating on you.'

'She bloody well was! My PI got pictures of –'

'She was *informing* on you. She was reporting to a Fed, you moron. She was an FBI asset. I don't know how long your wife's been passing on your every move,' Carlton said, 'but even if it was just this weekend, we're fucked.'

Mack felt his scalp suddenly prickle.

On Saturday evening, the club had covered a lot of ground. Many of their 'what if's had finally morphed into concrete plans. That evening, the Mulligan Club had stepped over a line and moved from a gathering of a dozen bitter men grumbling about the state of the world to fully fledged conspirators.

'The Feds know we meet,' Carlton went on. 'And I'm sure they have a strong suspicion as to why we meet.' He paused. 'What we have to hope is that your wife didn't manage to gather any evidence for them.'

*Shit, shit, shit. My Kerry? Pretty, blonde, clueless, I'm-here-for-the-pearls Kerry?*

'More to the point,' said Carlton, 'we have to hope she didn't manage to sneak anything she recorded out of your house.'

'She... she was spying on us?' Mack felt blindsided.

'Yes, Wakefield, she was *spying*. Eavesdropping. Recording whatever the hell she could catch. I spotted her holding a phone up to the lounge door.' He thought he heard Carlton sigh. 'She was a ridiculous amateur. Standing right outside the door while we discussed what we discussed, holding her phone up to the goddamned keyhole.'

'Jesus fucking Christ.' Mack dabbed at his clammy forehead with his shirt sleeve.

'She couldn't transmit whatever she managed to record, because of the blackout,' Carlton said. 'But the moment she stepped out of your grounds, we dealt with her.'

Mack felt his stomach fold over on itself. *Dealt with her?*

'You mean you *shot* her?' he gasped.

'Not personally,' Carlton said. 'But I used a guy.'

Mack let out a long ragged breath. 'Jesus.'

'And my concerns would have been put to rest,' Carlton growled, 'but for the fact that I've *now* learned that you've had a private investigator hovering around.'

'Listen, Carlton, he's just a boots-'n'-binoculars type, all right? He's not Sherlock bloody Holmes.'

'If he has anything, Wakefield – *anything at all* – he's a danger to us. Do you understand? A picture of any of us arriving at your place. A car, a number plate, a grainy photograph of the senator. Do you understand?

'All it took was one grainy image of his head poking out of a doorway to destroy your Prince Andrew. Proof of association is damning enough.' There was a long silence. Then Carlton spoke again. 'I need to know everything he has. *Everything.*'

'It's not much,' Mack replied. 'He managed to catch her meeting someone called Ryan, but that's about it.'

'Does he have photographs? Video? Audio?' Carlton asked.

As far as Mack was aware, all Jay Turner had accumulated so far were endless pictures of Kerry having a coffee with her friends, shopping, getting in and out of her car, and a brief muffled encounter with a good-looking man in a fancy garden.

'Just some pictures,' Mack replied. 'But, look, now Kerry's dead, I should pay him off and send him back home.'

Carlton took a moment to consider that. 'Yes. You do that, Wakefield. Let's get rid of your PI and as quickly as possible.'

## 35

J ay was just getting sucked into an episode of the original *Star Trek* when his phone buzzed beside him on the bed. He reached for the remote to pause the show, but remembered this was terrestrial TV. Instead he muted it and picked up his phone. He was surprised and relieved to see it was Mack. This surely had to be him giving Jay the all-clear to pack up and ship out.

'Mack, how're things going?' he asked.

'Fine,' Mack replied. 'Look, Jay, I've been thinking about it and there's really no point in you sitting around with your thumb up your arse.'

'So I'm good to go home?' Jay asked hopefully.

'Yeah,' Mack said. 'The police seem pretty sure it was some local perp who spotted a high-value car and an easy opportunity... It was just terrible, *terrible* luck for my Kerry.'

Jay realised that that was the first time he'd heard Mack express any sympathy at all for the poor woman.

'She didn't deserve that,' Mack continued. 'Now that this has happened, I don't think we need to drag her reputation through the mud. I'll take everything you've got on her and ditch it, all right?'

'Okay,' Jay agreed.

'And, yeah, I know what you're going to ask me next and I'll be good for the rest of that cash if you want to meet up at O'Connors. Tomorrow night good?'

Jay nodded. 'That's really decent of you, Mack. Thanks.'

'Yeah, well. A promise is a promise. Shall we meet at seven? You bring all your shit. I'll bring the money. We'll share a pint and bid *adios amigo*. How does that sound?'

Jay smiled. It sounded very good. 'I'll bring it all. Memory sticks. Logs, notes and her phone.'

'Her phone?' said Mack.

Jay mentally kicked himself. He couldn't let anyone see his photo on Kerry's burner phone. Mack might use it against him.

'Her phone?' repeated Mack.

'Uh... yeah. I had to retrieve my bugs and stuff – just to be, you know, on the safe side.... and I found her phone. It's pretty burnt up and useless. I was going to toss it into a dumpster,' Jay said.

'I'll need that,' said Mack.

*It could still be readable, Jay.* That's what Ronni had suggested. He was decidedly wary about letting anyone else have it until he knew for sure that the SD card inside was trashed.

'If you don't mind, Mack, I'm just going to toss it where it can't be found.

'Listen, Jay, you need to give me that phone, all right? No messing around with it – just bring it along with you. Relax. I'll make sure it's wiped clean,' Mack said.

Jay sat up. 'Mack, look, I'm not being funny, but I'd feel uncomfortable with anyone, even yourself, having that phone with a picture of me, seeing how she's been murdered. I'm sure you can see where I'm coming from.'

'I don't give a shit, Jay,' Mack said. 'I *need* that fucking phone.'

*Need.* The word spooked the hell out of Jay. The nagging suspicion returned – the persistent worry that Mack could be looking for a patsy. What if the police *weren't* actually pursuing the carjacker theory and were quietly circling Mack? What if they suddenly started reading him his rights? What then?

*Look, detective... My wife, she said something to me about catching some creep under her car. She said she even took a photo of him...*

'I don't want to sound like a dick here, Mack, but I need to hang on to it just for a bit. Until I know it's clean and I'm home.'

'I *need* that phone, Jay,' Mack repeated. His tone softened just a fraction. 'Look, *mate*, I don't want to sound like a dick either, but no phone, no cash.'

Jay mentally kicked himself again for mentioning the bloody thing in the first place.

'What do I care if your mug's on her phone, eh?' Mack chuckled. 'I just want to make sure there are no intimate photos of her and me on there? You can understand that, right?'

'Mr Wakefield, Mack... I'm sorry, but it's a no.'

The sound of Malcolm Wakefield's breathing ceased for a moment, then he spoke. The tone in his voice was different, the friendly tone suddenly absent.

'This isn't a request, Turner,' Mack said coldly. 'You will give me that fucking phone tomorrow or...'

Jay suspected the offer of sixty large for services rendered might be history now. Mack sounded pretty pissed off with him. More to the point, the '*or*' at the end of that sentence had sounded uncomfortably like a threat. His suspicion that he was being used as a patsy intensified.

He heard Mack's heavy breathing for a few seconds, followed by the rustle of sudden movement, then the call ended abruptly.

Jay lowered his phone and stared at the problematic nugget of plastic, metal and glass that was on the table.

Was Mack's doggedness about getting his hands on it only about sparing his blushes?

*Or is there something else going on here?*

---

## 36

**B**oyd rose from bed to the sound of the alarm going off and Ozzie licking his left ear. The crafty sod had managed to inveigle himself onto the bed during the night and had worked his way up between himself and Charlotte.

In reality, the alarm on his phone was superfluous. It wasn't so much Greenwich Mean Time that signalled that it was time to get up, it was more like Ozzie Meal Time.

'All right, mate, all right,' Boyd grumbled, pulling on his dressing gown and opening the door to let Ozzie and Mia thunder down the stairs.

As he approached the bathroom door, it opened wide and Dan strolled out, headphones on, butt-naked and towelling himself dry.

'Dan!' Boyd called out.

The lad stopped and spun round, his eyes wide. He wrapped the towel firmly round his waist, then pulled a headphone out from his ear.

'It's not your flat, Dan,' Boyd said. 'Clothes on, mate, eh? There's women around!'

'Ah, shit! Sorry, Mr B. I – I'm so sorry. I didn't… I wasn't thinking clearly,' Dan stuttered.

'It's okay.' Boyd smiled at his bumbling apology. 'I just don't want to give poor Charlotte an embolism.'

'I heard that,' Charlotte called from the bedroom.

Dan nodded to show he'd taken the advice on board, turned and hurried down the hallway towards Emma's room. From the shafts of sunlight spilling in from the hall window, Boyd was certain that he'd caught a glimpse of something on the lad that gave him cause for concern.

～

MID-MORNING, as Boyd took a break from sifting through his intray and watching Okeke constantly checking her phone for calls from Jay, he reflected on the marks he'd seen on Dan's upper arms. The faint ladder marks.

He was pretty sure that Dan had been cutting himself.

Boyd had seen those marks often enough to recognise them. They were a common sight these days, the marks almost as prevalent as Celtic swirl tattoos.

He presumed Emma knew about them. Were they old ones? And what the hell was it with that weird conversation Dan had had with him yesterday?

*Something's going on here.* Dan losing his flat, despite apparently storming Europe… Then asking whether he could join the police…

It took Boyd a couple of minutes to google the Mad Priests' website.

Dan wasn't mentioned in the band's line-up. There were plenty of pictures from their recent tour: four willowy young lads with mops of hair and wannabee beards, glistening with gig sweat. And none of them were Dan.

For a moment Boyd wondered whether he'd got the right band, but then he spotted their track list and a song called 'Wonderful Day'.

Dan's catchy song.

On the Contacts page, he found a phone number for their manager. A woman called Nikki Turkman. It was a London number. He dialled and got an answerphone message. Boyd left his name, number and the fact that he was a detective, the latter hopefully guaranteeing a call back.

'Morning, Boyd!'

He turned to see that Sutherland's cheerful round head had emerged from its glass fishbowl. 'Hatcher wants a quick chat with you.'

'Now, sir?'

Sutherland nodded. 'Yes, *now*.'

∾

'MA'AM, YOU WANTED TO SEE ME?'

Margaret Hatcher glanced up from her mobile phone. 'Morning. Yes, come in,' she said.

Boyd stepped into her office and caught a glimpse of her phone's screen as he waited to be offered a seat. She seemed to be playing Puzzly Words, one of Charlotte's favourite games.

'Just a moment,' she said, eyes still locked on her screen. Then a moment later came a whispered 'Dammit.'

'Did you lose?' Boyd asked, smiling.

She returned his smile, a little guiltily. 'Damned game. I can't ever seem to get into the second round. Wretched bloody thing. Take a seat.'

Boyd pulled the seat out and sat down.

'Now then, Bill... Can we talk candidly?' she asked.

Boyd glanced at her glass display cabinet. 'Is this a phones-away conversation?'

'Just an honest one.' She smiled again. 'Between colleagues who have accumulated a certain degree of, dare I say, *trust* in each other?'

'Trust' wasn't exactly the right word for it, Boyd thought. They had some compromising knowledge on each other. They both knew they'd been bribed by Rovshan Salikov; in Boyd's case, it was blood money – quite literally – that he was never going to spend.

He nodded. 'All right.'

'How are we doing with this local missing woman Audrey Hincher?' Hatcher asked.

So they were starting with Her Madge's version of small talk. 'Making some headway,' replied Boyd.

She nodded in satisfaction, then leant forward. 'I had a tap on the shoulder from Aubrey Dutton. He told me he read the riot act to you, DS Okeke *and* your families after you all ran off into the wilds of England to play at being spies.'

'Whistle-blowers,' he corrected. 'Not spies. And we ran because that boutique agency went rogue. Three innocent people were killed to keep this country's dirty little secret... secret.'

'Yes. He did mention that. The director, Warner, has been suspended and that division has been retired. He also mentioned he'd threatened the lot of you with being put on a travel watch list.'

'No more Costa del Sol holidays for me, then?' Boyd pulled a face.

'If he did, not without asking their permission first.' She checked a note she'd made. 'But DS Okeke's other half,

Jason Turner, appears to have flouted that. He's over in America, I believe?'

Boyd nodded. 'They had a big bust-up. I knew he'd stomped off somewhere.'

'Well, when he comes back, he may be in some trouble,' she said, adding, 'I don't know how far they'll want to go with that... To be fair, they have more important things to worry about.'

He looked at her. 'And this is a friendly, unofficial heads-up?'

She nodded. 'You might want to pass it on to Okeke. To pass on to him.'

'I will. Thanks, ma'am.' Boyd went to get up.

'One other thing,' she said. 'I heard from Ian that you're not interested in replacing Flack and heading up Rosper?'

He knew Sutherland was desperate to fill that slot.

'Correct,' he replied. 'I'm just... To be honest, I'm considering an early retirement. The last few years have been more than enough for me. Plus, I'm sure you've heard, I'm a grandad now and I'm keen to spend more time at home, not less.'

She smiled. 'Yes, I heard. Congratulations.'

'I've got more than enough plates to juggle right now,' he said – and that was putting it mildly. Emma was a stay-at-home mum without any kind of career. Something concerning was going on with Dan. And Boyd had had cancer just last year, and he was fifty-one. Not that old, but not getting any younger either. The idea of getting sucked into an operation without end definitely wasn't floating his boat.

'Fair enough,' Hatcher replied after a while. 'I have a shortlist of DCIs from other forces who *have* expressed an interest, so I think we can fill the gap quite quickly.'

'Good. That's good.' Boyd went to get up again, presuming the matter of Flack's replacement was the other thing she'd wanted to discuss.

'But...' she chimed in quickly, 'something has come up that *might* be of interest to you.'

He sat back down once again. 'What?'

'An opportunity,' she said. 'A somewhat *special* opportunity.' She reached into her intray and pulled out a sealed envelope. 'It's an invitation.'

She handed it over the desk to him.

'An invitation to what, ma'am?' he asked.

She shrugged. 'I imagine to have a chat.'

'With whom?' He raised his brows.

She replied with a sly smile and what appeared to be a mischievous glint in her eyes.

## 37

Special Agent Ryan watched the medical examiner through the window as he slowly paced round the autopsy table. Kerry Wakefield's body lay naked on the slab, her skin now a marbled and pale grey on the front and a livid purple on the back, where subdermal blood had pooled and clotted. The golden tan lines she'd once had were now just slightly paler stripes of blue-grey.

'First time?' asked Detective Angela Durrant.

'First time what?' Ryan said.

'Is this your first time at an autopsy?' Durrant asked.

He nodded. It was. But he'd seen more than his fair share of bodies. Before the FBI, he'd been in the Marines, and before that, a traffic cop. Ryan had seen bodies in all manner of condition: in pieces ('kit form' as they said in the Marines), seared like a griddled burger, or bloated from decomposition – and, on one occasion, flattened to the thickness of a doormat by an APC. Kerry Wakefield's body was in a comparatively good condition, apart from the discolouration of the skin and the tiny bullet hole between her eyes.

'No signs of restraint,' the medical examiner said, his voice carried to Ryan and Durrant via speakers. 'No signs of a struggle. No bruising around the thighs. No grab marks.' He turned to look at them. 'At first glance, I'd say she wasn't sexually assaulted.'

Special Agent Ryan nodded. *At least there's that.*

It appeared that she had been killed quickly and efficiently. Hopefully dead before she knew she was in trouble. But – and there was no escaping the truth – this was on him. His insistence, his *impatience* had put her on that slab. He'd pushed her into a situation she wasn't trained for and, at some point down the line, he was going to have to account for it.

'So?' Durrant said to Ryan. 'Are you going to explain to a cop who's been around a few decades, why the FBI's interested in this body?' She raised a brow. 'This obviously wasn't a random killing. She was hit by a pro. Is this an organised crime thing?'

Ryan shook his head. 'Worse.'

Durrant frowned.

'It's all corruption and politics. It's dirty stuff,' he said. But that was all he was going to give her. He'd been working this case for three years. Watching the Mulligan Club, as they called themselves. When a bunch of men went to great effort to meet in secret, it invariably meant they were up to no good. When a bunch of rich and politically connected men did so, it was worth a closer look.

The British businessman Malcolm Wakefield had joined the club a couple of years ago. Wakefield had been well on his way to becoming a billionaire and had appeared keen to insert himself into Florida's political ecosystem. The club gathered every three months or so, sometimes at a ski chalet in Utah, once at a hunting lodge in Denver, and in the past eighteen months meeting *more regularly* at Wakefield's Palm Beach mansion.

The secrecy and caution of the men attending these gatherings had initially flagged Ryan's interest. Their names even more so. There was a tech bro, a well-known senator, a former head of the NSA, a retired general...

Malcolm Wakefield's wife, Kerry, had been his lucky break.

He'd profiled her and discovered which gym she frequented. He'd signed up and, after a few days, he'd approached her with some tips on how to better use the cross trainer she was struggling with. After a few months of building up her trust, he'd asked her out for a coffee after a gym session.

It had taken him months of coffee, patience and an angle he could exploit before he'd felt he could come clean with her. She'd driven one of Malcolm's favourite vanity cars into a ditch, been breathalysed by a state trooper and found to be well and truly over the limit. Kerry had been more frightened about her husband discovering she'd trashed his precious car than the possibility of being charged with a DUI.

Ryan had been able to intervene and make that piece of paperwork vanish. The report indicated that she'd had a blow-out and veered off the road. Not her fault and nothing that Wakefield could punish her for.

Kerry Wakefield had been extremely grateful for Ryan's intervention, but it had come with a request.

A very *big* request.

## 38

S*hit. Shit. Shit. Shit.* This particular problem had kept Mack Wakefield awake all night. Not the absence of his wife from their king-sized bed, but his PI... Jay Turner.

The stubborn idiot had been ridiculously paranoid about his snapshot being on Kerry's phone – and he'd unwittingly turned himself into an issue that needed to be fixed. Mack hadn't been too worried that Kerry had caught Jay fumbling beneath her car, but now that he knew that Kerry had been spying, he was more than a little worried about what exactly Jay had inadvertently recorded on his wretched bug thing. And God knows how much of Saturday's conversation Kerry had managed to record on that phone. Thinking back, he and the club members had covered a lot of ground:

'*This needs to happen before June...*'

'*Neil, we can easily make it look like a lone wolf... a crackpot...*'

'*Some deranged NRA type with an unhealthy obsession?*'

'*Right.*'

'*No, Joe. It needs to be a headshot. We can't have him just wounded... He needs to be taken out; I mean it. We need a body bag, not a hospital gurney.*'

Christ – they'd been casually using each other's first names. Carlton had said that Kerry had been holding her phone right up to the door, recording audio. But what if she'd managed to take photos at some point, or had captured video evidence...?

There was too much at stake here. Far too much.

'Jesus,' whispered Mack. There really was no other way out of this mess. He finished his coffee and set the cup down on the breakfast bar; the noise seemed to echo deafeningly across the polished granite floors of his Palm Beach mansion. Without Kerry and her nineties pop music, clacking heels and inane squawking, the place was as still and silent as a monastery.

He picked up his phone and dialled.

'Mr Wakefield,' Carlton answered.

'Listen...' began Mack, 'I think we've got a problem with my PI.'

## 39

J ay had decided on the Mega Maple Pancake Stack with extras. Jorge had opted for a cheeseburger and milkshake. Sylvie brought the food over to them.

'One brunch special.' She winked at Jay. 'With bacon... and Heinz beans.'

'Thanks,' Jay replied.

'And for you, young man...,' She set Jorge's meal in front of him and pointed at the salad on the side. 'Greens first, then you can have the burger.'

Jorge rolled his eyes.

'I'll make sure he eats it in the right order,' said Jay, winking at Jorge.

His phone buzzed and he pulled it out.

It was Sam. He looked up at Sylvie, hesitating before swiping the screen and answering.

'Sorry... I've got to take this,' he said. 'Sam?'

Sylvie took the hint, turned and left them to their food.

'I called you a dozen times. Why the hell don't you answer?' Okeke began.

Jay nodded at Jorge to carry on eating. 'Your heard your

mum, lad – salad first,' he said, getting up from the booth and making his way to the doors.

'Who's eating salad?' asked Okeke.

'Jorge.'

'And how is Jorge?'

'I'm babysitting. Kind of.'

'Babysitting? What's going on?'

'The, uh... There's a waitress here – she's got a kid, and trying to work and be Mum at the same time. I'm just watching him for her.'

'*Waitress?*' Okeke suddenly sounded suspicious.

'Relax,' replied Jay. 'I'm just being neighbourly.' He stepped outside. 'So... sorry about that.'

Okeke sighed heavily. 'Whatever. What I'm more concerned about is where the fuck you've been! TWO DAYS I've been waiting for you to call. I thought you were dead!'

Jay looked around to make sure he was alone. He lowered his voice. 'I'd gone back to the lake when you called. To Kerry's burned-out car,' he said.

'Jesus! I told you to sit tight! Didn't I? To sit tight and –'

'I recovered Kerry's secret phone,' replied Jay. 'I couldn't just leave it there, Sam. The police could have found it, cracked it and wondered who the fuck I am!'

There was a pause, then she sighed. 'Okay, maybe it was the right move.'

'Well, yeah,' he agreed, 'except that I now think I've really pissed Mack off.'

'What do you mean?' Okeke asked.

'He wants Kerry's phone back. I mean, badly wants it back.'

'Okay. So give it to him,' Sam said.

'Well, I can't, can I?' he replied. 'Not with my face on her photo roll? What if he's setting me up? I've been thinking about it some more, Sam, and it's perfect for him. If the cops look his way, all he has to do is make sure they find the phone. If the data's still readable, or even if it did manage to upload to cloud storage somewhere? He could say that Kerry thought she was being harassed by someone from England! And if they do find a picture of me... I'd be fucked.'

Sam sighed. 'Okay, I see your problem. So what's your next move?'

'I think I'm going to try to just come back home. I'm not going to tell Mack I'm doing it, though. Sitting around here for another couple of weeks doesn't feel like the smart thing to do.'

'No. It doesn't,' Okeke agreed, sounding relieved.

'I'm gonna call the airline and book a flight, say I want to come home a week early. Hopefully I'll be back tomorrow night,' he told her.

'And what if you get stopped at the airport?' she asked.

'It didn't happen when I left the UK, did it? Or when I entered the US. I think the whole watch-list thing was just those MI5 people trying to spook us.'

'Jay?' she said.

'Yeah.'

'Do it *now*. Get yourself to the airport and see what you can get. Buy a new ticket if you have to,' she said, exasperated.

He huffed. 'I already have a ticket. Isn't that going to make me look super-dodgy? Relax. I'll call the airline and change my return booking.'

'And what about Mack?' she asked. 'Is he likely to do anything?'

'Like what? Come around and punch me?' Jay laughed.

'Love, be serious for a second,' she said.

Jay sighed. He'd had far too much time sitting alone in his room and was beginning to conjure up all sorts of paranoid theories. Was Mack going to send someone round to deal with him? Was there a little bit more to the bastard than met the eye? And what about this Ryan bloke? Who the fuck was he? What the hell had he been up to? Did this Ryan know who he was now, and was he going to pay a visit in the middle of the night?

Jay realised he was in danger of disappearing down a rabbit hole of paranoia and perhaps... perhaps... *hopefully*... the simplest answer was the most likely one.

'Look, Sam. I'm pretty sure he's just worried I've got a phone with loads of pictures of him with his dick out or something... That's why he wants the phone. He'll just have to live with it.'

## 40

S pecial Agent Ryan watched Malcolm Wakefield as he entered the interview room.

The officer with him stood up and offered her hand to the Brit. 'I'm Detective Angela Durrant, Martin County Sheriff's Office.' She glanced at Ryan – and there was no mistaking the disapproval in her glare. 'This is *Detective* Ryan.'

They'd had an argument about this as Wakefield was being driven over for his interview.

'You do realise misrepresenting yourself in the interview room may disqualify any evidence we unearth in there, right?' Durrant had said. 'Everything he says this afternoon could be inadmissible!'

'I know,' replied Ryan.

'He could come right out and say it: *I shot my wife*. And there's a chance that won't be allowed anywhere near the court,' Durrant said.

'Yes. I know,' Ryan repeated.

She'd been marooned somewhere between fury and bewilderment. 'So why do it? Why the false identity?'

'I can't have him getting a whiff that I'm FBI,' Ryan had replied.

Ryan was looking at the British businessman now, and reminded himself he was going to have to role-play a homicide cop. That meant dropping the agency speak.

He extended his hand to Wakefield as Durrant had. 'Thanks for coming in this afternoon, Mr Wakefield.'

'Well, I've got no choice, have I?' Wakefield replied. 'I want the bastard who did this!'

Ryan nodded politely and indicated a chair. Wakefield sat down. Ryan was surprised to see that Wakefield had come alone, without a lawyer in tow. He wondered if that was an attempt by the man to present himself as being wholly cooperative with nothing to hide.

Durrant started the interview recorder and called out the date time and those present in the room. She looked at Ryan and raised a brow that said, *This is your show... so you start.'*

'Mr Wakefield,' Ryan began, 'first of all, I want to offer my condolences...'

'Mack,' Wakefield replied. 'Everyone calls me Mack. And thanks. I appreciate it.'

Ryan nodded. 'Can my colleague get you a coffee or anything?'

Durrant shot him daggers.

'No, I'm good, thanks,' Wakefield said. 'Let's just get on with this, can we?'

'Sure.' Ryan pulled out the file of paperwork that Durrant had already started gathering for the investigation. It contained the trucker's statement, pictures of Kerry's body in the ditch, photos from the medical examiner's inspection and his report that stated a post-mortem would be forthcoming. That said, the cause of death seemed quite apparent: one very well-placed bullet.

'Now, you called the Palm Beach police after she didn't return home on Sunday, right? To say you were concerned about her welfare?'

'Yeah,' Wakefield replied. 'She said she wasn't going to be late back. And when she didn't come home, and I couldn't get hold of her on the phone, I decided to call the police.'

Ryan pretended to review the notes, then nodded. 'That's what we've got here. You called at 2.23 a.m. Monday morning to report your concern about your wife being missing. So, Mack, I'm going to lean into something straight off the mark, okay? Nine times out of ten a murdered woman is a victim to someone she knows. And in those situations, again, nine times out of ten… that's her partner.'

Ryan was expecting an explosion of pink-faced outrage from the Brit. But Wakefield simply nodded calmly. 'I know how it goes, mate. And that's fine. I've got nothing to hide. You ask what you've got to ask.'

'Great, I'm glad you're okay with that,' Ryan said, glancing at Durrant.

Mack nodded. 'It's fine with me. The sooner you can rule me out, the sooner you can focus on finding the bastard who done this to Kerry.'

'So, Sunday afternoon and evening, then,' began Ryan, 'can you give me an account of what you were up to?'

'Yeah,' Wakefield replied. 'I had a game of golf at the beach club; you'll be able to verify that. Then I had online calls with my business and logistics managers back in the UK, and an online call with my accountant into the evening. They'll all confirm that.'

'Sure,' said Ryan, pretending to make a note of all that.

He switched tack. 'Can I ask you about your relationship with Kerry?'

Wakefield shrugged, then nodded. 'Fire away.'

'Were things okay between you?' Ryan asked. 'Were there any stressors or points of friction in your relationship?'

'Nope,' Wakefield said. 'We were very happily married.'

'There's a notable age gap,' cut in Durrant. 'She was thirty-two, and you're...'

'I'm sixty-five,' Wakefield replied. 'What's that got to do with bloody anything, love?'

'An age gap like that brings its own stress factors,' Durrant said calmly.

Mack shook his head, irritated. 'We were very fucking happy, as it happens. Very fucking happy.'

Ryan nodded along with Mack, and gave an imperceptible shake of the head to Durrant, as though she'd just made a judgemental assumption.

'Did Kerry have anything she was worried about? Did she mention anything to you on Sunday that gave you cause for concern?' Ryan asked.

Wakefield's eyes narrowed, and his left hand – a big boxer's fist – came up to scratch his mottled pink cheek. It looked as though he was giving the question some serious thought.

*Of course Kerry was stressed*, Ryan reminded himself as he waited for an answer. *The poor woman was fucking terrified.* She hadn't wanted to go back on Saturday. She'd managed to escape the house under the guise of needing to get more scotch for the senator. She said she'd wanted to run for the hills.

'Well,' started Mack, 'now you mention it...'

Ryan cocked his head. 'Go on...'

'Kerry said something to me in England, not long before we flew back to the States.'

'Yeah? What was that?' Ryan asked.

Wakefield pressed his lips together in a display that Ryan suspected was his A-game attempt at expressing remorse, regret. 'Goddammit... I should have taken it more seriously. Taken *her* more seriously...' he added.

Durrant leant forward, eager to nudge him along. 'Go on, Mack... What did Kerry tell you?'

Wakefield's voice began to wobble slightly. Either he was channelling some kind of *genuine* grief from somewhere, or he was actually not a bad actor. 'She... she mentioned back in England... this... this bloke she kept seeing.'

'Seeing,' said Durrant, 'as in...'

'Not *meeting*, but... like... noticing. He was watching her,' Wakefield said.

'Watching her?' pressed Durrant. 'What do you mean? Harassing? Following? Stalking?'

Wakefield nodded. 'She said it was always from a distance, you know? Nothing too obvious. But...'

'But what?' Ryan asked.

'She said he was obsessive. Always watching,' Wakefield told them.

'Did she describe him?' asked Durrant.

Wakefield nodded. 'She said he was quite tall, quite bulky, you know... muscular. And white.'

Durrant wrote that down.

'He was a big man,' continued Wakefield. 'Possibly a Brit.'

Durrant added that to her notes, then looked back up. 'Mr Wakefield, this is a difficult question, but did you have any reason to believe that Kerry was cheating on you?'

## 41

Okeke fumbled for her phone on the sofa. She'd fallen into a fitful sleep while rewatching some old seasons of *Grey's Anatomy* to take her mind off Jay. The phone was buzzing insistently, lost beneath the cushions she'd piled up against the arm so that she could doze.

'Come on... Come on!' she hissed as she desperately tried to find the damned thing before it stopped buzzing. Finally she found it wedged down the back of the sofa and pulled it out.

'Jay?' she began hopefully.

'No, it's Karl.'

'Oh.'

Karl paused. 'Is this a good time? Bad time?'

She looked at her watch. It was gone eleven.

'I'm in bed,' Okeke lied. If this was a 'how're you coping?' call, she could do without right now.

'I've got some info,' said Karl.

She sat up. 'Go on.'

'So, I did some digging on Malcolm Wakefield,' Karl

said. 'It wasn't easy to do. He's kept his business affairs off the radar pretty well.'

'And?' Okeke prompted.

She heard Karl draw a breath. 'He's dodgy as fuck, Sam. A real piece of shit.'

'Let's have it,' she replied.

'He's almost a billionaire. Very nearly there. He made his first big pile of money out of Brexit.'

'How?' she asked. As far as she was aware, no one had done well out of that.

'Logistics contracts. Trucking goods,' Karl replied.

'But wasn't Brexit bad for trucks and –' she started.

'All with a bunch of US logistics contractors,' he cut in. 'They were all hungry for a piece of Britain, and Wakefield got in there early as the middleman. He went on to make his second big pile out of Covid. He did a Michelle Mone job on some large PPS contracts.'

'He sounds like an absolute wanker,' Okeke said.

'Oh, it gets better. He's on his fourth wife, the one Jay was watching. Kerry Wakefield, formerly Kerry Goldsmith.'

'What about his previous wives? Any history of violence? Abuse?'

'Nothing. Anyway, listen, Sam...' Karl continued. 'It's the company he's keeping right now that I think you should hear about.'

'Go on,' said Okeke.

'How up to speed are you on US politics?' Karl asked her.

'There's a lot of anti-Trump sentiment. Republicans are starting to see him as a huge liability. Either he'll lose them the election, or, if he wins, they won't be able to control him. Action groups are consolidating out there and it looks like Wakefield has cosied up with one of them.'

'Action groups?' she repeated.

'Conspirators.'

'Conspirators?' The dreaded C-word. No wonder Karl was sounding so excited – he loved a conspiracy theory. 'Conspiring to do what?' she asked.

'A Trump takedown? A sting? A stitch-up? A scandal? Something that completely discredits him? Who knows? Even an assassination attempt?'

'Shit,' whispered Okeke. 'And Jay's employer is...'

'Balls deep with one of these groups. Look... I'm not saying Jay has anything to do with whatever they might be planning, but...'

'By association, he could find himself in trouble,' she reasoned.

'Right,' said Karl. 'If they did do something crazy – let's say an assassination attempt. Or even if they've just started planning one and the Feds catch on to it... well, the authorities don't pussyfoot around with that kind of thing. They'll round up anyone with any kind of association. And Jay, being non-American, working undercover – and Christ knows whether he's even got a detective's licence – he's going to find himself in *big* trouble.'

Okeke dipped her head, and her left hand reached up to massage her temple.

*Oh, Jay, sweetie. What the fucking hell have you bumbled into?*

## 42

Boyd opened the envelope Her Madge had handed him as soon as her office door closed behind him. And she'd been right; it was a politely worded *invitation*. An invitation to discuss 'a unique strategic opportunity within the police force'.

The contact name at the bottom was one DCI Williams. Boyd wondered if it was Yolanda Williams from the CTU. He smiled – she'd really got under Okeke's skin when they'd been investigating the Eagle House fire. There were no other details. So, something off the records, then.

The language was intriguingly opaque and it was, to be fair, not an order. So, it was something he could at least hear out before respectfully turning it down. Intrigued, he was about to call the phone number at the bottom of the letter when his work phone buzzed in his hand. He answered it.

'DCI Boyd.'

'You left a message for me earlier today,' the voice said.

'Hmm?' His mind was blank for the moment.

'It's Nikki Turkman from ARC Talent?' she prompted him.

'Ah, yeah... right,' he said, scrabbling to switch tack.

'What can I help you with, Detective Boyd?' said Nikki.

'Do you manage the band Mad Priests?' he asked.

'Yes I do,' she replied. 'What's happened? Is one of my boys in a spot of bother?'

Nikki Turkman sounded like an old-school NHS matron. Boyd's mind conjured up a cross between Hattie Jacques and Vivienne Westwood.

He chuckled softly. 'No, it's nothing to worry about.'

'That's a relief. They've just come back from a tour, and I do worry when I send young bands abroad that one of them will try smuggling dope back, lose a passport or get some groupie pregnant. It's like trying to herd a pack of excitable Labrador puppies,' she said with a sigh.

'Have the Mad Priests had a Dan Elwood in the line-up recently?' Boyd asked. 'Or am I talking about a different band altogether?'

There was a long pause. 'Yes,' she replied after a while. 'Dan was in the band.'

'*Was?*' Boyd echoed. 'Until when?'

'Until five months ago,' she told him. 'I had to let him go a few weeks before they went on tour.'

'Can I ask why?' Boyd asked, stunned.

'Trust me, it wasn't an easy decision. Dan *was* the front-man, the singer and the main songwriter. He's a very talented young lad, to be honest with you. But he was also – how can I put this? – worryingly unstable.'

'Unstable? What do you mean?' said Boyd.

She took a breath. 'The other boys were getting *very* worried about him.'

Boyd's mind darted back to this morning's encounter outside the bathroom and the ridges of scars on the back of Dan's arms.

Nikki Turkman spoke again. 'For the love of God, please tell me, detective – he hasn't gone and killed himself... or someone else, has he?'

## 43

'Carlton, you fucking arsehole! You've dropped me into a right fucking nightmare!' Mack was on his second, very large G&T.

He'd needed it.

The interview with the two detectives this afternoon had badly shaken him up. 'There's no doubt about it, Carlton – those coppers think *I'm* responsible for Kerry's murder!' he raged.

'They actually *said* that they suspected you?' Carlton asked.

'Not explicitly,' Mack said. 'But, for fuck's sake, the questions they were asking strongly implied it.'

'What did they say?' Carlton asked.

Mack downed what was left in his glass, including the two large ice cubes, crunching them between his teeth, then gave Carlton a run-down of the interview.

Carlton let out a sigh. 'Well, listen, on balance, that's good news.'

Mack nearly choked on the ice in his mouth. '*Good news?* What the actual fu–'

'Relax, they're just cops doing their jobs. If they're going down that particular road, if they believe you're the jealous husband, then they're heading entirely in the wrong direction, aren't they?'

'Well, that doesn't really help me does it!' Mack pointed out. 'I swear they were about to read my rights and arrest me.'

'*Were?*' Carlton muttered the word softly.

It hadn't been Mack's intention back in the interview room to point them towards Jay Turner. He'd actually grown rather fond of the bloke, but Mack had been starting to feel the heat. The female detective had gone on to ask way too many questions about his marriage for him to feel comfortable.

Mack wandered over to his drinks cabinet. Dammit. He really needed another one.

'Yeah. *Were*,' said Mack. 'What's the problem?' He tossed a couple of ice cubes into his glass, poured a generous measure of gin and trickled in a little tonic for good form.

'*Were?*' repeated Carlton after a few moments. 'Past tense. Why does that concern me?'

Ignoring him, Mack took a slug of his third G&T of the evening. 'I had no choice.'

'What do you mean?' Carlton asked.

'I had to give them Turner,' Mack said. 'The PI. They were coming for me and I had to throw something else into the mix...'

'What did you say?' Carlton's tone was suddenly icy. 'Wakefield, tell me *exactly* what you told them.'

'I told them Kerry had said she thought someone was stalking her,' Mack replied. 'Some weirdo she thought might have followed her all the way over from England.'

'Jesus,' Carlton muttered.

'Calm down. I didn't give them an actual name. I just gave them a loose description.'

'You idiot!' Carlton hissed. 'I told you to get your PI out of the way!'

Mack bristled. The last person who'd spoken to him like that – admittedly thirty years ago – had ended up in hospital with a broken nose. If this wiry little gnome had been standing here in his kitchen, he'd have been tempted to do the same to him. Or worse. 'Listen, I wouldn't have needed to say anything if you hadn't fucking panicked and had Kerry *whacked*, for fuck's sake!'

Carlton was silent for a moment. 'She's dead because of *your* carelessness, Wakefield. If you'd vetted your tart thoroughly, then –'

'She's... she was my bloody *wife*, goddamit!' Mack spat. 'Have some fucking respect!'

'Respect?' Carlton laughed humourlessly. 'You're a desperate social climber, Wakefield. Far too concerned with appearances. Far too eager to please the Big Boys in the clubhouse. I had concerns all along about allowing you into Bowman's inner circle.'

'Oh, fuck off,' Mack yelled, disconnecting the call and throwing his phone onto the kitchen counter. 'Fucking bastard!' he screamed.

It took a few seconds for the last reverberation of his voice to finish echoing around his mansion.

*The Big Boys in the clubhouse?*

*Fuck him.* Mack had more money than most of them. He probably had more money than most of them *combined*.

*Big Boys, my arse.*

*He* was the bloody big boy. It was *his* place where they'd been meeting of late. Why? Because it was secure. Because it was tucked away from prying eyes. Because he had a big FUCKING WALL around his manicured lawn. That kind of privacy required money. And *he* had the money.

Not to mention he was the only one of them who had enough off-grid cash to pay the retainer for their hugely expensive professional – 'Ash' – for nine consecutive months. Senator Bowman and all the others might be wealthy, but they weren't wealthy enough to have several million *untraceable* dollars hidden away. If it hadn't been for *his* money, they'd be just another bunch of disgruntled old businessmen and political wannabees meeting regularly to moan about liberals and taxes.

His phone began to vibrate on the counter. It was almost certainly Carlton calling him back. Fine. The wiry little rat was going to get another piece of Mack's mind. Without his input, they might as well be a bunch of old men playing dominos.

He grabbed his phone. It *was* Carlton.

'What the fuck does your PI know, Wakefield?'

'Piss off. You can start by apologising, you twat.'

Carlton's one-word reply came far too easily to be satisfying. 'Sorry.'

There was a silence.

Then Carlton spoke again. 'Let's start again, shall we? How long has this PI been watching your wife?'

'Four weeks,' replied Mack.

'*Just* watching?' Carlton asked.

*Shit.* Mack realised a split second too late that he should have just thrown him a quick 'yes'.

'*Just* watching?' repeated Carlton.

'He put a bug on her, and a tracker on her car,' Mack said, with as much defiance as he could muster.

'Are you telling me...' began Carlton, his tone dangerous, 'that *your wife* was walking around all of Saturday, mingling with Senator Bowman, Noel Monke, Justice Hoffman and half a dozen nervous Congressmen... *with a bug on her*?'

Mack was getting irritated again with this little cunt's tone. 'It's none of your fucking business! Anyway, you jammed the internet, didn't you? What's the drama? My telephones were down –'

'The moment she drove out through your front gate, Wakefield, she'd have been reconnected to the world again,' Carlton said. 'Within seconds. And it's quite possible – almost a certainty, in fact – that anything your PI's bug recorded and stored would have been uploaded to him almost instantly.'

Mack felt his neck and his scalp prickling again. *Fuck.* She'd nipped out on Saturday to stock up on booze, hadn't she?

'Wakefield?' Carlton said. 'I already had a concern about your sugar-baby wife being present at the weekend. A concern that she might be a security risk. Then, for God's sake, I actually catch her spying!' He sighed. 'And now I learn she was being spied on in turn?'

'My PI wasn't listening in,' Mack said. 'I gave him the weekend off. And anyway... he had instructions not to listen in on us when Kerry was home!' Even as he said that, Mack realised how pathetic, even naive, it made him sound.

'Stop talking,' Carlton instructed him.

Mack's mouth clapped shut and the silence between them extended uncomfortably.

Finally Carlton drew in a long deep breath. 'You stupid, thick-headed British *prat*.' Carlton shuck out a dry, humourless laugh. '*Prat*... that's a word you guys use, isn't it?'

Mack found himself nodding. 'Carlton... I'm really sorry. I didn't think that –'

'Shut your mouth,' Carlton cut in, 'and listen. We're going to have to act fast. Give me the details of this PI of yours....'

# 44

Jay ordered another Bud and a bag of salted pretzels and took them back to his booth. Tanners – he'd discovered the other night – definitely looked the part from the outside: all neon cocktail signs and blinking lights in the small window, but inside the promise died. It was little bigger than a Maersk freight container. There was a bar down one side and booths down the other. At the end of the room, beside the door to the toilet, stood a jukebox and a flickering, jangling one-armed bandit. The wall behind the bar – cluttered with shelves of beer glasses and bottles of spirits – was mirrored, teasing the idea of another bar and a lot more space.

Jay and the barman, a guy with pebble-lens specs and a mop of curly auburn hair, had the place almost to themselves. On a stool by the front window was an old woman sipping a Coke, playing some time-waster game on her phone. Halfway along the bar, a solitary, bearded trucker wearing a MAGA cap was sipping beer from a glass and watching an American football game on the TV above the bar.

An ad break bounced onto the screen and the trucker's eyes drifted away, scoped the tiny bar and quickly landed on Jay.

He nodded politely.

Jay nodded back.

And that seemed to have been invitation enough. The man grabbed his glass and packet of nuts and took a few steps over to Jay's booth.

'Hey, man – mind if I join you?' he asked.

Jay smiled. *Why not?* 'Sure.'

The man set his beer on the table, then sat down. 'It's dead in here, yeah?'

'Uh-huh,' replied Jay. 'Dead as a dodo.'

The man grinned. 'You Canadian?'

'Uh, no. I'm from England,' Jay said.

The man's grin broadened. 'Hey... British!' He offered a hand across the table. 'Dean Fausner.'

Jay shook his hand and introduced himself in turn.

'Nice to meet ya, Jay,' said Dean. 'Whatcha doin' over here? Vacation? Work?'

'A bit of a road trip,' Jay lied. 'I've always wanted to take a few months off work and drift across the USA, east coast to west coast.'

'Right.' Dean nodded. 'Nothin' like cruisin' the open roads to find yourself, right?'

'Eh?'

Dean grinned. 'Your karma, mojo... Your spirit animal...'

'Right, I see what you mean.' Jay nodded. 'Yeah. I suppose so. What about you?'

'I drive trucks, man.' Dean raised a warning finger. 'But don't you dare call me a trucker, though.'

'Okay!' Jay spread his hands. Then: 'Uh, why?'

'Cos it's a lazy-ass stereotype. Fat, dumb, hairy-ass motherfuckers. Most of 'em fags. Look at me... Am I fat? Hairy?'

Jay shook his head. 'Nope. Not a bit of it.'

'I used to drive trucks in the Marines,' Dean added. 'Now I do it for Amazon. Watcha do when you ain't road-trippin', friend?'

'I'm a carpenter,' Jay replied. 'A furniture restorer.'

'Okay!' Dean nodded enthusiastically. 'A real goddamn job! A proper skill.'

Dean tossed the last dregs of his beer down, then pointed at Jay's nearly empty glass. 'Lemme buy you another?'

Jay had already sunk four this evening and was starting to feel it. But, hell, he wasn't driving anywhere tonight, his motel room was right in his eye-line just across the parking area. It was an easy stagger back.

'Go on then, mate,' he said. 'Thanks. Mine's a Bud.'

Jay smiled as Dean went up to the bar. There it was then: conclusive evidence that not all MAGA nuts were complete arseholes. He smiled as he imagined what Sam would have to say about that.

## 45

Jay returned to his motel room an hour and a half – and another four beers – later. Dean 'Don't Call Me a Trucker' Fausner had been a blast to talk to. They'd debated US vs UK football and which one of them truly was the beautiful game, Biden vs Trump, and which of the politicians was going to die of a heart attack first. Jay found out that, quite bizarrely, that Dean was a *big* fan of 'that crazy-ass *Blackadder*' and seemed to know virtually all the lines from every episode.

Shooting the shit at Tanners with Dean had been a much-needed distraction from worrying about his exit plan. The airline had been super helpful and he'd decided to ease back on his cash-only caution and pay for the ticket using his card. After all, to all intents and purposes, he was a just a tourist who'd been, done and seen all that he wanted to and was ready to come home. He was now booked on a flight leaving at five in the afternoon tomorrow. But he couldn't shake the suspicion that he'd be stopped from boarding at the last moment by some zealous official.

He'd left his phone in the motel room while he'd gone

across to the bar, partly because he just didn't want to have another arsey confrontation with Mack, but also partly out of a creeping paranoia. He'd been keeping his eyes on the car park, half expecting blue lights and a SWAT team to roll up outside his motel room.

He unlocked his door, flipped the light on and peered inside.

There were no waiting cops and no SWAT team.

'Idiot,' he muttered to himself. He stepped into the room and closed the door behind him.

Suddenly he felt dizzy. He'd had way too many beers on an empty stomach. He'd not eaten properly since his pancake brunch.

Jay stumbled into the bathroom and decided to run himself a bath. He tore open a sachet of bubble bath and poured in the granules. He'd have a good soak, then maybe call Sam. It would be late for her – or rather, *early* over there – but he was pretty sure once she'd finished moaning about the time, she'd be relieved to know he was going to be back soon.

And he had a final job to do tomorrow. He'd have to say goodbye to Jorge and Sylvie. Maybe he'd stop by Walmart first and buy them both a parting gift. Maybe he could get Jorge an iPad or some kid-friendly tablet. Jay had grown pretty fond of them both.

He stripped off his clothes and kicked off his boxers, staggering slightly as he did so, then he stepped into the scalding hot bath.

'Ouch! Ow! Arse!' he whimpered as he lowered himself down into the suds.

The tub was woefully small for him and his big feet ended up planted firmly against the grubby tiles above the tap.

~

ASH WATCHED the man stagger across the car park. He was going to be pretty easy to deal with. He'd been disarmingly merry and unguarded, completely unaware that Ash had been sipping Bud Lights while he'd been getting soaked on full-strength beer.

The plaza was virtually empty, and – apart from Tanners – the only place still open was the McDonald's, with a skeleton crew serving drive-through customers.

Ash's van was parked next to the motel. Hefting the Brit's unconscious body from the motel room would be a quick thirty-second fireman's lift and then Ash could drive off with him into the dark Floridian wilderness.

The instructions from Mr C had been pretty clear: *bring him to me alive.* His client wanted to ask a few questions. Ash would do all the messy work of extracting the answers. Then after show-and-tell was done, he'd get rid the body. He had the necessary kit in the back of his van – bone saw, tarp, duct tape – and there was plenty of time to mull over how best to dispose of the pieces.

Alligator bait perhaps...?

~

JAY FELT his troubles sliding off his shoulders and floating away into the bubbles. Tomorrow he'd be on his way back home to Sam and he still had twenty-three grand on him in American dollars. Sadly it wasn't the life-changing amount he'd been hoping for, but it wasn't a bad sum for a month's work. It might well be just about enough to set himself up. He could rent a small business unit for six months, maybe buy some advertising space on Facebook and print up some business cards: *J. Turner, Private Investigator – discretion assured.*

Then his mind drifted back to more immediate concerns. What about Kerry Wakefield's warped and cracked phone sitting on the table, under his money belt? Maybe he'd just toss the bloody thing into the swamp on the way to the airport. He really didn't want to bust his way into the thing and identify the bit of silicon that had his picture on it; he just had to make sure it ended up where no one was ever going to find it. The bottom of a swamp sounded like a decent plan. He didn't care about what else might be on the phone. It wasn't his business.

And, as to whether Mack had been responsible for her death or not, that wasn't his business either. That was the police's busi–

He heard a soft click coming from the bedroom....

*Shit.*

It wasn't one of the usual clicks and groans that he'd got used to. This old motel, he'd noted, was in the habit of reminding you it had been built back in the fifties, with a collection of creaks and clunks and gurgles to go with it, particularly when asked to draw a bath. The click he'd just heard... it was a new sound.

Jay held very still to allow the sloshing bath water to settle down. He waited in silence to see if the click had been a one-off.

*Click.* There it was again.

'Hello?' he called out.

Jay detected the whisper of light footsteps on a threadbare carpet and for a moment he wondered whether he'd left his motel room open and some wild animal had wandered in.

The door to the bathroom creaked softly as it swung open.

'Fuck!' Jay gasped, grabbing a flannel off the side to cover his groin.

It was the trucker from the bar. Dean.

'Look, mate,' Jay said, startled. 'I think you've got the wrong end of the stick. I'm not –'

'Oh, I know who you are, *Turner*,' Dean replied, now sounding completely different.

Jay stared, mouth open. There was a disconnect between what he was seeing – a bearded all-American trucker wearing a baseball cap – and what he was hearing, which was British grammar-school diction.

Dean smiled. 'You're pretty new to the freelancing game, aren't you?'

He held a gun with a long silencer on the end of it, and Jay couldn't take his eyes off the dark hole of the barrel.

'My first tip for you,' Dean continued, 'is that when some random stranger comes over and buys you a beer... you should probably wonder why.'

Jay's recollection of the 'Quick Disarm Technique' tutorial video he'd watched on YouTube weeks ago was somewhat hazy... Plus, the instructor *hadn't* been butt-naked and sitting in a bath for the purposes of said tutorial. Jay suspected that if he decided to make a move, his brains would be splattered across the tiled wall before the first of the bath water had sloshed out of the tub.

'Relax,' said Dean. 'There is going to be lots of time for questions. But, first, let's get out, get dry and get dressed, eh?'

Jay nodded. 'Who... who are you?'

'It sure as hell isn't Dean, but never you mind about that,' the man, Ash, replied. Only an amateur, like this Turner, would give his real name. He waggled the barrel of his gun. 'Come along, Turner – up you get. You've got a busy night ahead of you.'

Jay staggered to his feet. Ash reached for a towel and tossed it to Jay, who flinched but managed to catch it.

'Relax,' said Ash. 'I don't want you dead.' He pulled out a taser. 'Just compliant.'

'Compliant?' Jay repeated as he was ushered out of the bathroom. 'What is this? Why –'

'I told you: questions *later*.' Ash nodded at the clothes on the floor. 'Come on. Get dressed. We're going to take a little drive.'

*Christ.* Jay recognised him now. Why the hell had he not realised back in the bar?

This was the man who had torched and ditched Kerry's car. Except now his bald head was disguised by the cap.

'Where are we going?' Jay asked as he got dressed.

'To have a debrief. Don't worry... You're not in trouble.'

'Wait... Did Mack send you?'

Ash shrugged. 'Kind of. See, we're two different contractors with two different jobs. The problem is, there might have been some overlap.'

'Kerry?' said Jay, starting to understand.

Ash nodded. 'My clients are concerned that Mrs Wakefield may have inadvertently picked up info that she *shouldn't* have and, as a result, you may have too.' He shrugged. 'None of it's your fault, of course. We understand it was purely by chance, but –'

'Look, I'm just a PI.' Jay made a show of pulling on his sweat pants, while at the same time trying to work out whether he had a chance of trying an unexpected lunge for the gun. 'Wakefield paid me to snap some pics of her. He thought she was cheating on him. That's all. That's –'

'You see, if it was just a few photos, there wouldn't be a

problem. But you bugged her too. So we know you've got audio and video...'

'Mate, I never got anything more than photos,' replied Jay, lying. 'Honest to God.'

Ash smiled patiently. 'I'm afraid my clients need to take a good look at *everything* you've got. By *everything*, I mean your phone, any laptops, tablets, cameras, memory sticks...'

Jay lunged.

But far too slowly and far too clumsily.

A second later, he was flapping around uncontrollably on the bathroom floor like a large tuna in a small dinghy, every muscle in his body rigid. He was vaguely aware that he was screaming, sounding very much like a pig in a slaughter pen.

The electricity surging into his body finally ceased after what felt like an unnecessarily long time and he let out a long laboured groan.

'Please... fuck... not... that.... again...' he whimpered.

His face felt numb. His whole body felt numb.

Ash squatted beside him and leant in so close so that their noses were almost touching. 'Let's not do something like that again, eh?'

Bleary-eyed, Jay nodded. 'Okay...' he slurred.

Jay heard a muffled *clunk*, then in the next instant Ash was lying on the floor next to him.

# 46

Sylvie loomed over them both, an empty beer bottle in one hand, her eyes bulging with shock, her mouth an elongated O.

'I thought this man killed you!' she finally gasped.

'Um... I'm... 'live... shtill...' muttered Jay, struggling to get some control over his sluggish mouth. 'But... I... thing... think... he *was* planning to...'

He managed to prop himself up onto his elbows and knees.

'I need... to get out... of here,' he rasped.

Jay looked at the man lying on the floor. He wasn't dead, but he was definitely out for the count. For now.

'He'sh... going... to come round... shoon...' he said. His mouth still felt cotton wool.

'I will get your shoes,' said Sylvie, turning and hurrying out of the bathroom.

Jay staggered to his feet and steadied himself against the sink.

Two words were rattling around his head. *My clients.*

Plural. So not just Mack, then. Somebody else had sent this guy after him.

Sylvie with his trainers. Jay stepped over the unconscious body and took them from her.

He needed to gather his stuff and get the hell out of here. Fast. *Super* fast. If this guy 'Dean' knew where to find him, presumably so did his clients. And did this bastard operate alone? Or with a partner? Was someone waiting outside, ready to bundle Jay's unconscious body into a van?

'We need to get out of here, Sylvie,' said Jay.

'*We?*'

He nodded. 'You need to get Jorge! Quickly!'

'Why?' she asked.

'Because these are bad people,' he said, pointing at the man, before peering out of the motel's window. 'And the police, Sylvie... if the police turn up, what will you do?'

She nodded and ran out of the room. 'Police' was all she needed to hear.

Jay was still struggling to get his shit together. Beers and volts made for quite the heady mix. He needed to clear his head. Think straight. Act smart.

A groan emerged from the bathroom. The fucker was beginning to stir.

Jay could hear the scrape of movement on the bathroom floor. Decisions, decisions. Should he go back in there and smack his face in? Finish him off with his own gun?

Or just bloody run for it?

He chose the latter. Grabbing Kerry's phone and his money belt from the table, he charged out of the open door, then hurried towards Sylvie's room. She met him at the door with a sleepy Jorge in one arm and an overnight bag in the other.

'Can you drive?' he asked her as they descended the steps to the car park.

'No!'

He considered how far they were going to get with himself at the wheel. He was still dizzy; everything was a blur. The only saving grace was that there didn't seem to be many cars around. Maybe he should try to clear his head by driving around once around the plaza, before heading for the highway?

Jay bleeped his Pathfinder as they approached it. He jerked the rear door open and Sylvie placed Jorge on the back seat. Then they both got into the front seats.

'You okay to drive?' she asked as she belted herself in. 'Maybe you wait?'

Waiting wasn't an option. Jay glanced over his shoulder at the motel. Ash was now standing in the open doorway of his room.

Jay started the engine, jammed the gearstick into drive, slammed his foot down on the accelerator, and they lurched forward, leaving a twisting cloud of dust in their wake.

## 47

Ash watched the Nissan Pathfinder heading for the highway. He considered jumping into his van and racing after Turner, but he was seeing everything as a hazy double exposure. If he'd have been in a Loony Tune cartoon, he'd have had yellow canaries circling his head.

Ash gingerly touched the sticky, bloody back of his head. Whoever had cracked him from behind had split his scalp. He was going to need stitches at some point.

There was no need to panic. He'd placed a tracker on the Nissan. In fact, it would do no harm at all to let him think he'd got clean away.

Ash returned to the motel room and looked around. Jay Turner clearly hadn't come from a military background – the room was messy, with pants and socks dotting the floor. A pizza box and an empty beer bottle sat on a table. He pulled open the drawer of the bedside table and found the man's passport, a plane ticket and his driving licence. And next to the TV were two phones: an iPhone and a Samsung. Ash sighed at Turner's ineptitude.

Years of experience had taught Ash that you always – *always* – had your grab bag ready to go at a moment's notice. And that bag contained anything and everything essential.

'What a fucking idiot,' Ash muttered.

Inside the closet was a safe – which had been left wide open. Ash rolled his eyes. Scrunched untidily within it were a bunch of manuals and receipts.

He pulled them out and laid them on the bed, along with everything else he'd found.

Jay Turner had purchased a Samsung phone, a pair of car trackers, two micro trackers and a bug. Chances were that he *did* get some audio from Kerry Wakefield. Mr C would need to know that. Ash glanced at the gathered devices. He deduced that the Samsung would likely have been Turner's phone for the job, but Turner might also have backed it up on a memory stick or cloud storage.

The purchase receipts were in the name of Veronica Kirk, and had a billing address in Connecticut.

Ash stepped into the bathroom, tore several sheets of toilet paper from the roll, balled it up and dabbed it on the back of his head. There was enough sticky congealing blood to hold it there.

He noticed the idiot hadn't even thought to grab the gun and the taser when he'd had the chance.

Ash returned to the main room and sat on the bed. His head was throbbing. He needed another minute to recover before giving Mr C a call. The man was expecting to hear that Turner was trussed up in the back of Ash's van, ready to be delivered to him for interrogation.

Instead, Ash would have to explain that things hadn't *quite* gone to plan. It wasn't great for his professional reputation, but these things happened, even to the best.

Still, Mr C was not going to be happy.

~

CARLTON CURSED SILENTLY. Ash was supposed to be one of the best available.

'Who hit you?' he asked.

'I didn't get to see,' replied Ash. 'I think I heard a woman's voice.'

'You let a *woman* take you down?'

'She caught me off guard.'

'Did he have a hooker in there with him or something?' hissed Carlton.

'Maybe. I don't know. She split my scalp with a fucking beer bottle.'

Carlton was too pissed off to actually care. 'And Turner?'

'He's gone,' replied Ash. 'But I put a tracker on his car. And the idiot left pretty much everything behind. His passport, his phones. His driver's licence. I've got them all with me.'

'Well, why the hell aren't you after him?' snapped Carlton.

'Because I'm concussed,' said Ash matter-of-factly. 'I'm seeing double.'

'I don't give a shit how you're *feeling*! I want him contained!'

'Calm down,' Ash said. 'I can see exactly where he is right now... He's on the I-95 heading north. Look, we have more important things to talk about.'

'Go on,' Carlton said.

'He had bugging equipment,' Ash said. 'He would have been getting audio from her.'

Carlton closed his eyes. He knew that. 'Did you find any other devices?'

'Just his phones.'

'And Kerry Wakefield's phone?' Carlton asked.

'No, I don't think either is hers,' Ash replied. 'The wall-paper on one is Turner and some black woman. The other has his tracker and bug apps on it. They're both locked, but I can get someone to unlock them.'

'Do it. Wakefield said Turner had his wife's phone,' said Carlton.

'Wait. She had another? But she gave me her phone.'

'Well, apparently she had a second. Presumably that was the one I caught her using to spy on us. Wakefield says that Turner has it and isn't prepared to give it up.'

'Then he must be aware it's got compromising material on it.'

'My thoughts exactly.' Carlton balled his fist with frustration. Tonight should have been easy. Tonight should have been an end to it. 'You sure it isn't there somewhere?'

'No. I've turned the place over. Two phones. Both his.'

'Dammit.'

'All right. So then he's savvy enough to have taken that one,' said Ash. 'Which means he knows it's got leverage value.'

*But does he have any idea how much leverage?* wondered Carlton. He cast his mind back to when the club members had been gathered in Wakefield's lounge on that Saturday evening, enjoying whisky and cigars... Their tongues loose and with far too much bravado all round. And he'd spied Kerry standing outside... That fucking phone pressed against the key hole.

'I need Turner. *Tonight.* I need him bagged. And I need Kerry Wakefield's fucking phone!'

## 48

Half an hour later, Jay took the exit ramp off the I-95, towards a city called Port St Lucie, then took the first couple of turnings off the town's main road and found a small car park in front of a row of fast-food shops. They were busy with end-of-the-night drunks ordering burgers and pizzas.

He wanted busy. Somewhere too busy for a hitman to try his luck.

He turned the engine off and sank into his seat. A flood of adrenaline had sobered him up quickly and sustained kept him alert on the highway, but it was beginning to subside, leaving him feeling drained and shaken.

Sylvie twisted round to check on Jorge, who was still fast asleep on the back seat, then she turned to Jay.

'What happened?' she whispered quietly. 'Why was the man attacking you?'

Jay was still trying to process what he'd been told. The man was clearly a pro – and he was the same man who'd murdered Kerry Wakefield.

*And Jesus Christ... how fucking smoothly that bastard fooled me in the bar?*

What had the man been doing? Sizing Jay up? Working out how he was going to deal with him? Getting Jay pissed deliberately so he'd be easier to handle?

Sylvie grasped his arm. 'You did not tell me everything about why you are here.' There was a hard edge to her voice. 'You are not a tourist. You lie to me and Jorge. You put us in danger!' Her accent was thickening. 'This is to do with drugs? You are a gang member?'

Jay shook his head. 'God, no... no... no!'

And she was getting angrier. 'You are a *criminal*?'

'No, I'm not a gang member, not a criminal. I'm a PI,' Jay said.

Sylvie frowned. 'What is a Pee-Eye?'

'A private investigator. I was watching some rich guy's wife,' Jay explained.

'Why?'

'He thought she was cheating on him, but it turned out she was *spying* on him.'

'Spying? For who?' Sylvie demanded.

'I dunno.' Jay dug into the pocket of his sweat pants and pulled out Kerry's cracked, warped phone. 'But she was using *this* to spy on her husband.' He took a deep breath. 'I *think*, the rich guy's wife found out some really bad stuff about him. And whatever it was, it's on this phone. Now he wants this phone back...'

'And he wants you dead?' said Sylvie.

Jay nodded. 'I think that's... yeah, I think that's what he wants to happen. That's why he sent that guy after me.'

Jorge stirred and muttered in his sleep. Sylvie turned to glance at him, then looked back at Jay. 'So we are in danger now, yes?'

'Well, *I am*, for sure. But I guess you are now as well. I'm not sure who or what I'm dealing with right now.'

'Bad people?'

'Yes.' Jay nodded. 'Bad people. People happy enough to kill to get their hands on this,' he said, patting his pocket. 'Look, Sylvie, maybe I should just let you and Jorge get out of this shit sandwich here –'

'You cannot throw us out!' she said.

Jay didn't have the time or the mental bandwidth to argue with her. 'Look, I've got to work things out. I've got to get my head straight. I need...'

*I need to talk to Sam.* He reached into his other pocket.

'Shit!' he gasped. 'Bloody hell! Shitting, bloody bollocks!'

'What?' Sylvie asked.

'I left my phone behind!' he replied.

'You need a phone?' She pulled hers out of her jeans pocket. 'You can use mine.' She handed it to him. It was a battered old Nokia.

Jay sighed and took it from her. 'Thanks.'

'So, we stick together? Yes?'

Jay tapped in the first five digits of Okeke's number – the easy bit – then groaned as he tried to recall the rest. He spoke the first few numbers out loud, hoping it would trigger the remaining digits like some badly remembered song lyrics.

It worked.

Okeke answered after the third ring. 'Who's this?' she asked sleepily.

'It's Jay,' he answered.

'Jay! God! I've been so fucking worried! Karl got some info on Wakefield. I've been calling and calling. I've left you God knows how many bloody texts!'

'Sam, stop! Don't send me any more texts! You can't ring my phone again,' he told her.

'Why?'

'They've got it,' he replied. 'Listen, Sam... I can't believe I'm saying this, but Wakefield's hired a hitman to take me out. And he's just had a go!'

'*What?*' Okeke exclaimed. 'Where are you? What the fuck, Jay?'

'It's okay, babes. I got away, all right? I'm in a car. I'm parked up. I'm good for the moment.'

'What the fuck, Jay?' Okeke repeated. 'I mean, what the actual fuck?!'

'That's helpful,' he replied. 'Thanks, Sam.'

Okeke went quiet. Jay could hear her tongue clucking – the sound of her cogs turning. He found it vaguely reassuring. Someone else was doing the thinking.

'Okay,' she said eventually. 'So you're calling from a new phone?'

'It's not mine,' he said.

Another silence.

Jay glanced at Sylvie. 'You know the kid I've been babysitting? It's his mum's.' He paused. 'She's... uh... She's with me. Now.'

Okeke took a moment to digest this information.

'She's the one who saved my life. She twatted the guy who jumped me,' Jay explained. 'So... I couldn't just leave her.'

Sylvie leant towards the phone. 'Hello, Mrs Turner.'

Okeke cleared her throat. 'Jay, can we talk privately for a moment? Is that safe to do?'

'Sure.' He climbed out of the Pathfinder and closed the door. There was enough noise coming from Domino's and the neighbouring burger stand that Sylvie wouldn't be able to overhear his side of the conversation.

'Right. So where are you?' began Okeke. 'It's noisy.'

'I'm at some fast-food stop, off the I-95 somewhere,' he said.

'Tell me everything that just happened,' Okeke said. 'And don't leave anything out.'

Jay recounted the last couple of hours.

'Are you sleeping with her?' Okeke asked.

The question hit like an unexpected speed bump. He'd almost been killed and that was the only detail she was interested in?

'I'm sorry?' he said, '*What?*'

'You heard.'

'You've gotta be taking the piss, Sam?' Jay said, trying to control his temper. 'Look, now's *not* the bloody time!' Then he sighed. 'No, I'm not.'

'So what the hell was she doing *in* your motel room?'

'The guy fucking tasered me in the bath! He had a gun on me! I guess, she must've heard me screaming for my life. The bastard probably left the door open, didn't he?'

Okeke was silent for a moment. 'You've got the kid with you too?' she asked.

'Yup.' He huffed impatiently. 'So just to be clear... there's me, one woman and one small boy. And we all need some help, okay?'

'Okay.' He heard her take a drag of a cigarette.

'So, what's your plan?'

'I don't have one,' Jay confessed. 'I'm literally balls out here. My wallet, my phone, my ticket... shit, even my passport – they're all back in my motel room. And this guy will have them all by now.'

'Calm down, love,' Okeke said. 'Just... calm down.'

'I am calm, I am calm,' Jay replied. 'I just need some kind of a steer, okay? You said you got some info on Wakefield?'

'Yeah,' she replied. 'Karl did some digging. He's very rich, and it seems he's got some influential American friends. They're a bunch of nut-job politicians, senators, judges, generals even – and they're all up to something.'

'Up to what?'

'We don't know. Something big maybe. Karl's running hot with wild theories.'

'Such as...?'

'Somebody getting assassinated.'

'Shit.' Suddenly a lot of what had happened in the last few hours was making sense to him. 'Yeah, that fits,' replied Jay. 'The guy who jumped me mentioned something about *clients*, as in plural. So it's definitely not *just* Mack after me.'

'I agree,' she replied. 'When I spoke to you earlier, you told me that Mack was really pissed off about you hanging on to his wife's phone?'

'Yeah,' Jay said. 'I thought that maybe there was some very personal shit on there, right? But now you're thinking it's about something bigger?'

'Well, it could be. It's possible that Mack's wife discovered something about him and his friends. Maybe she had something on her phone, and *that's* why Mack –'

'Has gone all ape-shit on me?'

'Yeah. And that would also pretty much explain why she was murdered,' she continued.

'Thanks, love. That bit I already worked out.' Well, he'd realised it somewhat belatedly. 'I sprinted out with her phone and not mine.' Maybe if he'd left Kerry's behind, this nightmare would be over? Mack would have what he desperately wanted and be happy with that. But then again... maybe not.

'But this hitman now has your phones,' she pressed. 'If they have your phone, babe, they'll have all your contacts. And they'll know who you've been speaking to.'

'Yeah. I know I'm dumb all right. I just panicked and ran. What a complete –'

'Jay, stop!' she said. 'I'm thinking about your mate Ronni. She needs to be warned.'

'Shit,' he replied. 'I hadn't even thought of that.'

'What's her number?' Okeke asked.

Jay shrugged. 'Fuck knows. I can't remember.'

'What's her business called, then?' replied Okeke. 'I can look it up.'

'R. Kirk and... something... Hold on. R. Kirk and Partners, I think?'

'I'll look it up and I'll give her a ring. Is Sylvie's phone pay-as-you-go?'

'Yup. It's an old Nokia,' Jay told her.

'Okay. I'll get a burner phone and call you back later so we've got a clean connection. What're you going to do meanwhile?' she asked.

Jay gazed at the distant glare of headlights on the highway. 'I'm planning on heading north. I was thinking of driving to Ronni's, actually.'

'Well, *don't*,' Okeke cut in. 'It'll take them all of two nanoseconds to realise they need to watch her place if they're after you.'

'Okay, so what should I do, then?' Jay asked.

'Have you got money, Jay?' Okeke said.

'I've got most of Mack's upfront cash. Twenty-three grand,' he told her.

'Okay, so you can fend for yourself and stay off radar for a while?'

'Yeah. I suppose.'

'Listen, you should ditch the hired car, hun. If the people after you have clout, they may be able to tap into road cameras, license-plate recognition and all that.'

She was right.

'Look, just keep your head, okay?' she added when he didn't answer, sensing his anxiety. 'Stay calm.' She huffed out a laugh. 'Ask yourself, what would Jason Statham do?'

'Not funny,' he replied. 'It's not really the time for bants, babycakes.'

# 49

Ash turned onto the I-95 and followed the tracker. Turner was clearly oblivious to the fact that his car had been tagged. If he'd had a concern, he'd have pulled over somewhere by now and that peg on the screen would be in a ditch and going nowhere.

Just another indicator that this wally was all the gear and no idea.

Ash could happily say that he'd never been this clueless. Not even at the start of his freelance career. He'd entered this as ex-military and already trained. There was a lot to be said for the British Armed Forces. For the grunts, it was the perfect apprenticeship for a mercenary career; for the nicely spoken officers, the perfect network for executive job offers.

He could have gone the latter route and had a non-taxing career in a client-facing role at some large multinational with a six-figure salary, shares and benefits. But he'd chosen a far more lucrative path.

The problem with the job paying so well, however, was the temptation to keep doing it for longer than was prudent. A top-tier hitman was looking at a five- to ten-year window of opportunity to make all the money he'd need for the rest of his life before some diligent jobsworth from Interpol or the FBI assembled enough of a profile of you to make the job too risky to continue.

There was an awareness among the more experienced pros that the longer you worked, the longer the shadow you cast... and when you started to feel the tips of someone's toes stepping on it behind you, it was time to bow out.

Ash had had a good run: eight years and fourteen jobs. He'd started his freelance career with a triple hit for a drug gang in Essex. The crime remained unsolved, obviously, and had even become true-crime documentary fodder for a third-rate satellite channel.

Over the years, his reputation had improved, and his last job had been in Sharjah, capping a particularly troublesome prince who'd been shouting far too loudly about women's rights. Ash had done very well out of that one, but he'd also made a slip-up. On Interpol's website, just a few days after the job, the fuzzy, pixelated image of his undisguised face had appeared.

An image from the prince's dashcam.

The still had been taken moments after he'd killed the prince in his Ferrari. Walking away, he had stupidly turned to look back at it.

That picture had been a timely warning to bow out gracefully, and in this business you didn't get many of those. And he would have – *should have* – retired for-hire Diverr profile. But then he'd received a query that had sounded too good to turn down. Not only because of the money but because there was a good possibility that he might not even have to lift a finger. It was a retainer. A 'be ready and available on short notice' kind of offer. Job or no job – he'd be paid either way.

The target? Well, that would put his blurry, pixelated image on every news channel and the front page of every newspaper in the world if he were ever found out to be the culprit. He'd jump to number one on the FBI's Most Wanted and Interpol's Red Notices.

Retiring would no longer be a simple case of cancelling his VIP membership of Diverr. It would mean going off-grid – properly – for years. It was entirely doable, of course. There were plenty of countries in which a man could lie low for a decade, but they tended to be the sort of places he detested: shitty underdeveloped dictatorships with corrupt officials who could be bought cheaply at first, but, as the years passed, the price and the risk of being exposed steadily increased.

Ash very much wanted to spend his long early retirement at home in the UK.

In Devon, to be precise.

He'd had many wonderful childhood years in Devon. He had good memories of happy times. If his clients decided they *did* need him to follow through with the job, though, there'd be no Devon for Ash.

He was going to have to go full-on Lord Lucan.

However, as he drove north along the I-95, following the tracker on Turner's car,

the seed of a rather interesting idea was beginning to germinate.

## 50

'The problem I have with you, Ryan, is that your operation has raised enough red flags in the last week for me to consider shutting it down.' FBI Section Chief Gaetz looked up from his notes. 'You got a goddamn *civilian* killed! Kerry Wakefield should *never* have been put in that position without proper agency training!'

'Or reliable back-up,' added Director Coleman.

Both men scowled at Ryan across the conference table.

'The Bureau cannot afford another optics disaster,' continued Gaetz. 'If it turns out her husband killed her because he found out she was spying for the FBI, not only are we looking at a wrongful death lawsuit, but we'll be painted, again, as Deep State operatives meddling in civilian lives.'

Coleman nodded.

'And then,' continued Gaetz, 'there's the matter of you impersonating a homicide detective during a police interview!'

'I put the detective on the spot,' said Ryan. 'She didn't know I was going to do it, until I did.' That was a lie. He'd told Durrant beforehand, but there was no point dragging her into this. 'I *needed* to be in that room, sir. He had to believe it was a routine murder investigation. If he caught even a whiff of federal interest, he'd have shut down.'

'And you may have compromised the state's ability to prosecute,' said Coleman.

'I don't think he did it, anyway,' replied Ryan. 'He didn't plan it, nor even knew it was going to happen. It blindsided him.'

Coleman frowned. 'Excuse me?'

Gaetz closed his eyes wearily and sighed. 'The Mulligan Club.'

Coleman turned to Gaetz. 'Mulligan Club?'

'Special Agent Ryan has already spent over three thousand hours chasing shadows,' Gaetz said.

'Ryan? What's this?' asked Coleman.

Ryan hadn't been expecting to face Director Coleman this morning. If he had, he'd have been better prepared.

'Sir,' he began, 'I'm investigating a group of businessmen who hold extremist views –'

'What views?'

'Alt-right,' replied Ryan.

Gaetz shook his head. 'This is exactly what will get us shut down if Trump gets in: the perception of political bias.'

'Sir, they espouse dangerously radical views.' Ryan glanced at Coleman, hoping the director might be a little more open-minded about this. 'They've splintered off from the leading movement and have been holding clandestine in-person meetings for the last eighteen months. They call themselves the Mulligan Club,' explained Ryan. 'Mulligan's a golfing term. It means a replay if you've had a poor shot – a second chance, if you will.'

'And?' Coleman waved the agent on to continue, clearly not interested in the semantics of the club's name.

'Special Agent Ryan,' cut in Gaetz. 'There are Christ knows how many alt-right luncheon clubs out there, where disgruntled rich white businessmen bemoan

the liberal left and "wokeness gone mad". What makes you think this one's worth our time?'

'I have reason to believe they've hired a professional hitman,' Ryan replied.

Coleman cleared his throat. 'How certain of that are you?'

'I've been monitoring a dark-web platform called Diverr,' Ryan said. 'It's essentially a hitmen directory. A place where they post profiles, outline their hits. They also indicate whether they're available for new business or not. Initial direct contact is handled via an encrypted chatroom called the "date room".'

'*Date room?*' Coleman shook his head at the term.

'This gives the professional a chance to interview the client. If they're both happy with each other, further comms between them is down to whatever process they agree on. All we can monitor is who is available or otherwise. A lack of availability usually means an agreement has been made and the hitman is on a job.'

Gaetz turned to Coleman. 'The operators of Diverr, whoever they are, are aware that law enforcement agencies monitor, but access to the date room is membership only, which is granted through vetted recommendation.'

'So...' Coleman leant on the arm of his chair. 'What has this to do with the Mulligan Club?'

'I've been tracking an individual named Dominic Carlton,' Ryan explained. 'He's a fixer, a middleman. Ex-CIA. He was part of the group that hired Cambridge Analytica to swing the 2016 election and, before that, the Brexit refer-endum for the British. I traced a substantial Bitcoin transac-tion nine months ago, made by Carlton to Driverr. They take their fee, then pass the rest on to the professional. Within hours of that transaction, I noticed that a hitman marked himself as "off".'

'Who's the professional?' asked Gaetz.

'His Diverr account is KFH_50BTFOA_FI/10,' Ryan replied. 'KFH stand for killer for hire. Then 50BTFOA indi-cates that he operates on the basis of fifty per cent up front, paid in Bitcoin. The FOA stands for "fee on application".'

'And FI/10?' asked Coleman. 'FI/10?'

'Bragging rights,' Ryan replied. 'It means he's top-ten-listed on Interpol and the FBI website. He goes by the name Ash, but that's obviously an alias. This guy has been prolific for five years, but probably been doing the job for longer. He's been mid-level for some time: organised crime jobs, hits on rivals – that kind of thing. But he became of partic-ular interest to Interpol and the Bureau in 2023.'

'Because...' Coleman prompted.

Gaetz cut in. '*Political* assassinations.'

'We have a picture of Ash on our Most Wanted page,' said Ryan. He called it up on his government-secured laptop.

'Unfortunately, this is the best we could do,' he said, showing his superiors the pixelated image. 'It's from the dashcam of Prince Shahab Bin-Khurram's Ferrari. This image shows Ash walking away from the car just after he'd executed the prince. Not a great image, but it gives us some idea of what he looks like.'

Coleman squinted at the photo. 'So he's bald and white.' He sounded distinctly unimpressed. 'Well, that's most white men over thirty.'

Ryan nodded. 'That's true, sir, but the last time I met with her, Kerry Wakefield described a similar-looking man acting suspiciously next to her car.'

'And tell me why she is relevant to this?' Coleman demanded.

'Kerry Wakefield is the civilian homicide that Section Chief Gaetz mentioned,' Ryan explained. 'Her husband is a member of the Mulligan Club. He came to my attention because he's been hosting their recent meetings.'

'Ryan,' cut in Coleman, 'how the *hell* did you manage to recruit this woman to spy on her husband?

'I used a little *leverage*,' Ryan said.

Coleman scowled. 'Please don't tell me you used entrapment or blackmail.'

'She wrecked her husband's precious Jag while she was DUI,' replied Ryan. 'She was more afraid of him finding out than having it on her record.'

'So you spared her the criminal charges and asked her to spy on her husband?' Coleman said.

He nodded. 'She's been working as a source for several months now. When I flagged Carlton's Driverr transaction and saw that Ash had gone off-market, it was pretty clear: the Mulligan Club was transitioning from planning to operational. We needed someone on the inside.'

'And how good has her intel been?' asked Gaetz.

'She gave me some names,' Ryan said. 'The biggest one being Bowman.'

'*Senator* Bowman?' Coleman's brows shot up.

Ryan nodded.

'Jesus.' Coleman looked at Gaetz. 'He's a president-maker.... or breaker. He's also one of those bastards baying for the FBI to be defunded.'

'Did you get anything we could use?' said Gaetz.

'I believe a key meeting was held last weekend,' Ryan replied. 'They're getting ready to launch something.'

'Like what?' asked Gaetz.

Ryan shook his head. 'If Kerry hadn't been compromised, we'd have the intel.'

'You think they rumbled her?' asked Coleman.

He nodded. 'I'm certain. And I'm pretty sure that Malcolm Wakefield was not aware of the instruction to "deal with her". Also, there was nothing on her when she was found. No phone, no bag, no ID. It was made to look like a robbery. The car she was driving is still missing.'

Gaetz and Coleman glanced at each other. This meeting had gone from a dressing-down to something very different.

'I know something's in the works,' said Ryan. 'I know they've taken initial steps. They've hired a professional hitman and now they know they're being watched.'

Coleman looked at Ryan. 'I presume you have an ask?'

'Resources, sir. Manpower. If this is going to be a big hit – a domestic terror attack, or something worse – we need to move, *now*.'

'Worse?' said Gaetz.

Ryan met his gaze. 'What if they're planning an assassination attempt?'

## 51

Okeke took another pull on her fag and tried the number again.

It felt weird phoning the woman she'd spent the last few months suspecting of being Jay's secret fuck buddy. But he'd been adamant that there was nothing going on and that she was just a useful contact. Anyway, now it seemed he had some other woman, and her kid, in tow. So maybe he *had* been telling the truth about Ronni Kirk.

Okeke had found contact details on the website for Ronni's agency. It was a landline number, which she could imagine, right now, was causing some dusty old analogue telephone with a rotary dial to ring in a dingy smoke-hazed PI's office above a Chinese launderette.

There was no answer.

It was just after 1 p.m., which meant it was after 8 a.m. for Ronni. Maybe it was still too early to call. The answer-phone message came on. '*R. Kirk and Partners Detective Agency. This is Ronni Kirk's line. If you're an existing client, you already have my cell number. If not, leave your name and number and I'll get back to you.*'

Okeke hadn't left a message the previous time she'd called because she'd used her own phone. Which had been careless. This morning she'd picked up a cheap-as-chips Motorola and SIM card on her way into work.

'Hello, Ronni. My name's Samantha Okeke,' she said. 'I'm Jay's other half. I'm not sure if you're aware he has another half or, uh, that he's in big trouble. I'm presuming he hasn't shared that with you yet, though.' She paused, hoping that Ronni might be at her desk and screening the call, deciding whether or not to pick up.

'So he's basically on the run,' Okeke continued. 'The woman he was hired to watch – she's been murdered. Not by some random guy but a hitman. Jay thinks he's been set up. He's left behind his phone, wallet, driver's licence, passport. All he's got is cash and he needs some help. Call me when you pick this up.'

Okeke decided to take a risk, read out her burner number and ended the call. She stubbed out her fag just as the double doors to the station swung open. Warren and Rajan emerged, both fumbling in their jacket pockets for their vapes.

Rajan nodded. 'All right?'

'Not particularly,' she replied.

Warren's vape burbled as he took a pull on it. 'Jay trouble?'

She was tempted to tell him to bog off and mind his own business, but the question seemed to be asked with a touch of genuine concern.

She nodded.

'What's he done?' asked Warren.

She sighed. 'Too much bullshit to go into now.'

Or ever. Not with Warren. She wandered away from

them, heading towards her Datsun. She unlocked the door and climbed inside.

She really needed to speak to Jay.

## 52

J ay watched the flat countryside roll past the coach's broad windows. Florida's relentless green quilt was passing on the left, while on the right the sea glinted fleetingly between ordered rows of palm trees and a roofscape of terracotta tiles and faux Spanish Colonial turrets. At one point he caught sight of a distant and enormous tower of scaffolding and realised the Greyhound was passing one of NASA's famous launch sites: Cape Canaveral.

Sylvie and Jorge were in the seats behind him. The boy was throwing question after question at his mum, and Jay could hear the growing exasperation in her voice as she replied in Spanish. He could almost translate it from the tone alone: *Just stop asking me, Jorge, please! I don't know!*

Jay had bought a notebook and a pen at a 24-hour convenience shop, before he'd doubled back for West Palm Beach, for the Greyhound bus station. He'd spent the last hour writing down everything he could remember since his first meeting with Mack Wakefield in Kent two months ago. He now had several pages of jumbled notes.

He scanned the first page:

MALCOLM 'MACK. Wakefield: transport business, rich guy. Dodgy? Crime money or straight?

Ex-Eastender. Home in Kent, home in Florida. Anywhere else?

Has business manager back in Kent – name? Can't remember.

Business links in States – lots. Rich guys etc.

Kerry W – spying with a 'Ryan'. Is that his real name? Is he a copper/fed/crook?

THEN, of course, there was the stuff that Sam had told him last night. Questions that needed some answers quickly.

ALT-RIGHT TYPES. Conspiracy/big plan? Something very soon? Maybe.

Did Kerry have some intel on them? So murdered to shut her up? Almost fucking certainly.

Does her phone have that stuff on it? Yes almost certainly. Mack and others want it badly.

THE BOTTOM LINE was that Mack and his friends had decided that Jay was now a problem. That the data on Kerry's fire-damaged phone was important enough that Mack and his buddies were happy to hire a hitman and they weren't concerned about leaving bodies on the ground. More specifically, *his*.

Added to that, the police might well be looking for him too if – as Jay suspected – Mack had decided to set him up for Kerry's murder. He'd left everything behind in the motel room. If the hitman hadn't taken anything, leaving it all in the room – maybe trying to frame him as some obsessed stalker – then by now the police would know his name, his nationality and what he looked like. As soon as they unlocked the Android phone, they'd see he'd been taking pictures of Kerry for the past month. Invasive pictures, close-up pictures. The kind of pictures that a twisted, dangerously obsessed stalker might take. He realised he'd been dumb, again. As soon as he'd discovered Kerry was dead, he should have purged his phone of all that stuff. And, for that matter, binned those notes he'd made in his notepad – his handwriting listing her every movement and all the places she'd frequented around West Palm Beach.

He was in a 'right pickle', as his first foster mum, Jeanette, used to say.

As far as a plan went, all he had was this:

1) Go to Ronni.

2) Beg her for help.

3) Don't get killed.

He was woefully out of his depth here. Sam had said that Mack had influential friends. What the hell did that mean? Was he cosy with a police chief or something? A governor? Or did she mean local crime bosses? Or was Mack just a popular guy down at a private club for filthy rich Floridians? He had bugger all idea what level of shit he'd stepped into, other than it involved Mack... somehow... and Mack maybe wasn't the affable take-me-as-you-find-me geezer that Jay had thought he was.

He was now Harrison Ford in *The Fugitive*, Tom Hanks

in *The Da Vinci Code*, Jason Bourne in *The Bourne Identity*: on the run while trying to decode a tricky-as-fuck puzzle.

Eventually his looping and increasingly frantic thoughts were disturbed by a tap on his shoulder. He turned round to find Sylvie's face squished between the seat's headrests.

'Your lady is calling,' she said, and handed him her phone through the gap.

He answered. 'Sam? Did you get through to Ronni yet?'

'Not yet,' she said. 'I've left a message on her answer-phone, though. I'm guessing she won't pick that up until she turns up at her office. Where are you?'

'On a Greyhound heading up to New York,' he told her.

'*New York?* Why New York?' she asked.

'She's based up there, right? Connecticut?' replied Jay. His mental map of America had been inked by *The Sopranos*, *Breaking Bad* and Stephen King.

'Jesus, Jay. Connecticut is in another state entirely,' she said.

'Yeah, but it's still *up* from Florida, right? So I'm heading in the right general direction.'

'I'm really not sure finding Ronni is a good idea,' replied Okeke. 'If they know she's your contact, they could be zeroing in on her right now.'

'But she's the only other person I know. I mean, what the fuck else do I do?' said Jay.

'I'm sure she can help you, Jay, but, honestly, I'm not sure you should meet face to face. They're probably expecting you to head straight towards her.'

'Well, *where else* do I go?' he growled quietly.

'I don't know,' she said. 'I need to think.'

Jay sighed. 'You warned me this was too good to be true. I'm a complete bloody idiot,' he said sulkily.

'Look, don't start beating yourself up, love. You need to stay positive. Stay calm.'

'How am I going to get back home, baby? I've got no passport. No ID. No nothing.'

'Karl and I are going to figure something out,' she told him.

'Maybe, I should go to, I dunno, a British embassy? There's gotta be one in New York, right?'

'I don't know, Jay. I'm not sure,' Okeke said. 'Aren't they all in Washington, where the White House and other government stuff is?'

'Or maybe I *should* just hand myself over to the police?'

'No. No! Don't do that. Just... just keep low. You've got over twenty grand on you, right?' Okeke said.

'Yup,' Jay replied.

'Okay, so you're good for a while.'

'Good for a while doing what?' Jay said. 'Endless laps of America on a frigging coach?'

'Just find somewhere random, *anywhere*,' Okeke said. 'Somewhere you can lie low. Me, Karl and the guv will put our heads together and figure something out.'

That gave Jay more relief. Karl and Sam might make a good Mulder and Scully, but Boyd was a solid brick wall of savvy.

'What's my best bet?' he asked. 'What does Boyd think?'

'Maybe you can sneak into Canada or something?' she ventured.

'*Canada?*' Jay exclaimed.

'We're just throwing ideas around, Jay,' Okeke said snippily. 'All you've got to do is stay calm and, as I said, lie low.'

'I still think the police should be an option,' he murmured. Over the last hours, the idea of walking into a police station voluntarily, hands raised and fully cooperative, had started to make sense.

'*Don't* go to the police!' Okeke snapped. 'If they're after a quick suspect for Kerry's murder, you'll be it. Or it could be worse,' she added ominously.

'Worse! How?' Jay asked.

'One of Wakefield's friends might lean on them,' she said. 'Listen, just sit tight and find somewhere to hunker down while we try to work things out our end. You're lucky you've got a wad of cash on you. And nothing – I mean *nothing* – that's traceable, yes?'

'Uh-huh. I'm distinctly old school right now, Sam,' he said. 'I'm actually making notes on paper.'

'Do me a favour, Jay – ditch Sylvie's phone and get your *own* burner, would you?' she said.

He smiled. 'Jealous?'

'No,' she replied sharply. 'It's just that I'd like to know for certain that what you're holding in your hand is completely vanilla and off-radar.'

'It is. She's an illegal.'

Okeke tutted irritably. 'Just get your *own phone*, Jay, okay?'

'Okay.' He glanced out of the window. The sunlight was now glittering on a rucked carpet of waves, lapping on to a silt-grey beach. 'What do I do about the coach? Stay on? Get off?'

'Stay on it for now,' said Okeke. 'I'll do some research and see if I can find you a good place to head to.'

'And Ronni? If she's in danger too...'

'I'll keep trying, love,' she told him.

'Good, cos she needs to know.' He paused for a moment. 'I'm sorry about all this, babycakes. I'm really –'

'When I get you back, there'll be some stern punishment,' she said mock seriously.

He grinned. 'Can't wait.'

'I'd better go,' she replied. 'Love you, you muppet.'

'You too.'

The call ended and Jay handed the phone back to Sylvie. She took it from him, then said, 'Your lady, she is very bossy, no?'

'Very,' he replied.

Ash ducked down and retrieved the tracker from the front left wheel arch of the Nissan Pathfinder. Turner had left it in the car park between West Palm Beach's Tri-Rail and Greyhound stations. If Turner had even an ounce of wits, he wouldn't have broadcast his intentions quite so obviously.

*Good old Greyhound buses: the time-honoured escape route for transient criminals, escaping teenagers and doomed lovers,* was the thought that had crossed Ash's mind.

At his motel last night, it had taken Ash a total of thirteen minutes, a crypto transaction of a grand and one brief phone call to a Norwegian hacker to get Turner's phone unlocked remotely. Ash deduced that Turner was heading north. The only US contact on his phone was someone called Ronni. It was clear from their text messages that she'd introduced him to Wakefield. Ronni was Turner's go-to resource while he was in the US.

A simple reverse number search told Ash that she was Veronica Kirk and that she ran a small PI business based in Connecticut. How the hell had Wakefield wound up doing business with a PI based all the way up there and hiring some muttonhead all the way from Hastings?

Ash stepped into the Greyhound bus station, adjusted the beanie on his head and marched to one of the two open ticket windows. He reached into his jacket as he approached, then pressed his fake FBI badge against the Perspex.

'I need your help,' he said authoritatively. 'I'm Special Agent Rick Hoffner.'

The ticket agent squinted through her thick-lensed glasses at his badge. Her eyes popped wide as she realised she was looking at a Fed.

'How can I help you, sir?' she asked.

'I'm tracking an active one-nine-seven,' he told her.

'A... a what?' she asked.

He grimaced, as though he was mentally kicking himself. 'Sorry, ma'am. I mean the abduction of a minor. The suspect is a British male, white, bald, bearded and tall with an athletic build. The female is Hispanic and in her twenties or thirties. There's a child with them. A boy. They were here this morning.'

'Oh my goodness!' the woman gasped. 'Yes... yes! They were here!'

'Can you tell me *which* bus they took?' Ash asked her.

'No, sir, I can't,' she replied apologetically. 'This terminal only issues tickets. I can't access details of previous ticket sales on here.'

Ash huffed impatiently. 'The woman and the minor are in extreme danger, ma'am.' He glanced at her nametag. 'Flora-Anne, time is *critical*. Is there a manager I can speak to?'

'I'm the shift lead here, sir,' she said. 'But I still can't access something that's not there.'

Ash cast his eyes around the station and spotted several CCTV cameras. 'What about the cameras? Do you have access to those?'

'Yes, those I do, sir.' She nodded at a row of flickering screens on the wall behind her.

'Then do you mind if I come through and have a look?' he asked.

She paused for a moment, then nodded again. 'Sure. Come over to the door on the left – I'll let you in.'

∽

TEN MINUTES LATER, Ash had identified the coach they had boarded: the 7.30 a.m. to Orlando, due to arrive there at 11 a.m. In the meantime, Flora-Anne had managed to remember more details: '*The woman* did *seem very nervous, and the child, he was quiet as a ghost!*'

By far the most useful piece of information she could recall was that Turner had paid $870 for the three of them and had the cash, right there on him.

'So they were travelling further than Orlando?' he'd asked her.

'Oh, definitely. They were going to New York,' she'd replied firmly.

The coach journey was a long one: thirty-two hours in total, with three stop-and-transfers along the way in Orlando, Atlanta and Washington. Flora printed out a travel itinerary for him. At each station there'd be a one-hour wait, which was helpful. He could get ahead of their coach on each leg of the journey and be waiting for them at each stop. Then he could watch to see if they were actually taking the next coach, or whether that final New York stop was a clever red herring. Turner may have managed to arrange a rendezvous with his colleague Kirk. Ash wanted them all together and, ideally, somewhere not public.

'You need me to call the Orlando shift manager?' asked Flora-Anne.

Ash shook his head. 'I'll call the Orlando field office.' He smiled reassuringly at her. 'Agents there will be ready to intercept him. Thank you for your swift and efficient coop-eration, ma'am.'

❧

ASH MADE good time and arrived at Orlando's bus station only ten minutes after the coach. He was relieved when he saw Turner leading the young boy into the men's restroom. The Hispanic woman – presumably the bitch who'd whacked him from behind – remained at the stop for their next coach, anxiously checking around her.

Turner returned with the boy a few minutes later. He glanced at his watch, then nodded at a McDonald's across the road. From his van, Ash watched them enter the fast-food restaurant. While the boy played on a tablet fixed on the counter beside them, Turner and the woman talked as they took seats at the window.

## 54

'Y̶ou're a detective?' Sylvie whispered.

'It's okay. I'm not with the police,' Jay replied. 'I'm a private detective .'

She frowned. 'Like Magnum PI?'

Now *he* frowned, until he remembered the old eighties show – Tom Selleck with his big old fanny-tickler moustache, the nice Ferrari and those dodgy Hawaiian shirts – and he nodded in reply.

'So this businessman hired you to watch his wife because she is cheating on him?' asked Sylvie.

He nodded again.

'But you find out *she* was spying on *him*,' she said.

'Then on Sunday I found her. She'd been *murdered*.' He whispered the last word so that Jorge wouldn't hear. 'And last night Sam told me that the bloke who hired me is friends with a bunch of powerful men – and that it was probably *them* who arranged for Kerry to be killed.'

'These men, you say they are powerful.' Sylvie glanced at him and he nodded once more. 'How powerful?' she asked.

Good question. 'I think she said there's a senator among them.'

She pursed her lips. '*Very* powerful, then. And this dead woman's phone. They want it, right? So why not just give it to them?'

'If only it was that easy.' He sighed. 'I think they're worried that I know what's on this phone already.'

'What *is* on it?'

'That's the big question, right?' He huffed. 'I wish I knew. Well...' He corrected himself, 'I'm happy *not* to know. But they don't know that, nor are the fuckers likely to believe me if I told 'em that.'

Jorge's head shot up from the tablet. He watched his mother, waiting for her to issue a sharp reprimand.

'Yes, Jorge...' She sighed listlessly. 'He said a bad word.'

❧

*KEEP A COOL HEAD.* Ash cautioned himself as he watched them. *Let's keep a cool head and there are multiple wins to be had out of this.*

Turner and the woman were chatting animatedly. From the expressions on her face he was telling her everything. What Turner didn't realise was that he'd just painted a target on her face. Effectively signed her death warrant. Perhaps the boy too.

*Or perhaps not*, Ash thought.

The kid seemed engrossed in the tablet. Ash might be a cold-blooded, killer but he wasn't particularly keen to have the blood of a child on his hands. That said... during his time in Afghanistan, he'd called in strikes that had caused significant collateral damage. If he was brutally honest with himself, he'd had a hand in blasting many civilians, including children. There was no point trying to whitewash the past.

Nonetheless, directly capping a kid wasn't something he particularly wanted to do.

But Mr C wanted a clean slate. That meant adding them all to the list, including Ronni. He'd wait until they were all together. He could swoop in, no small talk, just *pop-pop-pop-pop*, grab that wretched phone and exit.

Or he could be smart and strategic.

Ash wanted his damned profile scrubbing from those FBI and Interpol lists. More than anything, he wanted his name erased. Watching Turner tuck into his Big Mac, the seed of his earlier idea was beginning to bloom, to take shape... and Turner fitted the role perfectly.

## 55

Special Agent Ryan now had the full backing of his boss and the FBI Director, which meant that Detective Durrant and the Martin County Sheriff's Office were going to have to go along with the charade a second time and quit whining.

Ryan nodded at the bullish British businessman as he stepped into the police interview room, with Detective Durrant at his side.

'Thank you for coming in again, Mr Wakefield,' he said.

'Do you have any more news about Kerry's murderer?' Wakefield asked. 'Have you got a suspect yet?'

'Mr Wakefield,' began Ryan, 'I'm not going to waste time this morning sugar-coating this for you.'

Wakefield suddenly straightened up.

*Was that a prickle of concern on Wakefield's face?*

'Mack, we *know* you did it,' stated Ryan.

Wakefield recoiled in his seat. 'What?'

'We know you were behind your wife's murder,' Ryan said.

Wakefield shook his head vigorously. 'For God's sake! Why the bloody hell would I have my own wife killed?'

'We've interviewed your wife's friends and they say she told them that you were controlling and abusive,' Ryan lied. 'They said you were extremely jealous. She also told them you'd accused her of cheating on you and that she was afraid you might do something to her out of a jealous rage.'

Ryan could feel Detective Durrant's eyes burning holes into the side of his head. None of that was true. Clearly she was pissed that he was following a path that might be deemed to be coercive, which would put them on legally shaky ground if Wakefield confessed anything at all.

'That's not true!' blurted Wakefield. 'That's outrageous! I've never been violent or abusive to her or threatening!'

Ryan stared at him. 'We have witnesses who say otherwise.'

'You'd better tell me who these bloody witnesses are!' Wakefield raged. 'Because that's slanderous!'

'I'm afraid I can't share that information with you, Mr Wakefield,' Ryan responded. He, of course, had no such witnesses.

Wakefield folded his arms. 'Okay, this is crazy! It's ridiculous! I came in today because you said you needed some more help from me. I'm here because I want you people to find the bastard who killed Kerry.' He glanced at Durrant, then back at Ryan. 'What I *didn't* fucking expect was to walk in and be accused of her murder!'

'Listen, Mr Wakefield, we could have sent uniforms to arrest you,' Detective Durrant told him. Ryan could see she was uncomfortable saying that. MCSO didn't have enough yet for a warrant.

'But,' she went on, 'we wanted to see whether you'd

cooperate willingly, or attempt to flee.' She smiled at him. 'Clearly you made the right choice.'

'Right!' Wakefield nodded.

'And that will be noted by your defence,' she continued.

'But –'

'But,' cut in Ryan, 'right now it's not looking good for you and if you want to call in a lawyer, then you should. Be my guest.'

'This is... this is insane!' Wakefield had gone from looking prickly to petrified. He stood up and Detective Durrant stood up with him.

'We have a warrant for your arrest,' she told him. 'If you leave this room, we'll have no choice but to take you into custody.'

'Please sit, Mr Wakefield,' said Ryan.

Wakefield slumped into his seat and buried his face in his big hands.

'We're on a path, Mr Wakefield,' said Ryan. 'And it's leading to court and a conviction. Unless you have any information that steers us elsewhere.'

Wakefield slowly lifted his head. 'I told you that Kerry thought she was being stalked, right?'

'Yes, you said she thought he'd followed her over from the UK,' Ryan said, unimpressed.

'And I gave you a description,' Wakefield said. 'He was a Brit. Bald, scrappy beard. Tall, muscly. You really should be looking for him.'

Ryan's mind suddenly jolted. 'Did you say *bald*?'

That last time he'd met her, Kerry had talked about a man fumbling around under her car – white, tall, muscular. Adrenaline surged through his veins. She'd never mentioned that he was bald.

A piece of the puzzle clicked into place. Ryan had

considered the possibility that the incident was some punk trying his luck at stealing it. It was a Lotus Elise, for crying out loud. There was every possibility that Kerry's death had, in fact, been some random, unfortunate coincidence – but for that one last descriptive ingredient. Had Wakefield actually just described KFH_50BTFOA_FI/10, aka Ash, seventh on the FBI's Most Wanted list?

Had that been Ash scoping her out?

If so... that meant that somebody in the Mulligan Club had already been on to her.

He'd sent her to Wakefield that Saturday and she must have *already* been burned.

*Jesus.* He'd sent her back to face certain death.

'This interview is terminated.' Ryan turned off the interview recorder.

Durrant glanced his way, surprised.

'Mr Wakefield,' said Ryan, standing up. 'Detective Durrant and I are going to step outside for a moment.'

'Can I go?' Wakefield asked hopefully.

Ryan shook his head. 'Stay right where you are. We won't be long.'

He led Durrant outside and closed the door behind him.

'Uh, that was kind of sudden. What the hell did I miss?' she asked.

'We're done here,' he told her. 'This is now an FBI interview.'

She raised her brows. 'And how does that work?' she asked.

'There'll be no interview recorder. No lawyer. And, I'm afraid, no you,' Ryan told her.

'Excuse me? You're ejecting me?' She glared at him. 'You can't do that.'

Ryan smiled. 'I'm sorry, but I'm afraid I can. This is now a federal matter.'

'Screw you,' she replied, her patience finally exhausted, and she marched off.

Ryan returned to the interview room.

Wakefield looked up at him, worried. 'What the hell's going on, detective?'

'I'm not with Homicide,' Ryan replied as he sat down. 'I'm FBI.' He noted the flicker of alarm on Wakefield's face. 'Which means, Mr Wakefield, that it's just you and me – we can speak off the record.'

'Wh-what the hell are you talking about?' Wakefield blustered.

'I'm going to tell you what I know,' Ryan said. 'I'm going to tell you about the Mulligan Club. I'm going to tell you about Senator Bowman, Dominic Carlton, Noel Monke, Justice –'

'*Oh God,*' Wakefield whispered.

'I know you gentlemen hired a professional hitman,' Ryan continued. 'I know he's here in Florida right now. Paid for by the Mulligan Club.'

Wakefield glanced at the video camera in the corner of the ceiling. The red recording light was off.

'Yeah,' said Ryan. 'That's switched off too. It's just the two of us, buddy.'

Wakefield looked at him. 'Why would I... Why should I tell you anything?'

'Because Kerry has been my asset for months,' Ryan replied.

'Oh fuck,' Wakefield whispered, his face reddening.

Ryan nodded, 'Oh fuck, indeed...'

## 56

Over the tired croak of the wipers and the rain drumming on the windscreen, Okeke saw her phone wink to life in its dashboard holder. She glanced at it. It was Karl.

She tapped the screen and the speaker icon. 'Yup?'

'Sam, I've got a plan for Jay,' he said.

'Do I want to hear it?' she asked warily as she pulled out of her parking spot at the station.

'Well, given the current circumstances, it's all I can think of,' Karl replied.

'Is it legal?'

'Not entirely. No,' Karl admitted.

She turned left onto Bohemia Road, downhill towards the seafront. As she was heading home, she felt fractionally less guilty having this conversation.

'Is it anything to do with a fake passport?' she asked.

'Yup,' he confirmed. 'I know someone who can knock up a decent passport pretty quickly.'

'You know someone?' she said.

'Okay, not personally,' Karl said. 'It's through a some-what dodgy site. Payment in crypto, natch.'

Okeke stopped at a pedestrian crossing and watched a young mother walk past, pushing a buggy with one hand and dragging a toddler with the other.

She sighed. 'Are we really going down this route?'

'We don't have a lot of options, Sam,' Karl pointed out. 'She's good, she's quick and she's discreet.

'How do you know?'

'Her reviews are all five-star.'

'Five-star reviews from the criminal underworld?' Okeke snorted. 'What could possibly go wrong?'

'It'll cost five thousand in Bitcoin,' he said, ignoring her, 'and should only take a day or so to FedEx it direct to Jay.'

'Shit. I don't have five thousand,' Okeke replied.

'It's okay – I do, and it's already in Bitcoin,' said Karl. 'Jay, can pay me back later.'

'He already owes you,' she said as she eased off the brake and continued down Bohemia Road.

The shitshow in Brighton the year before last, involving Rovshan Salikov's wayward son going rogue had resulted in Karl's rented apartment being burned to the ground along with all his possessions. Not to mention the fact that he'd very nearly been killed.

'Yeah, well, he's all I've got in the way of fam,' Karl said.

'And what if this fake passport doesn't cut it? What if it triggers something when it's scanned? He'll be in even bigger trouble.'

'But he won't be dead, which is more important, right?' Karl countered.

Okeke shook her head. This was getting out of hand, but she *did* want him home...

'All right, okay.' She sighed. 'Let's do it. Do you need a passport photo of him?'

'If you've got one lying around,' Karl said. 'If not, she said she can use AI to reconstruct one from a Facebook pic.'

Okeke turned right at the seafront junction, the wind and rain battering her car. 'I'm not sure I want her doing that. Let me see if I can find one. I know he had to sort out a new pic for his gym pass recently.'

'Don't worry if it's not quite passport standard,' replied Karl. 'She can change the background or remove anything that would disqualify the photo.'

'I'll have a look when I get home,' said Okeke. 'I'll call you later.'

~

OKEKE TURNED the kitchen and back room upside down, looking for Jay's gym-pass photo. She pulled out drawers, emptying them onto the kitchen table, and gutted their small filing cabinet. She spread out the folders, hurriedly flipped through each one. Nothing was organised. Every folder had a Sharpie-scrawled label on it that bore absolutely no resemblance to its contents.

She finally remembered she'd taken a few DIY passport photos on her phone just over two years ago. Back when they'd had to update Jay's passport online, to get it sorted months before a cheap-as-chips Ibiza holiday they'd booked. They never went, of course. A new DCI had arrived at Hastings by the name of Boyd, and life had been a pretty relentless game of whack-a-mole ever since.

She scrolled back through her thousands of photographs, guessing multiple times at the year and month. At last she found what she wanted: seven attempts at a photo that the passport portal would accept as valid.

Okeke picked the seventh attempt and WhatsApped it to Karl.

He called her a minute later. 'I've sent it and she's already working on it.'

'Okay,' she whispered, stepping into the kitchen to slap the kettle on.

She needed a coffee and a fag. They were actually going ahead with a fake passport. Okeke pushed the illegality of it out of her head. Right now, her priority was Jay.

'So how do we get it to Jay?' she asked.

'We'll need a PO Box,' replied Karl. 'You can set one up online in a couple of clicks. We just have to make sure it's one that Jay can get to.'

'Don't forget he's relying on public transport at the moment,' Okeke reminded him.

'I know. And heading towards New York, right?' Karl said.

'Uh-huh.'

'Well, it won't be a problem getting a PO Box set up,' Karl said. 'Let me check...' There was a moment of silence. 'Yup, there's a post office near Times Square. Nice and central – easy to find and get to.'

'I'll call Jay and let him know what we're doing,' Okeke replied.

'Before you go, Sam, the forger needs a name for the passport. Do you have any suggestions?'

She patted her pockets for her cigarettes while she thought it over. The first name really needed to be his – Jay or Jason – so that he'd be comfortable responding to it if he was randomly pulled aside for questioning, for whatever reason. The surname, though – that should be something bland, instantly forgettable. Or was that something that immigration officers looked for? The Steven Smiths and the Jack Joneses?

'Jason something,' said Karl, as though reading her mind. 'Statham? Bourne?' He suggested. 'Bond?'

'How about Collins?' said Okeke.

'Why Collins?' Karl asked.

'Louie Collins, his mate. The one that got murdered,' Okeke said.

'Ah right. Yeah,' replied Karl. 'That's probably a good shout. Jason Collins, it is then. There are other details too – place of birth, date of birth, NI number... I can give her some random stuff.'

'No. Give her Jay's real DOB and place of birth. He'll need to know those if he's quizzed. The NI number can be anything, though. Who knows their actual NI number anyway, right?'

## 57

B oyd had had a full twenty-four hours to mull over what Nikki Turkman had told him over the phone about Dan.

'Look, Detective Boyd,' she'd said. 'Dan's one of those rare things, a genuinely talented musician that I'd call an actual artist. He's everything in one package, both singer and songwriter. He's a good-looking, charismatic boy, a great frontman for the band. His lyrics are deceptively deep. He's prolific, profoundly driven... He's everything you'd want.'

'But...' Boyd had prompted.

'But artists like Dan have a habit of imploding. I don't think I'm exaggerating when I say I'd group him with the likes of Kurt Cobain, Amy Winehouse and Ian Curtis. Artists who went off the deep end. Dan's *extremely* talented but also extremely volatile, and the other members of the band were growing concerned about his behaviour.'

'I spotted the scars on his arms,' Boyd said.

'Then there were the voices,' Nikki had told him. 'I mean, obviously I'm no expert on this kind of thing, but

Rory – the lad who's now fronting the band – said Dan had told him he was hearing voices.'

'Hearing voices? What do you mean?' Boyd asked.

'Dan was hearing voices in his head,' Nikki repeated.

'Christ, so this isn't just an artistic angst phase, then?' Boyd said.

'He needs professional care,' Nikki replied. 'And a formal evaluation. To be honest, for his safety and anyone else, I think he might need to be sectioned.'

'Do you know if he's doing drugs?' said Boyd.

'I don't know. I'm sure they all do a little bit of this and that,' Nikki said. 'But, look, can I ask you how he's of particular interest to you? Has he been in trouble with the police? Has he been arrested?'

'My daughter's his partner,' Boyd explained. 'She's just had his baby. He's living with us right now.'

'I see.' Nikki Turkman paused. 'If I were you, Detective Boyd, I'd get him some help. And very quickly.'

## 58

S pecial Agent Ryan had struck gold. Malcolm Wakefield had been very forthcoming and cooperative. Ryan was now in possession of some incredibly useful information. To begin with, there was a chance he had the real name for KFH_50BTFOA_FI/10, aka Ash.

Wakefield's description, coupled with the date of his flight over from the UK, had given Ryan a passenger manifest, a list of names and their passport photographs. The passenger travelling alone, sitting in 27C, was undoubtedly his man.

*Jason Turner.*

Ryan had assumed, at first, that the name was another alias, but after a detailed online search he suspected that this was an authentic identity. Jason Turner's Facebook page wasn't a recently set-up fake with AI-generated pictures of him at parties and weddings; it was seventeen years' worth of posts, photos, memes and social interactions.

The Jason Turner in the photos was a consistent person, changing slowly over time. Scrolling through the years,

Ryan followed Turner from the young man's receding hair-line to a buzz cut and the more recent straightforward shaved head.

Ryan was pretty confident he was looking at Ash's actual identity. Which, of course, begged the question: why the hell would he have slipped up and given the Mulligan Club his real ID?

It made absolutely no sense. As a professional hitman, he'd left nothing behind him – not an ounce of forensics, not a bullet casing, not a fibre, not even a cigarette butt. All the FBI and Interpol had on him was that one grainy dashcam image of his face.

*Then all of a sudden he takes a job under his real name? Why?*

The only conclusion that made sense to Ryan was that Turner was bowing out of the game. He was organizing his exit strategy. This was almost certainly going to be his last job and when he was done he was going to surrender that name, that ID, and live the rest of his life under a brand-new one. Presumably an alias he'd been carefully curating and nurturing, ready for his retirement.

One final job with a payout that would tide him over and allow him to reinvent himself as a legitimate law-abiding citizen.

It appeared that Turner was over here for something big. Something spectacular. And while Wakefield had been extremely helpful, he'd played decidedly dumb as to what it was.

'*Look, mate, I don't know what they're planning. It's on a need-to-know basis. I provided some capital and a place to meet, but that's all I can tell you. The plan? That's for the Big Boys. I'm just a new recruit.*'

It was bullshit, of course, and Wakefield knew that he knew it. Clearly he was holding that card, until Ryan brought him something cast iron that he could scrawl his name on.

An immunity deal.

## 59

'Pint of shandy for you, Danny boy,' said Boyd, setting the glasses on the table, 'and some smoky bacon crisps, as requested.'

He sat down on the other side of the table with his Caffrey's. He'd picked a table upstairs at the Pump House, where it was a bit quieter. Where they could talk.

'Thanks,' said Dan, taking a sip. 'Hey, I just wanna say thanks for letting me move in.'

Boyd nodded. 'No problem.'

He'd asked Dan out for a pint after dinner, making it sound as casual and innocuous as possible – the first of many friendly drinks down at the local. But this was going to be a very different kind of after-dinner pint.

'So, I'm curious, Dan – what's made you suddenly want to give up being a rock star and join the police?' he asked.

Dan shrugged. 'I dunno. The whole rock-star thing feels kind of pointless. It's just songs, right? None of it really amounts to anything important.'

'You're not enjoying it?' Boyd prompted.

Dan shook his head. 'Not any more. I've had enough of writing inane pop songs.'

'What about your band mates, though? You get on pretty well, huh?' Boyd's questions felt disingenuous, given what he knew, but he wanted to see how much Dan was prepared to open up to him.

'Yeah. Sure. We get on fine,' Dan replied.

'But after the tour... I suppose you're feeling burned out, eh?'

Dan nodded. 'That's it, I guess.'

'But you're okay apart from that?' pressed Boyd. 'No problems? No issues?'

Dan nodded again. 'Nah. Burned out's a pretty good way of putting it.'

Maybe he wasn't going to open up after all.

*What do I do?* mused Boyd. *Just go for it? Tear the plaster off?* There certainly was no way they were walking back home without discussing this. It was now or never.

'Dan, I spoke to Nikki Turkman yesterday.'

Dan's eyes suddenly rounded with panic.

'So,' continued Boyd, 'I know the band toured Europe without you.'

Dan's cheeks flashed pink.

'What've you been doing while they were over there for all that time? What was it four, five months?'

Dan raised a hand to his mouth and started nibbling at the corner of his thumbnail absently.

'Dan?' Boyd prompted gently, but the lad wouldn't meet his eyes. 'What's going on, mate? Why did you lie to us?'

'I... I'm sorry,' Dan said miserably.

'I don't need you to be sorry, mate,' Boyd said. 'I just want to know what the hell's going on with you.'

'I couldn't go. I just can't do it any more,' Dan mumbled.

'You can't do what?' Boyd asked. 'Write songs? Gig? Be in a band? Come on, tell me... What's going on in that head of yours?'

'I can't do the writing any more.' Dan resumed gnawing at his thumbnail.

'Why? The song-writing's the fun bit, isn't it?'

Dan looked at Boyd. 'I have to *think* to do it. I have to sit still *and think*. And *create*.'

Boyd smiled. 'Uh, yeah. That's the job. And as jobs go, it's got to be better than – I don't know – delivering parcels, order-picking in a warehouse...'

Dan seemed to perk up for a second. 'I'd totally do *that*. I'd do it – just to keep my fuckin' head empty. Just to keep from actually fuckin' *thinking*!'

The swearing was new. Dan probably swore all the time, but so far never in front of Boyd.

'Okay, mate,' he replied. 'Take it easy.'

Dan went back to chewing his thumbnail. That was also new.

'What is it? The creative pressure? Is that getting too much for you?' asked Boyd.

Could it have been the creative pressure –on top of whatever dormant fracture lines already existed in their troubled minds – that had been too much for those musicians Turkman had mentioned? They'd been just kids still, probably already mentally fragile for one reason or another, then suddenly asked to come up with the creative goods as success suddenly came knocking.

Dan shook his head. 'I can make the tunes – that's easy.' He glanced again at Boyd. 'It's the words...'

Nikki Turkman had mentioned that the tone of Dan's lyrics had gone pretty dark. She'd told Boyd she was old enough to know that a bad acid trip could produce some weird shit, but the notebook of lyrics that the band had shown her had some pretty disturbing stuff in it.

'The words?' repeated Boyd. 'What do you mean by that?'

'Dark stuff.' Dan cracked a desperately unhappy grin. 'Existential distress. That's what head doctors call it, right? Or something like that.' He shook his head. 'I don't want to say it's not me. But... it's not me.'

*Not me.*

Nikki Templeton had mentioned voices. If Boyd revealed to Dan that he knew about the voices, would it trigger something? Denial? An aggressive outburst? Shame?

*We're not going home without talking about this*, Boyd reminded himself. Nikki Turkman had said that Dan needed professional help. She had also begun their conversation yesterday by asking whether Dan had harmed anyone.

'Dan, your manager told me...' Boyd began tentatively, 'well, she said you were actually hearing voices?'

Dan looked down at the packet of bacon crisps and started flattening it, his hands cracking the crisps within to granules.

'Dan, mate, is that true?' Boyd pressed.

Dan nodded, and Boyd felt his gut sink. Creative burnout or depression was one thing, psychosis was quite another.

'Okay.' Boyd was uncertain as to what to say next. 'All right. So these voices, what sort of things are they saying?'

Dan continued to crush the crisp packet.

'Mate,' Boyd said gently. 'What sort of –'

Dan smacked his palm down on top of the flattened packet. 'To kill myself!' He glared intensely at Boyd through his fringe. 'You know, open a wrist or something.'

'Does Emma know about any of this?' Boyd asked, shocked.

Dan shook his head frantically. His angry glare morphed into a pitiful plea.

'Please... Please don't tell her!'

Boyd felt out of his depth. He had no idea how to handle this. Charlotte would have probably found a better, more indirect way to coax the truth out of him, but she wasn't there and it was down to him.

'Have you tried yet? To kill yourself?' asked Boyd. 'Has this gone any further than just *ideation*?'

Dan shook his head.

'Are you on any drugs that could be fuelling this?'

Another shake of the head.

*Shit.* Boyd was well outside any level of competence on the subject. It was a Thursday night and he had no clue who he should call to get advice this late.

'Listen, Dan, we need to get you some help,' he said, somewhat lamely, as Dan drew invisible lines across the flattened packet with his index finger. 'If I can get you some help, will you take it?'

Dan shrugged.

'Dan!' said Boyd sharply.

Dan nodded. 'Yeah. Maybe...'

There was no way, absolutely no way, that Boyd was going to take Dan back home with him tonight. Not with Emma and Maggie under the same roof.

'Dan, listen, I'm going to help you out. Tomorrow we're going to get you some help, okay? But tonight...'

The young man looked up at him. 'You're going to say I can't come stay, aren't you?'

Boyd nodded. 'I'm so sorry. Just for tonight, could you stay at your mum's?'

~

'WHAT THE HELL'S GOING ON?' asked Emma.

Dan finished stuffing his overnight bag with clothes and headed to the bathroom to get his toiletries.

Boyd was standing on the landing at the top of the stairs. 'He's staying over at his mum's tonight.'

'What? Why?' Emma demanded.

'I'll explain later,' Boyd told her.

Emma wasn't having any of it. 'What's going on? Have you guys had a fight or something?' she asked, bewildered.

Boyd shook his head as Dan emerged from the bathroom clutching his toothbrush, a can of Lynx and a flannel.

Emma stopped him. 'Dan? Have you two fallen out?'

'No, Ems,' he mumbled as he shoved the toiletries into his bag. 'I'm just gonna stay over at Mum's tonight, that's all.'

'Oh, for God's sake!' She turned to face Boyd. 'Dad!'

'I'll said I'll explain later,' he snapped. 'When I get back.'

~

DAN DIRECTED Boyd up the hill towards Ore.

'Mum lives on...' He pointed through the windscreen at the next turning on the left. 'Down there.'

'Markham Avenue?' Boyd asked.

'Yeah, that one.'

Boyd signalled and turned into a narrow street lined with terraced houses on either side.

'It's number thirty-seven,' Dan said.

Boyd scanned the houses as they crept up the avenue, squeezing between cars parked nose-to-arse on both sides. Finally he pulled up outside Number 37. There were no lights on.

'Is she not home?' he asked.

'She'll be at bingo,' Dan replied sullenly, clutching his overnight bag. 'She'll be back soon.'

Boyd turned to look at him. 'Listen, Dan. We're going to get you sorted out, okay?'

He shrugged.

'This is not me kicking you out,' said Boyd calmly. 'This is for tonight only. I'll come over tomorrow morning, we'll call some people and get you the help you need, okay?'

'I don't want to be sectioned,' Dan mumbled.

'I'm sure you won't be,' Boyd said. 'But you're going to need to talk to someone, someone professional who can help, perhaps with counselling or drugs to help you stabilise what's going on in your mind.'

'Okay,' Dan agreed.

'We'll make those voices shut the fuck up, eh?' said Boyd, patting his arm gently.

'Right.' Dan looked at him. 'Then I can come back home?'

*Home.* That word made Boyd's heart ache for the lad. He'd been with them just four days and already 30 Ashburnham Road was his home.

Boyd smiled. 'Sure.'

As Dan opened the door to get out, Boyd grabbed his arm.

'You going to be okay tonight?' he asked. 'Promise me you're not going to do anything stupid.'

'I won't,' Dan replied.

Boyd let go and Dan climbed out.

'Tomorrow, all right,' said Boyd. 'I'll be here at nine and we'll make some calls, okay?'

'Sure.' Dan gave Boyd a furtive wave, then shut the door.

As Boyd drove down Markham Lane to the junction at

the end of the road, he was already rehearsing how he was going to explain all this to Emma. He glanced in the rear-view mirror to see Dan still standing on the pavement outside his house.

Still waving.

## 60

J ay stirred from his sleep. Someone was tapping his shoulder. It was Jorge, his grinning face squidged between the headrests.

'Jay, it's your lady from England.' He dangled his mother's phone over the top of the seat and Jay took it from him.

Jay had managed to pick up a burner phone and a fully juiced grab-and-go charger at a CVS in Orlando. He looked down at his lap – it appeared that he'd fallen asleep on the coach before he'd even managed to remove the phone from its packaging.

'Hey, babycakes,' he whispered.

'Where are you?' she asked.

'On our way to Atlanta. We're transferring there,' he told her.

'Me and Karl have a plan for you,' she announced.

'Yeah?' Jay said hopefully.

'Karl's getting you a fake passport. Made in Taiwan, would you believe?' she said. 'He's going to have it sent over to you.'

'Sent where?' Jay asked.

'To a PO Box,' Okeke replied.

'For fuck's sake!' he hissed. 'How am I supposed to –'

'Calm down. It's fine,' she told him. 'You're heading to New York, yeah? Karl's going to book you one in the Times Square Post Office – it'll be easy to get to.'

'Yeah, but I can't hang around in New York waiting for something to come from Taiwan!' Jay pointed out.

'It'll only be for three days,' she replied. 'It's not His Majesty's Passport Office we're talking about. We're FedExing it to you.'

'Okay, fine,' he whispered. Then realising he was being bit of a dick: 'Sorry, love. I'm just a bit strung out.'

'And your name,' she continued, 'will be Jason Collins. You're thirty-seven and you were born in Kent,' she continued.

'All you've changed is my *surname*?' he asked, surprised.

'That's all we *need* to change, baby,' she said calmly. 'It's best to keep it simple.' She paused. 'I thought you'd like to have Louie's name.'

He nodded. 'Yeah... yeah, I do. Good choice, Sam. Good choice. So three days?'

'Three days. You've just got to lie low in New York until Monday. Then you can pick up the passport and get a flight home.'

'Right,' he said. 'So I'm thinking I could hook up with Ronni. Maybe we can hide at her place.'

Okeke sighed. 'I told you. I'm not so sure that's a good idea, Jay. The hitman, if he's a pro, will have hacked your phone by now and got her number – I'm assuming she's your only American contact. It's likely she'll be on his radar.'

'I'm going to call her when we get there,' Jay said confidently. 'She's a pro. She'll shake off anyone following her.'

'You're putting a lot of faith in her, aren't you?'

'She's had training, remember. We both have,' he added.

'Right.' He heard her sigh again. 'You've had a three-day course.'

'Wait. Shit. I haven't got her number on me.'

Okeke sighed. 'I have.' She read it out to him, and he scribbled it down on his notepad.

'Have you managed to speak to Ronni yet?' he asked her.

'I left a message,' she replied. 'I gave her the gist of what's going on and asked her to call me back ASAP.'

'Shit. Could you keep trying please? I'm getting worried about her,' he said.

'All the more reason not to meet up with her, love,' Okeke advised.

'She needs to be warned,' said Jay. 'And if she needs to be off-grid too, then she might as well be with us. Two pairs of eyes are better than one, right?'

'Hmmm... maybe,' replied Okeke.

'How about Karl? Has he had any luck finding out who that Ryan guy is?' Jay asked.

'No. But Karl thinks he might be FBI. If Kerry was spying for him, he could have been her handler.'

'Ryan might be his last name,' said Jay.

'True. But how many Agent Ryans are there in the FBI?' she pointed out.

'Could Karl hack their records and find out?' Jay asked.

'I wouldn't put it past him,' she said. 'But...'

'What?'

'There might be an informant line for you to ring or something?' she said thoughtfully. 'I'll see if there's some kind of website or phone number for that kind of thing.'

'Yeah. Good thinking. If I've got something they want, maybe they'll look after me,' Jay said.

'Let's hope so,' Okeke replied. 'In the meantime, we need to focus on keeping you off the radar. What time are you due into New York?'

'Tomorrow, half three in the afternoon.'

'Good. It'll be nice and busy,' she said.

'Yeah. If you do speak to Ronni, let her know too.'

'I'll try,' she replied. 'But don't forget: her phone might be tapped. For God's sake, get your own burner when you stop at Atlanta, will you? You can't keep relying on other women.'

'I got one,' he replied, looking down at the unopened packaging. 'I just haven't got round to setting it up yet.'

'Then may I suggest you do it?' she snipped.

'Yeah, yeah,' he grumbled, then again realised how ungrateful he was sounding. Without Sam orchestrating things at her end, he'd be running round in circles.

'Listen, Sam... I... uh... I'm –'

'Is this you saying thank you or sorry?'

He smiled. 'Both, actually.'

'In that case, *you're welcome* and *don't do it again*.'

## 61

C arlton smiled as the door opened. 'Good evening, Mack. Mind if I step in?'

Malcolm Wakefield checked his watch. 'For crying out loud, it's nearly midnight,'

'It's important,' Carlton replied. 'Very important.' He tapped the Walmart bag he was carrying. 'I've brought a gift. A gift. A nice bottle of Jack Daniels.'

Wakefield frowned.

'Fine,' he said, and stepped back into the cavernous interior of his vulgar Palm Beach mansion.

It was all faux marble and Doric columns, fighting with Spanish Colonial trimmings. Carlton sighed inwardly. In his opinion, taste took three generations to acquire and another three to curate.

Wakefield led him through the entrance hall to the large dark oak doors where Carlton had spotted Kerry spying. They stepped into the main lounge. In this very room on Saturday the Mulligan Club had mapped out the final revisions to their grand plan. They'd talked boldly and openly.

Too openly.

Carlton spoke first. 'There are some important matters we need to discuss, Mack.'

'Let's keep it short. I'll have *one* drink with you,' Wakefield said, 'then I'm going to bed. It's been a long fuckin' day.'

Carlton smiled. 'I know. I watched you enter the police station and I watched you leave.'

'Christ.' Wakefield turned to him in surprise. 'You've been spying on *me*?'

'Yes. We're concerned you've got heat on you.'

Carlton pulled out a glass tumbler from the drinks cabinet. He took out the whiskey he'd brought, poured a double measure and handed the glass to Wakefield.

'Have a drink, Mack – you're going to need it.'

'Why? What's the news?'

'Drink,' Carlton instructed.

Wakefield stiffened at the command, but he took a sip.

'The police *allowed* you to leave,' said Carlton. 'An unsettling fact for us.'

'They didn't have enough to hold me,' replied Wakefield.

'That, or you gave them something,' Carlton said.

Wakefield's eyes widened. 'What the actual fuck?'

'Sit down,' said Carlton.

'No, I won't bloody well sit down!' Wakefield replied.

'SIT!' Carlton snapped.

Wakefield relented and slumped into an armchair. 'Mate, I didn't tell the cops anything if that's what you're getting at! I pulled the wool over their eyes and I pointed them in Jay Turner's general direction. Problem sorted.'

'Mack, Mack... *stop*,' said Carlton, shaking his head. 'Were you aware that one of the homicide detectives interviewing you was, in fact, an FBI agent?'

'Huh?' Wakefield attempted to look shocked.

Carlton smiled. It was a pretty impressive reaction. Worthy of an award.

'In my experience,' he said to Wakefield, 'an FBI agent letting you walk usually indicates you have something to offer and a deal might be on the table.'

'What? No! As far as they're aware, they're chasing down a druggie,' Wakefield tried.

'The FBI don't eat that far down the food chain,' said Carlton. He reached into the Walmart bag and pulled out a gun. 'We need to know exactly what you've told them, Mack.'

'I haven't said *anything!*' Wakefield pleaded.

'If you'd been honest and told me that you'd been interviewed by a Fed this afternoon, I'd be more inclined to believe you. But...' Carlton shook his head again. 'You didn't even reach out to me once you were home – and that makes me feel very twitchy indeed.'

Wakefield set his tumbler down heavily. 'Look! Put that fucking gun away! I'm not having this conversation with you while you're waving that bloody thing around.'

'What information did you give them?' Carlton asked once more.

'*Nothing!* I gave them nothing!' Wakefield shouted.

Carlton took out a tea towel from the bag and calmly wrapped it round the gun. 'This is every bit as effective as a silencer for muffling a shot, Mack. And far cheaper too.'

'Fuck's sake, Carlton!' snapped Wakefield. 'That's enough! Why the hell would I give them anything? I'm as involved in this as you are!'

'Did they promise you an immunity deal?' Carlton demanded.

'No! Because they don't think I'm guilty of anything!' Wakefield said. 'That's why they let me come home!'

'Did you mention Kerry's phone?' Carlton asked.

'What?'

'You heard me. Did you mention it?'

'No! Of course I didn't mention it!'

Carlton sighed. 'How about I start with your kneecaps? One bullet in each.' He smiled. 'That's how your old IRA liked to do it, isn't it?'

'I told them,' Wakefield suddenly blurted, 'that Kerry thought she was being stalked! I said she told me she'd caught a bloke following her, taking pictures of her. She was spooked. Thought he might be a weirdo. You know, dangerous.'

Carlton didn't doubt that he'd said that, but it wasn't enough to warrant the presence of a Fed, though.

'You've really screwed us over, Mack. Big boys – *sensible* boys – don't bring their girlfriends to business meetings. They send them off on a nice holiday. They don't keep them hanging around to show them off and to spy on everyone.'

'I had no idea that Kerry –'

'That's right,' said Carlton. 'You didn't. And that makes you a careless fool. I'm giving serious thought to advising Bowman and the others to pull the plug on the whole operation. They're not going to be happy about that. So I'm going to ask you one more time.' Carlton levelled the gun at him. 'And I really need to believe your answer this time, understand? *Do they know that there could be recorded evidence on Kerry's phone?*'

'I told you *no*! I didn't mention it!' Wakefield whispered. 'They don't even know about her bastard phone!'

Carlton waited a beat to see if Wakefield would say any more. He didn't. Carlton nodded. 'All right.' He lowered the gun.

Wakefield let out a long ragged gasp. 'So that's it? You fucking believe me now?'

'There are two sides to my job,' Carlton said. 'The fun part, of course, is making big things happen. The less rewarding part is fixing mistakes. I'm afraid you have turned into the latter.' He sighed. 'The trick is spotting the moment you can make a fix while it's still easy to do.'

'Make a f-fix?' Wakefield spluttered. 'There's nothing to fix. It's going to be fine. Ash will find Turner, recover the phone and we're all good. Just tell the others not to panic, for fuck's sake! This isn't the time for anyone to start losing their shit and- –'

'Malcolm, Mack...' Carlton sighed ruefully. 'I've been far too slow to act before. I should have dealt with Epstein *before* they arrested him. Do you have any idea how difficult it was to arrange his death in custody? With the world looking on?'

Wakefield stared at him. 'Fuck? That was you?'

Carlton smiled, raised the gun and fired.

Wakefield flopped into his chair. Carlton wiped the gun down and placed it in the man's lap. He grabbed one of Wakefield's big hands and smeared his finger over the handle and barrel. Next, he poured whiskey into Wakefield's open mouth, wiped the bottle and set it down next to the tumbler.

Finally, he looked at the dead man and cocked his head.

'Yes, that was me,' he said.

---

## 62

From the comfort of his van, Ash watched the coach pull into Atlanta Bus Station. He'd parked opposite, on Brotherton Street, beside a charity-run soup kitchen where there was a steady flow of bedraggled patrons going in and out.

Turner, the woman and her child alighted the coach and stretched their arms and legs. It looked as though they might be the only passengers waiting around for the overnight bus to Washington.

It was decision time. Ash could make a move on them right here and now: pull up and, at gunpoint, hustle them into the back of his van, dispose of them in a remote forest. Or he could let them continue on to New York. If Turner was planning to meet Kirk, Ash would have them all together, rounded up in one spot.

Nice and tidy.

Ash's phone buzzed in his lap. It was Carlton.

'Ash,' he said as he answered the call.

'Wakefield's dead,' as Carlton's greeting.

That didn't surprise Ash one bit. The man had been a

squeaky wheel from the very beginning. There was no one quite as mouthy as a rich Brit abroad. Particularly one from the East End. Ash had grown used to clients who met discreetly in gentlemen's clubs in Belgravia, who spoke very softly in a highly nuanced language.

'You should never have let him into your inner circle,' said Ash.

'It wasn't my decision,' replied Carlton. 'Bowman and the others were dazzled by his money.'

'How did you stage it?' asked Ash.

'Wakefield was feeling guilty about hiring someone to whack his wife and he drank too much whiskey,' said Carlton dryly. 'It was all too much for him. He shot himself. Where are you with Wakefield's PI?'

'I've got eyes on him. He's taking Greyhounds up to New York. I suspect he's trying to meet up with his colleague, Veronica Kirk.'

'What's your plan?' asked Carlton.

'I'm going to let them meet. If they've figured out the kind of mess they're in, they'll go to ground somewhere. Which is fine with me. I can deal with them all together.'

'Let me reiterate,' Carlton said, 'I need to know whether Turner has Kerry's phone on him. Turner and Kirk being silenced is all very well, but if that phone ends up in the hands of someone who can crack it open...'

'Relax,' Ash said. 'I'm pretty sure he has it on him still. He hasn't had a chance to pass it on to anyone and he hasn't dropped off any packages.'

'Good,' replied Carlton. 'Now, I have some bad news.'

'What?'

'The main job is off.'

Ash took a moment to digest that. 'May I ask why?'

'Wakefield was interviewed by the FBI. I have no idea

how much he's given them. He could have completely rolled over for all we know. I conferred with the others and it's agreed. It's far too risky to go ahead with our plan.'

'Pity,' replied Ash.

'So, I'm afraid, once you've dealt with Turner and the others, your services will no longer be required.' Carlton said.

'I see,' Ash replied.

'Listen, I'm sorry to mess you around. I hope this doesn't sour our relationship.'

'As long as you pay the abort fee, we're good,' Ash said.

'We will,' replied Carlton. 'And I may want to call on you again in the near future. My people are still keen to get the result they want come November.'

'I may be off the market by then, permanently,' Ash replied. 'I've done my time and I'm done.'

'Well, that's sensible,' replied Carlton. 'The smartest players know when to quit.'

'Exactly,' Ash agreed. 'Plus, if Wakefield squealed, they'll know you've hired someone. And they'll work out it's me.'

'Yes, you could well be right.' Carlton drew a breath. 'Then I think you and I are pretty much finished here. Let me know when you've dealt with the problem.'

'I'll have it sorted by Saturday. You want me to send the phone to a PO Box?' asked Ash.

'God no. I want it in my hands. Deliver it in person.'

'I never meet clients,' Ash said. 'What I can do is conceal the phone somewhere and text you a What3Words location. And if Wakefield gave them your name, you could be being watched yourself.'

'I understand,' replied Carlton. 'We'll do it your way. Once I have it in my hands, I'll pay your abort fee.'

'Good.'

'Goodnight, and I wish you a pleasant retirement.'

Ash ended the call and sighed with frustration. The main fee was money he'd been relying on. He'd set aside most of the money he needed to buy a lovely old mansion outside Salcombe in Devon with over a hundred acres of farmland. This job would have cinched it. The $500K abort fee was a joke, chump change.

*Shit.* Maybe he wouldn't be able to retire from the business just yet. Perhaps he'd have to take one more job. That, or rethink his retirement plans.

*Focus on that later.*

For now, he had some rough corners to sand down and make good for the client. More importantly, he needed to think carefully how he was going to stage his exit. How was he going to convince the FBI that they had the dead body of Number 7 on their Most Wanted list?

## 63

Special Agent Ryan exhaled a cloud of breath into the cool morning air as he swung left to jog through the Japanese Gardens – so called because there was a solitary thicket of bamboo canes among the gladioli and rose beds of Munsen Park. It was 6.30 a.m. on Friday morning and the only other people he usually encountered at this time were other fitness addicts getting in their five miles before a day at work.

Ryan didn't have a partner or kids, family or friends. He'd scored highly on the Weiler/Reynolds OCD chart, and incredibly poorly on empathy. It made him a somewhat selfish human being, with an unhealthy fixation on a singular goal.

Diverr member KFH_50BTFOA_FI/10.

Aka Ash.

Aka Jason Turner.

For the last twenty-four hours he'd been forensically picking through the man's social media history, his employment details and his past. Ryan had read up on Jason Turner's family, his friends and even his medical records. Either

Ryan had been trawling through the most meticulously assembled false identity he'd ever encountered, or he was looking at a real person.

Right now, he was leaning towards the latter. Jason Turner had established a very credible alternate life. He'd been a nightclub bouncer, a furniture restorer, and more recently employed by a private investigation firm based in his home town of Hastings, England.

Jason Turner was in a relationship with a British police officer called Samantha Okeke and his name was on an MI5 case file. They were obviously looking at him too. The clever sonofabitch was burning up his real identity for this job. Which meant only one thing. He was checking out of the business, leaving his old identity behind and migrating to another.

That was smart. Fucking smart. So many pros in this game were either addicted to the big pay cheques or addicted to the kill. And that figured, as so many of them were ex-military, damaged irreparably by PTSD, trained to do only one thing.

But Turner wasn't a *broken* army vet. He was clearly a pro.

And the slippery bastard was playing a very, very smart game. Ryan turned out of the park and onto the beachfront walkway. The first of the early-bird open-air gym users were already out flexing their shaved, waxed torsos, muscles popping like walnuts.

Wakefield was due to arrive at the Fort Pierce station at 10 a.m. this morning. Ryan could have arranged for the interview to continue in his FBI field office, but the longer this looked like a simple homicide department case, the less suspicious Wakefield's collaborators would be.

Wakefield had said that he had a lot of compromising

material to offer, but would only share it if he had a cast-iron immunity deal.

And guaranteed protection.

Immunity. That would depend on the usefulness of Wakefield's intel. Protection, though? That was going to be difficult. Ryan would need to check with Gaetz about what incentives and protective measures might be available to convince Wakefield to cooperate and start spilling what he knew.

## 64

The Greyhound coach disgorged its tired passengers onto the busy sidewalk. Jay and the others stepped out into the bustle of New York. He looked around the drop-off. It was a busy intersection with the entrances to Madison Square Garden and Pennsylvania Station diagonally opposite, and a huge, impressive white building on the other side of the road. Jay's attention was also caught by the appetising-looking Mexican restaurant and Starbucks on the final corner of the intersection.

Considering it was Jay's first time in the Big Apple, it was a pity he couldn't just be a regular tourist, with a 'Things to Do and Places to See' map in his hands. Shaking that fantasy out of his head, he switched on his new burner phone. Paranoia had got the better of him and he'd turned it off immediately after texting Sam his new number. It buzzed to life. There were a couple of messages from her.

Okay. Thanks. Logged. Xxx

Then at 4 a.m.:

Just spoke to Ronni. She'll meet you at the stop. Told her

she could be being watched too. Said she'd be super careful. Also no more using Sylvie's phone! xxx

And then one only five minutes ago.

You there yet? Is Ronni there? X

Sylvie tapped his arm and held out her phone. She'd just turned hers on too. 'I have a message from your lady.'

Jay took it.

Karl's booked you a box at Times Square PO. Number is P-239. Passport will be there Monday afternoon. You set up new fucking phone yet????

He smiled at her multiple question marks. Sam and her long-distance nagging. He was about to reply to her when his phone buzzed.

'Hello?'

'It's Ronni.'

'Where are you?' he asked, looking around.

'Watching you,' she replied dryly. 'To be clear, I'm not about to come running over arms spread for a hug until I know for sure that *you're* not being watched.'

'I don't think I am,' Jay said.

'*I don't think so* doesn't cut it. Take a stroll up 8th Avenue, past Madison Square Garden and Penn Station. Go to the halal shop and turn into the side street for me, would you?' Ronni asked.

He nodded and turned to Sylvie and Jorge. 'Follow me.'

They walked along the street, past the halal wholesalers, and turned right into the next side street.

'Okay?' Jay said to Ronni on the phone. 'What next?'

'Stay put.' He could hear Ronni breathing heavily, then finally she replied, 'All right, I can't see anyone acting funny. Come back to the Starbucks. That's where I am.'

'I presume Sam told you I've got two civilians with me,' said Jay as he made his way to the Starbucks.

Ronni laughed at his use of 'civilians'. 'Yeah, you don't like to make it easy for yourself, do you? See you in a sec.'

With that, she ended the call. Jay glanced at Sylvie and her son. Jorge's eyes widened as he gazed up at a giant billboard that featured Ryan Gosling posing in a grubby vest and sunglasses for *The Fall Guy*. Which felt strangely ironic.

They stepped into the Starbucks and Jay immediately spotted Ronni. She'd staked out a table by spreading her coat and a bag across it and was warding off any potential seat-stealers with a challenging glare.

Jay led Sylvie and Jorge over to her, and she got up.

'Now I can hug you,' she said, wrapping her arms around him and planting a kiss on his cheek. She looked at the other two. 'Now who the fuck have we got here?'

∾

ASH WAS RATHER impressed with Turner doing his little surveillance check. Clearly he'd had some training, then. Turner returned with the woman and child and ushered them into Starbucks. Inside, Turner embraced a short, slim woman with dark hair cut short.

Her face matched the photo on her website and her LinkedIn page. It was Veronica 'Ronni' Kirk.

They sat down together at a table while Ronni went to the counter.

Ash's van was parked in the halal wholesaler's delivery zone. He hadn't been hassled yet to move along, but he had his FBI badge on the dash and was ready to flourish if needed.

*Meet and greet done. Coffees and pastries all round. Then what's the plan for today, folks?*

~

'So you need a place until Monday?' Ronni asked.

Jay nodded, wiping the pastry flakes from his lips. 'FedEx are dropping my passport off in the afternoon and then I'm catching the first UK flight I can from whichever airport's closer. JFK or LaGuardia?'

'LaGuardia,' Ronni replied.

Jay nodded. 'Then I'm heading home and back to the Land of Normal.'

Ronni's eyes darted to Sylvie, then back to him. The unasked question was blindingly obvious. *What are we doing with them?*

Jay sidestepped that for the moment. 'Sam said going back to yours might not be such a smart idea.'

'And she'd be damn right, given the situation,' replied Ronni. 'I've got an Airbnb place over in Williamsburg, just by the bridge. It's usually busy, but we're in luck: the folks who are in it vacate today.' She checked her watch. 'They've left and my cleaner should be arriving about now. Which means we've gotta hang out here till four thirty. Then we're good to crash there until Monday morning.'

'Thanks,' Jay said.

Ronni smiled. 'Yeah, well... I kinda owe you after getting you into this mess.'

Jay shrugged. 'We both got me into this. I should have realised it was too good to be true.'

'And I could've done some more due diligence on the guy.' Ronni sighed. 'But all I saw was an easy job and a fat pay cheque.' She looked at Jay. 'A teachable moment for the both of us, eh?'

## 65

Boyd knocked on the door of 37 Markham Avenue at nine o'clock sharp, as promised.

His phone had pinged a couple of times with texts from Okeke. No doubt an update on the current state of Jay's ongoing troubles. She was going to have to wait, though. His priority was getting Dan some professional help. This morning hopefully, if not by the end of the day.

Emma, after a lot of tears and shouting, had come to that same realisation too. She'd wanted to come with him, but Boyd had promised Dan he wouldn't tell Emma the worst of it and now wasn't the time to betray his trust.

The door opened and he was greeted by a young woman with a fractious and grizzling baby cradled in one arm.

'Yeah?' she said.

'Is Dan in?' Boyd asked.

'Who?'

'Daniel Elwood,' he clarified.

The young woman frowned. 'Sorry, love, I think you've got the wrong house.'

'Mrs Elwood lives here, though?' he said, confused.

She shook her head. 'Sorry. No Elwood here. Like I said, you got the wrong house.'

With that, she closed the door.

'Shit.' *What the hell you playing at, Danny Boy?*'

Boyd recalled catching Dan in his rear-view mirror. On the pavement. Just standing there like an abandoned bloody puppy.

'Oh, fuck.'

He called Emma. 'He's not here,' he said.

'What do you mean, he's not there?' she asked.

'I mean the address I dropped him off at *isn't* his mum's address.'

'It's in Ore, right?' Emma said.

'Markham Avenue, Ore,' Boyd replied. 'But there's no Dan and no mum here either.'

'Well, I haven't been to his mum's,' Emma said. 'I've actually not met her yet...'

'You've never met her?' repeated Boyd.

'He said they didn't really get on. So, no.'

'Does he even have a mum?' he asked.

Emma sucked in a breath. 'Oh God, did we just throw him out onto the street?'

'I think he's been feeding us bullshit, Ems,' Boyd replied. He was beginning to wonder if anything Dan had told them since Emma had first introduced them two years ago had any truth to it.

'And you haven't heard from him?' he asked.

'No. He's not replied to any of my texts,' she said.

'What about his bandmates. Have you got any of *their* phone numbers?'

'I might. I got a text off one of them – Rory, I think his name is – last year.'

'Can you find it, Ems? I need to talk to him.'

'Yeah. Yeah, I'll dig it out. I'll text it to you.'

He hung up. He needed to get to work. He was already late and there was only so much Sutherland/Hatcher good-will he could exploit. As he climbed back into his Captur, Boyd felt like the meanest, most cold-hearted, bloody bastard in the world.

He'd turfed a vulnerable, deeply troubled young lad onto the street.

## 66

Special Agent Ryan stared at the body of Malcolm Wakefield. Detective Angela Durrant and the forensics technician were crouched over it, inspecting the corpse.

'It's clearly *not* a suicide,' she replied.

Wakefield was slouched in an expensive leather armchair, a single bullet wound just above his left eye. His head was tilted backwards, mouth wide open and containing a small pool of congealing dark liquid.

'That's a mixture of blood and whiskey,' said the forensics tech.

'You're sure it isn't suicide?' asked Ryan, ignoring the technician.

Durrant nodded. 'There are no muzzle burns to the skin. You turn a gun on your face, even just a handgun and you'll need about a yard clearance to avoid burns and residue.' She looked again at Wakefield's face, eyes open, wide and now milking over. 'This was staged as a suicide. And not particularly well.' She looked up at him. 'I'm presuming this is the direct result of your off-the-record interview with him yesterday?'

Ryan had been certain that he'd done enough to maintain the appearance of a straightforward homicide case for his Mulligan Club investigation. He'd considered arranging overnight protection for Wakefield, but had decided it might spook the man into clamming up, and also that it would likely draw attention from Wakefield's associates.

Now the man was dead.

'Steve?' Detective Durrant tapped the tech's arm. 'Give me a time of death, roughly.'

The technician pulled his mask down. 'Late last night. Midnight is my guess. I'd say he's been dead at least twelve hours.'

Ryan gazed at Wakefield's cloudy eyes. *They must have been watching him yesterday.* If so, then it meant that they knew the Bureau was on to them. And, if that was the case, the members of the Mulligan Club were probably already burning, shredding, deleting all evidence that they'd been up to anything. Deleting evidence that they'd ever even met each other, other than at some C-PAC fundraising event.

With Wakefield dead, Ryan had just lost any chance of taking the really big scalps. Whatever that bunch of fuckers had been conspiring to do was vapour now, for sure. Even if Kerry had managed to record anything damning on her phone over the weekend, it had probably been erased by now.

She was dead. Wakefield was dead, and when he wrote this up for Gaetz and Coleman, all he'd be able to say was that some suspicious influential men had been planning something bad. Not the kind of report that would do him any favours.

The only positive addendum he could add was that he now, almost certainly, had the true identity of Ash. But if Number 7 on the FBI's hit list was about to go dark and retire for good, it was, to paraphrase Alanis Morissette, *a death row pardon, two minutes too late.*

## 67

R onni tapped in the PIN code for the door of her apartment.

'There are two bedrooms. Sylvie and Jorge, you guys can have one.' She looked at Jay, one brow ever so slightly raised.

'I'm happy with the couch,' he replied.

She laughed and led them inside. Sylvie and Jorge gasped at the luxurious furniture and the shiny, chrome kitchenette, then hurried over to the floor-to-ceiling window and marvelled at the view. Ronni's flat was on the third floor of a new building amid traditional brownstones with a clear view of the East River and the Williamsburg bridge in the distance, and the Jenga-block skyline of Lower Manhattan.

'Nice,' agreed Jay.

'I used to live here when I worked on Wall Street,' said Ronni.

Jay looked at her, impressed. 'Like stocks 'n' shares?'

She smiled. 'Yeah, Turner, like stocks ' n' shares.'

He joined Jorge and his mum at the window.

'Bloody hell, 'Jay muttered. 'I'd love a place like this.' He turned to Ronni. 'What made you give up *this* for PI work?'

'Well, it wasn't the money,' she said.

'What was it, then?' he asked.

'It's a long story,' she replied. 'You folks wanna grab some food?' She looked down at Jorge. 'How about a milk-shake, young man?'

Jorge's head bobbed up and down. 'Yes please, Miss –'

'Call me Ronni, sweetheart,' she said with a smile. 'I know a great place around the corner.'

～

THE GREAT PLACE was a Chinese buffet restaurant with a retro games arcade at the far end. Jay spotted foosball, air hockey and Space Invaders. He and Ronni watched as Sylvie and Jorge took their time examining the hotplates and working out which dishes to try.

'I thought Wakefield was just another rich idiot with heaps of small dick energy,' said Ronni. 'Loads of money and a deep insecurity complex over his glamorous young wife.' She gave him a guilty look. 'Your Sam has been doing the due diligence I should've done. Seems that Wakefield's been trying hard to establish himself over here. Trying to surround himself with a bunch of useful friends. Influential friends'

'He's already rich,' muttered Jay. 'What's the point?'

'There's a lot of wriggling around in the States right now,' Ronni commented. 'The markets are all over the place, trying to figure out whether there's going to be a Trump 2.0 come November. And if so, what the hell's that going to look like? Every congressmen, businessman, sena-tor, governor, every CEO is wondering who they want as friends and who they can afford to make as enemies.' Ronni chuckled. 'Sam's right – you picked a bad time to get involved in America.'

He looked at her. 'How long did you two talk for?'

'Dunno. A while.' She smiled. 'I think we bonded.'

'God help me.'

'She said someone called Karl...'

'My brother – *half*-brother, actually.'

'He's been doing some more digging. Found details about some super-secret private club – and they seem to be getting up to some bad things,' said Ronni. 'Any idea what?'

Jay shook his head. 'Nope. Something shady obviously.'

'She said there was a governor involved, some tech bro, some judges...?'

'Honestly, Ronni, I've got no fucking idea what they're up to. But Kerry? She was spying on them for someone – I'm sure of it.'

'Who's the someone?'

'I dunno. I'm now thinking maybe the FBI? That Ryan guy could have been an agent. Mack said he had loads of meetings that weekend she was murdered. So, it could have been that private club, right? Maybe she overheard something she shouldn't have?'

'Kerry's phone. You think there might be stuff on it that they're worried about?' Ronni asked.

Jay nodded. 'Wakefield got really shitty with me when I told him I'd recovered it.'

Ronni pulled a face. 'Uh, probably *shouldn't* have told him that, then?'

Jay nodded. 'Yeah, I realise *now* that wasn't the smartest thing. I was trying to be, you know, *professional* about things at the time,' he replied. 'I didn't know he and his cronies were going to send someone over to whack me for it!'

Ronni shook her head. 'Christ. You're too straight for this job.'

'I prefer the word *professional*,' Jay said, a little stung. 'Anyway, I had my own reason for wanting to hang on to it, remember? My face on her phone.'

Ronni shook her head and tutted. 'Getting caught out like that? Rookie error, Turner, rookie error.'

'Yeah, well,' he grumbled, 'I'm still learning. Anyway, the last thing I need is for that to fall into police hands while they're investigating her murder, right?'

'So you've got this phone on you?' Ronni asked.

He patted his hip pocket. 'I'm not letting it out of my sight from now on.'

'Okay,' she replied, 'so *that's* why they want you so bad.'

He sighed. 'I mean, would this be a whole lot easier for everyone if I just, I dunno, invited Wakefield and his guys to some ceremonial throwing-of-the-phone into the sea?'

Ronni laughed. 'Right and you'll all share a toast, some cucumber sandwiches and head your own ways?'

'Come on. Don't take the piss,' he grumbled.

She patted his hand. 'Your naivety is so damned sweet.'

Sylvie and Jorge were on the far side of the buffet counter, nearly done and ready to return to their table.

'What're we doing with them?' Ronni asked.

'I don't know.' He sighed. 'Sylvie saved my life.' He explained how she'd whacked the hitman over the head from behind with a beer bottle. Ronni nodded approvingly. 'They couldn't stay there... and I can't just abandon them now. I *won't*.'

'Relax. I can put out some feelers,' she replied. 'I've got a friend who runs a support group for illegals. Was Jorge born in the States?'

'I don't know. I don't think so,' Jay said. 'Maybe.'

'If there's no record, then that could be fudged. If we can do that, then there *is* a way to legalise them.'

Jay looked at Ronni earnestly. 'If I'm shooting off on Monday, can I trust you to...?'

'Take care of them?' she asked.

He nodded.

'Sure. I got this.'

## 68

Ash followed them back to Kirk's apartment on foot. At one point he'd carelessly allowed himself to drift close enough that he was only a dozen yards behind. If Turner had chosen that exact moment to turn round and check to see if they were being followed, he would surely have spotted and recognised Ash.

But he didn't. Turner was distracted with the boy, holding his hand like some big dumb uncle, and chatting animatedly to the kid. They paused outside the glass doors to the lobby as Kirk fumbled for a pass to unlock. They went inside and he lost sight of them as they stepped into the lift.

Ash withdrew across the street to a board-games store with a café. The sign on the door said it stayed open till nine on Fridays, which meant it would probably be flooded later with sweaty nerds rolling twenty-sided dice and chugging Red Bulls and root beer.

Fine by him. Busy was good.

He went inside, and found that the café was on the first floor. He picked a table with a clear view of the apartment block opposite. A light on the third floor winked on and Ash caught a glimpse of Turner pulling the blinds across the window.

Ash almost felt sorry for the man. In a world full of ruthless, conspiring, self-serving wankers, he seemed like a decent enough chap.

Pity.

## 69

Ronni took out a cigarette and offered the pack to Jay as they stepped out of the lobby, onto the street.

He hesitated. 'I've been trying to switch to vape,' he said.

'I've tried many times,' she replied. 'Doesn't stick with me.'

Jay relented and took one, and she lit them both. For a couple of minutes, they silently watched the games store opposite empty out and the lights go off in the café above.

'How much longer?' asked Jay. He was getting hungry for his pizza.

She checked her watch. 'Luciano's are pretty prompt. It'll be any time now.' She pulled on her cigarette. 'So tell me about you and Sam...'

'We've been together nearly five years now,' he said.

'She sounds pretty hard-ass,' Ronni said. 'I like her.'

They watched a group of young men emerge from the games store carrying bags of rubbish. One of them stopped to lock the doors.

'When I reached out to you for this job, it sounded like the two of you were having some problems,' Ronni pressed.

Jay huffed. 'I think it was just me really. There's been some pretty heavy stuff that's happened over the last two or three years. I'm not going to go into it, but it made me re-evaluate everything in my life. Made me rethink a lot of things.'

He patted the money belt around his waist, under his sweatshirt. 'The money Mack was offering, it was too fucking good to walk away from.' He glanced at Ronni. 'What was your commission, out of interest?'

'Twenty K. Just to set up the hello.'

'Jesus.'

She smiled. 'Not bad for a couple of phone calls.'

A Deliveroo cyclist wearing a face mask, with a thermal bag strapped to his back, pulled up at the door.

'Chinese for apartment 4A?' he asked.

'Not us,' replied Ronni.

She and Jay moved away from the front doors so that they could continue to talk in private.

'Anyway, Mack only paid me half that intro fee,' she continued. 'He said he'd pay the rest when you were done.'

'You gonna chase him up for it?' Jay asked.

'Hilarious. I'm staying the fuck away from him. As far as I'm concerned, this job never happened. I never hooked you two up. I know nothing.' She nodded at something across the street. 'Ah, here we go.'

A young man hurried across the road, carrying a stack of pizza boxes. 'Ronni?' he said.

'That's us,' she replied, and handed over several twenties. 'Keep the change.' She turned to Jay. 'Here. Make yourself useful. You can carry them.'

They stubbed out their cigarettes, then Jay took the

boxes and they returned to the front doors. It was being held open by the guy from 4A as he checked through the plastic bags. 'Where's the duck? I don't see any.'

'Not my problem, bro,' replied the Deliveroo guy. 'I just pick up and deliver.'

Jay and Ronni stepped into the lobby and left the two men to work it out.

'Let's eat,' said Ronni. 'I'm starving too.'

～

ASH STRODE past the two men arguing in the doorway, his eyes firmly on Turner and Kirk. He was just a few feet away from them now. If Turner turned round, the disguise of a beanie and shades probably wasn't going to cut it. Ash would have to act fast.

For a moment it looked as though they were going to linger in the lobby and wait for the lift. He busied himself beside the post boxes, making a show of fumbling for some keys, but then he heard footsteps. In the reflection of the glass doors, he saw that they'd given up waiting and taken the stairs.

*Good.* He waited a moment longer, continuing to check his pockets. Behind him, the dispute over an order of crispy duck seemed to have resolved itself and the Deliveroo guy had left.

Ash quickly pulled a flyer from the shelf next to the post boxes and slapped one of the post boxes as though he'd just slammed it shut.

The guy with the Chinese delivery walked past him, chuckling. 'What an idiot.'

Ash looked his way. 'You got shafted?'

'No, I just found the duck at the bottom of the bag,' the man confessed. '*I'm* the dumbass.'

Ash smiled. 'Ouch. Hate that...'

'I know. I'll have to double-tip him next time.' The young man hit the button for the lift. 'You want up?'

Ash shook his head. 'Nah, I'm good with the stairs, man.'

## 70

'Mr Boyd?'

Boyd checked the time on his bedside clock. It was 2 a.m. Who the fuck was calling at this ridiculous time?

'Yeah. Who's this?' he grunted.

'It's Rory Taylor. You, uh, you left a message on my phone about Dan?' He sounded like Dan, polite, hesitant and a little vacant. 'Sorry... it's late, isn't it?'

'It's early actually,' sighed Boyd.

'Sorry. I just got back in from a party and I read your message.'

Boyd sat up in bed. He checked Charlotte; she was still fast asleep.

'Just give me a moment, Rory.' He got up, slid his feet into his slippers and headed downstairs to the lounge.

'You still there, Rory?' he said.

'Yeah, man. This about Dan?'

'Yup,' Boyd replied. 'I'm concerned about him. About his state of mind.'

'Yeah. We all are. I've been trying to get in touch with him ever since we got back.'

'I spoke to your manager, Nikki,' Boyd said.

'Yeah, she mentioned.'

'She told me that you and the other lads were getting uncomfortable around him.'

'Yeah. I mean, before we left to go on tour, his behaviour was becoming increasingly weird. And none of us felt right about spending four months with him.' He paused. 'Honestly, I felt Dan was, like, a bomb waiting to explode.'

'Jesus. Was he that bad?' Boyd asked.

'Uh-huh. I mean, I'm the closest to him. I've known him the longest and he was all right pretty much until the end of last summer.'

'Did anything significant happen then?' said Boyd.

'Nothing I can think of... but, you know, that's kind of when our bookings and downloads were started to ramp up. I thought maybe it was, like, the pressure of things that might have started him off.'

'I wonder if it's more deep-seated than that,' said Boyd.

'You're Emma's dad, right?'

'Yeah.'

'He's just had a kid with her, hasn't he?'

'A daughter. She's twenty weeks old.'

'Well, he was stressing about that *a lot* last year. He was terrified about becoming a dad. I thought maybe it was that and the band that pushed him over the edge.'

Boyd shook his head. 'I'm not sure what he's going through is caused by stress alone. I'm really worried about him, Rory. We had a chat on Friday night. And *some* of what's going on in his head came out. I told him he had to stay with his mum until we got him some help –'

'His mum?' Rory cut in. 'I'm pretty sure he doesn't have one.'

Boyd sighed. 'I know that now. He got me to drop him off outside some random house.'

'Ah, shit.'

'Yeah, I'm guessing he slept rough last night and is doing it again tonight. I need to find him. That's why I got in touch. I just wondered if you knew of any other family he might have. Any mates he has that he could be couch-surfing with.'

Rory sucked in a breath. 'No. I mean, none really. Maybe some old mates from school or something, but for the last three years it's only been me and the others in the band who've been hanging out with him.'

'Right.'

'Did Nikki mention the voices?' Rory asked. 'Fuck, man, that's what spooked me the most – sorry about the language. That's what kind of decided things for us. I mean, we all knew he was struggling. He has running conversations, like, arguments, in his head, but...'

'But?'

'I overheard him one time, when he thought he was alone...'

Something about the way he paused left Boyd feeling a chill. 'And?'

'I heard him mumbling and whispering. But then there was this angry outburst. I mean, not super loud, but it was clear. Like he was giving some shit to someone in the room with him.'

'What did he say, Rory?' Boyd asked.

*'I don't want to kill anyone.'*

## 71

Ronni cut the huge pizzas into smaller slices, while Jay dealt out plates, then uncapped some beers and popped a can of Coke for Jorge.

Jay looked at his beer and realised he needed the loo.

'I'm just going to use the...' He thumbed in the direction of the bathroom.

Sylvie raised her beer bottle. 'I want to thank you, Ronni, for all the kindness you have shown Jorge and me.'

'No problem,' Ronni said. 'Listen, Sylvie, I know some good people in Brooklyn who can help you two out. There's actually a sort of legal route out of your current situation if Jorge was born in the US...'

Jay left them talking about immigration law. He went into the bathroom, snapped on the light and closed the door behind him. The room was windowless and an extraction fan began to hum loudly. He unbuckled his jeans and sat down with a long sigh of relief, glad that the noise of the fan was going to spare his blushes.

The chaos and the unrelenting stress of the last forty-eight hours had played havoc with his guts. He'd been nursing a persistent ache that he was pretty sure was the start of a stomach ulcer or something.

He could still hear Ronni's voice faintly over the hum of the fan. It sounded as though she was giving poor Sylvie chapter and verse. Apparently, there was a lot more to Ronni Kirk than a hard-faced PI with a mouth on her. So she'd worked on Wall Street, eh? He'd have to ask her about that. Had she been a trader? Some arse-kicking Gordon Gekko type?

*She's a good one to have your back*, he told himself. He felt pretty certain she'd be a useful lifeline if Mack's gang of creepy cronies decided to reach across the Atlantic to find him. Having that damned phone on him was like carrying a nugget of radioactive waste. But it might turn out to be the one bargaining chip he could use to keep them at bay. The first thing he needed to do when he got back home was to get Karl to hack it. His brother had a circle of tech contacts – surely one of them was bound to know how to extract its data? And then there'd be options, right? If there was incriminating shit on it, he could do the responsible thing and hand it over to the Feds... after making sure he'd deleted his face from Kerry's photo roll.

Or he could do the smart-as-fuck thing and blackmail Mack's club. They had money, or Mack certainly did. Maybe giving over what he had to the FBI would be a dumb move. If the Mack's friends were *that* worried about what was on Kerry's phone and found him but he *didn't* have that bargaining chip any more...

*Fuck it. Fuck them.* Even if there was bugger all on there that could be used, they didn't know that. What he had in his pocket was kryptonite for them. When he got back to Hastings, Jay resolved that he was going to call Mack, tell him he'd hacked it and listened to *everything*. And that it made for some very interesting listening.

Then, perhaps, they could agree a price.

He finished his business, sorted himself out and flushed the chain. He opened the door and switched off the light. The extractor fan ceased its humming and he realised the apartment was strangely silent. He couldn't see the dining table, because the kitchenette wall was in the way. He stepped out of the bathroom, rounded the wall and stopped dead in his tracks.

'And there you are.' Ash smiled. 'It's nice to see you again, Jay.' The man had a gun trained on the others, who were all seated at the dining table. 'Well, we can make this a quick meeting, and you can get back to your pizzas. Where's the phone?'

*Right here in my pocket.* Jay could only hope it wasn't producing an obvious outline.

'Not here,' Jay replied. 'I stashed it somewhere.'

Ash smiled. 'I know you're lying. I've been watching you very closely since Orlando. I know you have it here, so let's cut the crap. Hand it over and I'll let myself out.'

'Jay,' said Ronni. 'It's not worth it. We should just tell him who we gave it to.'

Ash's eyes flicked to her briefly. 'Nice try. Now, Jay, I know you've got it. My patience has pretty much run out. Hand it over.'

'It's not here, mate,' said Jay obstinately. 'Do you honestly think I'm that stupid?'

Ash sighed wearily. Without warning, he fired a single muffled shot. Jay expected to hear something shatter over in the kitchenette. But then Sylvie started to gurgle, a tiny, perfectly round hole in her forehead, just above her eyebrows. A trickle of dark blood weaved its way down the side of her nose. Her eyes rolled left to look at Jorge, before her head slumped forward onto the table.

And Jorge screamed.

Ronni, closest of them all, leapt out of her seat and lunged for the gun. She managed to wrap one fist around the end of the silencer and swung her other fist at Ash's face. A glint of light in the sudden movement caught Jay's eye and he realised Ronni had managed to palm the pizza knife.

Ash raised his other hand at the last moment and the knife sank into it, the blade poking out the other side. The two of them were fleetingly frozen in a bizarre pose, her hands raised, matched with his as if they were about to tango, their faces almost close enough to kiss.

Then Ash headbutted Ronni and she dropped to the floor, unconscious. He straightened his arm, angled his aim downwards and put a bullet in her head. Then he swung his aim to Jorge, who was now crying and desperately shaking Sylvie by the shoulders.

'For fuck's sake, Turner!' Ash snapped. 'This is where your kind of stupid get us! I'll ask one more time, and – so we are clear – the next one's for the boy.'

'Okay, okay!' Jay pulled out Kerry's phone from his pocket and held it out. 'Here! Here it is!'

'On the table,' Ash commanded. 'Slowly!' He grimaced. The knife was still rammed through his left palm.

Jay nodded and raised his hands to show he had nothing stupid left in him. He stepped forward and set the phone on the table, pausing to glance at Ronni. She was dead. There was no doubt about it.

'You! Kid, shut up!' barked Ash.

Jorge's screaming had given way to sobbing. He was mumbling, 'Mama,' over and over, still shaking Sylvie gently in the desperate hope she'd stir.

'You bastard,' whispered Jay. 'You didn't need to fucking kill them!'

'Clearly I did,' replied Ash, looking Jay in the eye. 'You didn't need to lie. Now see what's happened.' His gaze flicked to Jorge. 'Boy, come here. I need you.'

'If you touch him!' Jay hissed.

'Relax, what kind of monster do you think I am? I just want this fucking knife out of my hand.' He glanced at Jorge again. 'Boy, come here.'

'Are you going to let us go after he's done that?' asked Jay. He nodded at the phone. 'You've got what you came for.'

Ash grunted and gave a nod of assent. Jorge looked from his mother to Jay.

Jay nodded. 'It's okay, Jorge. It's okay. He's going to let us go,' he said gently. 'The man needs you to pull the knife out. Then he's going.'

'Yes,' said Ash. 'Then Mr Turner here can call an ambulance for your mum and your friend here, okay?'

Jorge let go of Sylvie and slowly rounded the table.

'Grab those napkins,' said Ash.

Jorge clutched a fistful, then approached Ash.

'Now listen... *Jorge*, is it?' said Ash, and the boy nodded. 'You hold the knife's handle tight and I'm going to pull my hand free, then you're going to wrap those napkins round my hand really quickly. Got it?'

The boy nodded once more.

Ash's gaze flicked to Jay. 'And you, sit on the floor with your hands on your head.'

Jay complied. 'Just so you know. I've got no idea what's on the phone. You can see how fucked up it is.'

'Yeah, yeah.' Ash's priority right now was his bleeding left hand. 'Jorge, just hold the handle steady.'

The boy wrapped both hands around the handle. Ash

took a deep breath, then slowly eased his hand up the blade, wincing as he did so. The tip emerged, and blood began to flow from his palm.

'Napkins,' said Ash. 'Quickly!'

Jorge remained where he stood, holding the blade, frozen.

'The napkins!' Ash shouted.

Jay glimpsed a snapshot of the future: seconds from now Jorge would be dead on the floor. Terrified though he was, the boy was going to do something foolish – Jay was sure of it.

'Do as he says!' barked Jay. 'He's bleeding out!'

Jorge twitched at the sound of Jay's voice. The boy turned to him and Jay saw the look of rage in his red-rimmed eyes.

*Oh, shit. He's going to-*

Jorge turned back to Ash, and with a speed and strength that surprised them both he plunged the knife into the man's thigh.

'You little shit!'

Ash aimed the gun at Jorge, as Jay got to his feet and lunged. The gun pumped a muted shot a heartbeat before Jay could grasp the hot barrel. His weight and momentum were enough to knock Ash to the floor, with Jay landing heavily on top of him.

It was all about the gun now and who could wrestle control of the fucker.

Jay had one hand on the burning hot metal of the silencer and was trying to savagely twist it to break Ash's trigger finger. With his other hand, he fumbled down the man's side, trying to find the protruding knife handle.

The kid was dead. It was just Jay now, and it really didn't

matter how much jujitsu training or experience this bastard had, Jay had two good hands and he had only had one.

Ash swung his left elbow into the side of Jay's face, cracking something. A cheekbone? His nose? Then he doubled down, letting go of the gun, and punching Jay in the face with his good hand.

The two blows, a second apart, were enough to knock Jay senseless. Ash rolled them both over so that now he was sitting astride Jay, but the gun flew out of Jay's limp grasp across the room somewhere.

Ash reached down to his thigh, pulled the blade out and held it to Jay's throat.

'Christ, you're a such a fucking lightweight,' he snarled.

Once again this *amateur* had managed to get the better of him – almost.

'Please... pleashe... don't...' Jay rasped. Blood gushed from his nose, flowing into his mouth and down his throat, making his words gargle. 'I... won't shay... anything...'

'Have some fucking balls, Turner,' hissed Ash. He pressed the tip of the blade into Jay's Adam's apple. 'The kid had bigger balls than you...'

The kid, though, wasn't dead.

He rose into Jay's peripheral vision with a beer bottle raised in one hand. He swung it down hard on the back of Ash's head, targeting the bloody scab of the wound that had been dealt by his mother.

Jay shoved the stunned hitman off him and scrambled to his feet.

'Where's the gun? Where's the bloody gun?' he yelled.

Jorge looked down at the floor.

'Where's the fucking gun?' Jay glanced in all directions. Where had it gone?

Ash was groaning and shaking his head, recovering far too quickly.

*Jesus.* Jay wondered what the hell his head was made of. Then he noticed the hitman getting to his knees, the knife still in his good hand.

Jay grabbed Jorge's arm. '*Run!*'

## 72

They emerged onto the street, hurried across it and ducked into a twenty-four-hour convenience store.

Jay led Jorge to the back. He squatted down beside the boy, making it look like they were checking out something on the bottom shelf together, their backs to the entrance. He tried to think of the best thing to say to reassure Jorge, but then he realised that the boy hadn't made a sound. As Jay looked into his eyes, he found that Jorge appeared to be the calmer of the two of them.

Jay hurriedly checked him over. He could see no gun wound.

'You didn't get shot?' he asked.

Jorge nodded. 'I ducked.'

Jay embraced him. The boy had saved his life. Ironically, in exactly the same way his mother had.

Jay released the boy and said, 'Listen, we're in big, big danger, Jorge.'

'I know,' Jorge replied, adding. 'You've got blood on your face.'

Jay swiped at the sticky gunk under his nose. The blood had stopped flowing, thankfully. 'We've got to get away from here...'

'I know,' Jorge said again.

'We can't go back to see if your mum's okay,' Jay said.

Jorge acknowledged his words with a stony, red-eyed face. In that moment he looked a good ten years older. He *knew*.

'That man wants to hurt us both,' continued Jay. 'So this is going to be like a game of hide-and-seek, okay?'

Jorge raised a brow. 'I'm seven. Not a baby.'

Jay smiled. 'Sorry, mate. But look... we have to move quickly.'

Jorge nodded.

'We need to find somewhere to hide,' said Jay, 'then I can figure out what we do with...' He fumbled in his pocket. *Fuck! Kerry's phone!* He'd left the damned thing on the table. 'Shit, shit, shit.'

'S'okay, Mr Jay,' replied Jorge. He dug into the pocket of his shorts and pulled it out. 'I picked it up for you.'

Jay took it and shoved the warped device deep into his pocket. It was the only bargaining chip they had. He squeezed the boy's shoulder 'Jorge, thank fuck for you.'

Jorge raised disapproving eyebrows at him.

'You're right,' Jay said. 'No more swears.'

❧

ASH FOUND THE GUN. It had skittered across the floor and was lurking beneath the dining table. His head was throbbing. For the second time in the space of forty-eight hours he'd been knocked senseless. He was going to have a brain bleed, for sure. The scab on the back of his head had been ruptured and blood was tricking down his neck. Again.

'Shit!' he wheezed. Taken out *again*, and this time by some grubby Mexican rugrat, for God's sake.

He sat down at the dining table and wrapped some more napkins tightly round his hand. Incredibly, no arteries had been severed. There was blood everywhere. From the women, from his hand, from Turner's broken nose. There was no point even starting to clean the place up; he could be scrubbing for days and still there'd be forensics left everywhere.

He looked on the table for Kerry Wakefield's phone.

It was gone.

'*Fuck!*' he snapped. *That bastard amateur fucker!*

He needed to gather his wits. There was no point charging outside to try to find Turner and the boy; his bloody hand and head would attract attention. Someone would call a cop.

Turner could wait. What he needed to do was run a quick risk assessment here. This apartment was going to be covered in cops at some point, and he had an opportunity to influence the narrative. The apartment block's CCTV would clearly show Turner entering the building with two women, who were now dead, and a boy. And of course leaving in a hurry. With the boy.

How long did he have before the cops turned up? Had any of the neighbours heard anything?

*Think. Think.*

The cops and their forensics bunny men would be swarming this apartment by tomorrow. They'd collect Turner's DNA from the blood on the floor and Ash's DNA from the knife wounds. Conclusion: two dead women, two others

ALEX SCARROW

and a child were here. They'd be scouring the CCTV
footage within hours.

*Priorities. Come on, think. Think.*

*The phone.* Screw the sodding phone. That was Mr C's
concern now, not his.

Turner was the priority. Turner could describe him. And
how long before the FBI got involved? Was the bastard
going to head straight to the nearest police station? And
what would he tell them?

*The man's British. Yeah, I'm pretty sure.*

*Was he this guy, Turner? Take a close look at this dashcam
footage.*

*Yeah... that's him.*

*Any distinguishing marks? Tattoos? Scars?*

If Turner had been observant enough, he might just
have spotted the small, faded winged dagger tattoo on Ash's
forearm. And the motto: WHO DARES WINS.

How long would it take the FBI to work out his identity?
Scott Ashworth. Former sergeant in the SAS. Former officer
in the Royal Marines. Two tours in Helmand. Distinguished
service award. Educated privately at Plymouth College.

*Think.*

He had two options: pack up his shit, return to England
and hope that no one came knocking on his door. Or track
down this idiot before the cops found him, and – third time
lucky, for Christ's sake – finish the fucker off.

## 73

J ay gazed out of the coach's window. They were on yet another Greyhound coach, this one heading west towards Pittsburgh, Pennsylvania. It had been the first one to leave New York. He watched as dawn lit the sky a mottled amber over Lower Manhattan, the tension cables of the Lincoln Bridge flitting past as they headed across the Hudson River, in the direction of New Jersey.

The past few hours – in fact, the past few days – had become one impossibly long smear of time. The last day that had felt vaguely normal had been their Tuesday trip to Disney World. Ever since then, he'd been floundering.

Sylvie's phone was back at Ronni's place. Luckily, it wasn't a smartphone, but Ash would be all over it and he'd know that Jay had been waiting for a passport to arrive at a PO box at Times Square Post Office. He'd also have Sam's number. Her new one. He quickly tapped out a text on his burner.

Sam – Sylvie's phone compromised. DONT answer any calls from it x

His phone buzzed a moment later.

What's happened??

Long story. Hitman caught up. Ronni dead. Sylvie dead. Me and Jorge now on a coach.

Wtf?

Killer knows who I am. Knows everything about me. Will know about you too. I can't get the passport. Im kinda fucked right now

Can you talk?

Call you later at next stop – public phone OK?

Are you safe, baby? Are you sure he isn't still following you?

Don't know. I ran. Safe for now. I think. Got to sleep. Get my head straight.

Call me asap. It's going to be OK. Just keep calm. Keep your head on. Going to talk to Karl/Boyd OK? X

Yeah. Plz. I need advice. I need help.

We'll get heads together. Are you OK? Hurt? Xx

Fine. A broken nose. I think. But OK.

Jorge?

In shock. Saw his mother shot dead!

Jesus

Gotta sleep. Will text. Love you xxx

Jay turned off his burner phone. Proper off. Just in case. He turned to Jorge. The lad was wide awake. Watching him.

'We're gonna be okay, Mr Jay,' he whispered, patting his arm.

It wasn't a question. The boy was trying his best to reassure him.

Jay felt tears pricking his eyes.

'Yeah, mate,' he replied, squeezing Jorge's hand. 'Yeah, we've got this.'

## 74

T he old man was flapping his hands and switching between a foreign language and broken English. 'Very much noise last night. Shout. Scream. I hear child scream.'

'You heard a *child* scream?' asked Sergeant Luis Rodriguez.

The old man nodded vigorously.

Rodriguez turned to his partner. 'That's enough to force entry if they don't open.' He said that loudly as they climbed the stairs, not just for the rookie he'd been lumbered with this morning but for the benefit of his chest cam. Goddamn it if they didn't have to announce every decision, every thought process like a bingo caller.

They stepped onto the third-floor landing.

'Which one?' Rodriguez asked.

The old man nodded to the door on the left.

Rodriguez stood before it, cleared his throat and then knocked heavily on the door. 'Police! Open the door!'

There was no answer.

He tried again. 'Police. Open the door or we will force an entry!'

He shouted it one more time for the camera on his vest.

Still no answer.

He turned to the rookie, young and fit and definitely not suffering from back problems. 'Kick it in, Kemp.'

Officer Sean Kemp nodded, took a step back, lifted one boot and gave the apartment door a sharp kick beside the handle. The door splintered around the brass doorknob.

'And another one should do it,' said Rodriguez, resting one hand on his gun, which was in its holster.

The young officer kicked again and the door juddered inwards.

Rodriguez could see a body in the lounge beyond the narrow hallway. He pulled his gun.

'Police! Entering!' he shouted.

He led the way inside, gun aimed, checking the corners and for any side doors that might take him by surprise. Then he reached the apartment's lounge.

'Jesus Christ,' he muttered at the sight of the two bodies. One was slumped forward on a dining table, the other one on the floor. Both were women.

Kemp joined him, gun raised. 'Fuck!'

There was a *lot* of blood. On the table were a stack of pizza boxes. Several were open, revealing cold pizzas, sliced and uneaten.

'Let's check the rooms,' said Rodriguez.

It was evident that whoever had killed them had departed. And, thank God Almighty, there was no dead child to be found.

Rodriguez lightly touched the cheek of the woman on the floor. She was cold as a fridge.

Kemp crossed the floor to check the other woman. He left a boot print in a pool of coagulated blood.

'Kemp, careful! That's forensics you're stepping in,' Rodriguez snapped.

He keyed his radio. 'Twenty-three Sergeant to Central. We got a couple of 10-54Ds over at Kent Avenue and South 2nd Street.'

## 75

Dominic Carlton wasn't the type of man to lose his head. Getting twitchy solved nothing. Panicking fixed nothing. Better to do nothing than to panic. Whoever coined the phrase 'move fast and break things' was an asshole.

But Ash should have texted him that location by now. He'd said 'by Saturday'. Did that *include* Saturday? It was getting late in the day. Bowman had already sent several texts to check everything had been 'tidied up' so that he could relax with his family this weekend.

Against his better judgement, Carlton called Ash. If the man wanted his half-million, then he'd better pick up the damn phone and give him an update.

'Mr C?'

'Why the hell haven't I heard from you yet?' Carlton snapped. 'What the fuck's going on?'

'The complications have developed complications,' Ash replied.

'What's that supposed to mean?'

'Ronni Kirk is dead, and Turner escaped.'

Carlton closed his eyes and breathed deeply. 'Please tell me you recovered the fucking phone.'

'He took it.'

'FUCK!' Carlton screamed, ignoring the painful strain in his vocal cords. 'Jesus Christ, Ash! You're supposed to be the fucking elite!'

'Turner got lucky. Luck's a factor from time to time.'

'When I pay crazy money for a job to be done, I don't expect luck to be a goddamn factor!' Carlton hissed.

Ash said nothing.

Carlton took another deep breath to settle his nerves. 'So what's your next move?'

'I'm going to stay on Turner. I need him dead just as much as you do. He could ID me.'

'What do you think he's going to do?' Carlton asked.

'I don't know. We're not dealing with a seasoned pro. He's an amateur. He's probably shitting bricks right now. He's got a kid with him too.'

'A kid?'

'Some Mexican kid,' Ash said. 'The cops are all over Kirk's apartment. Their priority will be the child. There'll be an APB out. I've got to get to them before the police do. I'm heading to the Greyhound stop near Penn station. Turner is an open book. I'm guessing he grabbed the first bus available.'

Carlton sat down, feeling far too old and weary to be dealing with a fire this size. 'What a fucking mess,' he muttered.

'That's a fair description,' Ash agreed.

'Since our interests are still aligned, what can I do to help?' asked Carlton.

'Do you have any contacts with a link to the Feds? It would be helpful to know if they're on to him.'

'I can call in some favours.'

'Do it. If you want me to track him down fast, I need intel.'

'I'll see what I can do,' replied Carlton.

## 76

Another flipping early-morning call. Boyd really needed to get into the habit of switching on his phone's 'Do not disturb' mode, if only for Sunday mornings.

He fumbled for it on his bedside table. The offending phone, buzzing away in his hand, was his work phone. Not his personal one.

Boyd sighed. It was Minter. *For fuck's sake.* It was seven in the morning and he wasn't even scheduled to go in today. What the hell did he want?

'Yup?' Boyd answered irritably.

'Sorry, boss. I know it's your day off but –'

'But what?' Boyd snapped.

'I wouldn't have called you otherwise, see,' Minter continued, 'but I know you've been looking for Emma's fella, Dan.'

Boyd sat up, suddenly wide awake. That sounded ominous.

'Go on,' he said, his heart starting to race.

His abrupt movement caused Ozzie and Mia to leap off

the end of the bed, in hope of an early breakfast. Their claws, scratching loudly on the wooden floor, roused Charlotte. She opened her eyes and stared at Boyd, quickly reading his face as he listened to Minter.

She sat up with him. *Is everything okay?* she mouthed.

He turned to her. 'It's Minter. A body's been found on the tracks beyond St Leonards.'

# DCI BOYD RETURNS IN

A GUARDIAN ANGEL available to pre-order
HERE

# ALSO BY ALEX SCARROW

**DCI Boyd**

SILENT TIDE

OLD BONES NEW BONES

BURNING TRUTH

THE LAST TRAIN

THE SAFE PLACE

GONE TO GROUND

ARGYLE HOUSE

THE LOCK UP

THE ARCHIVE

A MONSTER AMONG US

THE VANISHING

**Thrillers**

LAST LIGHT

AFTERLIGHT

OCTOBER SKIES

THE CANDLEMAN

A THOUSAND SUNS

**The TimeRiders series (in reading order)**

TIMERIDERS

TIMERIDERS: DAY OF THE PREDATOR

TIMERIDERS: THE DOOMSDAY CODE

TIMERIDERS: THE ETERNAL WAR

TIMERIDERS: THE CITY OF SHADOWS

TIMERIDERS: THE PIRATE KINGS

TIMERIDERS: THE MAYAN PROPHECY

TIMERIDERS: THE INFINITY CAGE

**The Plague Land series**

PLAGUE LAND

PLAGUE NATION

PLAGUE WORLD

**The Ellie Quin series**

THE LEGEND OF ELLIE QUIN

THE WORLD ACCORDING TO ELLIE QUIN

ELLIE QUIN BENEATH A NEON SKY

ELLIE QUIN THROUGH THE GATEWAY

ELLIE QUIN: A GIRL REBORN

# ABOUT THE AUTHOR

Over the last sixteen years, award-winning author Alex Scarrow has published seventeen novels with Penguin Random House, Orion and Pan Macmillan. A number of these have been optioned for film/TV development, including his bestselling *Last Light*.

When he is not busy writing and painting, Alex spends most of his time trying to keep Ozzie away from the food bin. He lives in the wilds of East Anglia with his wife Deborah and five, permanently muddy, dogs.

Ozzie came to live with him in January 2017. He was adopted from Spaniel Aid UK and was believed to be seven at the time. Ozzie loves food, his mum, food, his ball, food, walks and more food...

He dreams of unrestricted access to the food bin.

For up-to-date information on the DCI BOYD series, visit: www.alexscarrow.com

Printed in Great Britain
by Amazon